MOOREWOOD FAMILY RULES

A Novel

HELENKAY DIMON

AVON
An Imprint of HarperCollinsPublishers

MOOREWOOD FAMILY RULES. Copyright © 2023 by HelenKay Dimon. All rights reserved. Printed in the United States of America. No part of this book may be used or reproduced in any manner whatsoever without written permission except in the case of brief quotations embodied in critical articles and reviews. For information, address HarperCollins Publishers, 195 Broadway, New York, NY 10007.

HarperCollins books may be purchased for educational, business, or sales promotional use. For information, please email the Special Markets Department at SPsales@harpercollins.com.

FIRST EDITION

Designed by Diahann Sturge

Library of Congress Cataloging-in-Publication Data has been applied for.

ISBN 978-0-06-324052-0
ISBN 978-0-06-329714-2 (hardcover library edition)

23 24 25 26 27 LBC 5 4 3 2 1

For Suzanne, my roommate during our London semester in college, the maid of honor at my wedding, and a lifelong friend who loved the color pink, New York City, her incredible family, Broadway shows (we saw Les Misérables *together three times), meals with friends (so long as she picked the restaurant), vacationing in Nantucket during the off-season, finding the perfect lipstick (and demanding I go buy one before I did another Zoom interview), her days at Mount Holyoke College, picking up an amazing black purse, and all (non-work-related) travel. You adored every book Elin Hildebrand wrote. While I'm not her (but envy her book sales), I promise this one isn't a thriller. Consider this my final gift to you, my amazing friend. I still can't believe I live in a world without you in it.*

MOOREWOOD FAMILY RULES

CHAPTER ONE

MOOREWOOD FAMILY RULE #4: *Maintain the public facade. Keep family arguments private.*

JILLIAN MOOREWOOD WAITED THIRTY-NINE MONTHS AND seven days to make a spectacular and unexpected entrance. A simple car and driver wouldn't do. That left a yacht, splashy yet sure to draw attention, or dropping down from above into a sea of stunned faces via helicopter. Clearly, the latter won.

She scanned the target area from the window next to her seat. From this angle she could see the expanse below. A gated entrance. Towering trees hiding a wall that outlined every pristine inch of the property. Not one pool but two . . . because, of course. Didn't every house need two?

This house had a name because that's what people around here did. They baptized their sprawling estates as if they were precious children. This one—Hideaway. A completely nonsensical description of a forty-five-acre oceanfront estate that could accommodate five hundred guests for a sit-down dinner in the second-floor ballroom. Every building awash in weathered-looking-but-not-really gray shingles, and the whole thing plunked down on prestigious Ocean Avenue, just a short, chauffeur-driven ride from Rhode Island's historic Newport Country Club.

The whapping and rattling grew louder the closer they got to the ground. Mere feet from landing, Jillian could make out the faces of the dozen or so people standing at the bistro tables set in a careful pattern around the larger, cascading pool.

A party. How convenient . . . for her, not them.

The landing skids hit the ground and almost in unison the people milling around stopped sipping whatever fancy drinks they carried and stared in horror. No one came running to greet her. They'd have to close their mouths and stop blinking first. Exactly the type of *what is she doing here* welcome she'd expected.

Tense silence descended on what looked like a once-lovely garden party, complete with a string quartet playing in the corner of the upper flagstone deck. Women decked out in expensive dresses, wearing the obligatory uncomfortable shoes. Men dressed as store mannequins.

The pilot helped her down from her seat. The second her heels hit the grass a wave of unexpected anger crashed over her. The history. The broken promises. The lies.

Ah, family.

She shoved a creeping sensation of doom aside and plastered a smile on her face that she hoped telegraphed a fraction of the you-bitches-are-in-trouble emotions surging through her.

Uncle Jay—Jayson Oliver Moorewood, to be exact—made the first move. He mindlessly handed off his glass of champagne to the woman hanging on his arm. She was just his type. Pretty in an understated, wouldn't-dare-wear-too-much-makeup kind of way. Likely in her fifties, because Jay had a thing for *women of a certain age*, that *certain age* being any woman who had lived long enough to collect impressive trinkets and stockpile money.

"Jillian. How wonderful!" he called out for all to hear as he closed the gap between them.

He didn't touch her. *Wise man.*

"Uncle Jay." The warmth in her voice surprised even her. Lying might be fused into the Moorewood blood after all.

"Right. Well. You're here. Absent a call so we could prepare. Typical," he said, and then, without warning, reached out and gave her a hug that went on just long enough for him to whisper in her ear, "Do not make a scene."

"Don't tempt me," Jillian whispered back.

"We're in the middle of an important party." He stood back far enough to keep a hold on her arms, likely aiming for some sort of loving *look at you* gesture to impress the assembled crowd. The perfectly tanned and vacuumed skin on his forehead didn't move as he performed his devoted uncle act.

"You should ease up on the Botox." Okay, not nice. The words slipped out but, in her defense, she'd been holding in years of pent-up sarcasm. That sort of crap was bound to spill over sooner or later.

To his credit, and as a result of a lifetime of practiced pretending, he didn't show any sign of surprise or anger at her unexpected presence, even though both had to be festering inside him, screaming to get out. Only a slight twitch in his cheek hinted at his annoyance. "Never tried it."

She pulled out of his hold, disconnecting from him while wearing a smile that threatened to crack her back teeth from the force of it. "Totally believable."

He looked like he'd stepped out of the most recent edition of *Healthy Living for Rich White Dudes* magazine, something she assumed existed. Tall and totally put together. Trim from riding ponies, or wrestling them, or whatever he did with ponies.

His navy blazer even had a crest on the pocket. She'd bet he paid someone to create a fake family emblem and already had a story about being related to a regal landowner in England. Likely insisted he was a distant cousin to the queen because Uncle Jay would not settle for anything less than royal lineage.

He had a story for every occasion. That's what he did. He made shit up. The whole family did. Sure, they dressed in linen and silk and threw on flashy hats when an event called for them. They gave a good show, because a good grift required that sort of thing.

Always *on* but never genuine. That could be the family motto.

Uncle Jay's gaze searched Jillian's face as if he expected to find an answer there for her sudden appearance. "No one—"

"Warned you?"

"*Told* us today was the day. We could have sent a car to pick you up." He looked ready to corner his kids and demand an explanation but schooled his expression a second later.

"Hello." The woman who hung on Jay's arm earlier rushed over. "We weren't expecting more company."

We?

The other woman looked as put together close-up as she did from a distance. Short dark hair cut in the sort of bob that looked good on women with long necks and strong collarbones, and this woman possessed both.

She wore one of those flowy silk dresses with a matching silk blazer in a slightly different color. Add in the diamond loop earrings and she managed to look casually rich, which was not an easy social status to pull off.

Clearly, this was Uncle Jay's newest target. The poor thing, though Jillian doubted *poor* described the woman in any way.

"And you are?" Jillian asked, bracing for a name that would likely make her choke.

"Yes, of course. Please forgive my terrible manners. I was just so excited to see you." Jay placed a gentle hand on the other woman's lower back. "This is Catherine Isadora Folger-Green."

And there it was. Jillian managed not to roll her eyes, but only barely.

"I go by Izzy."

Of course you do. Jillian looked at Izzy's hand. At the diamond and emerald tennis bracelet. At the shoes that cost more than some small cars. Mostly, Jillian was stunned no one in the family had come up with a creative way to steal at least one of those items yet . . . but give them an hour.

Jay cleared his throat. "Izzy, this is my niece Jillian."

A huge smile broke out on Izzy's angular face, making her look much more approachable than her name would suggest. "The world traveler. Jay told me you had"—Izzy leaned in and whispered—"an incident."

"Did he?" Jillian hadn't been sure which backstory to expect—cancer, breakdown, divorce. Jay was a wealth of untrue stories. The more tragic, the better.

"It's nothing to be ashamed of." Izzy reached out for Jillian's hand but never made actual contact. "We all have times when we need . . . rest."

The unnecessary whispering made the discussion all the more ridiculous, but Jillian couldn't help but be intrigued. "Where did he say I went?"

Jay cleared his throat, which was his usual way of telegraphing that it was time to shut up. "Jillian, I think we should—"

But Izzy was off and running. "You were last in Morocco, I believe?"

"Yes." Jay turned his megawatt smile on Izzy. "Darling, I think we need to have a quick family chat. Do you mind mingling with our guests for a bit without me?"

Our?

"Of course." Izzy kissed Jay on the cheek, then she was off. Rushing to a nearby table, laughing as she walked.

Jillian waited until the other woman was out of hearing range. "Thanks for not having me die in a horrifying accident. That would have made my appearance today difficult to explain."

Jay's adoring gaze centered on his newest girlfriend and never wavered. "Too risky since you're not the type to go away and never return. You tend to linger."

"Jillian." One of Jay's daughters, cousin Astrid, used the brief break in the private conversation to race over while the other lurkers inched closer, but not too close.

Before Jillian could brace for impact, Astrid charged in, all arms, air kisses, and dainty sniffles. She hummed as she hugged. Probably from nerves, at least Jillian hoped so. Seeing this usually high-performing, always-stay-calm-in-public family fall apart was the point.

"I don't get it." Astrid pulled back and gave Jillian a once-over just as her father had. "No one told us you were . . ." She stopped to clear her throat. "Coming today."

Out. She clearly meant *out* but stopped herself.

"I wanted to surprise Anika. You know, since we're so close." Jillian looked past Astrid to her equally blond, beautiful, petite, and perfect fraternal twin, Anika, as she spoke. "There's a rumor you're engaged or about to be."

Anika stood anchored against the side of an I-played-lacrosse-at-my-private-boarding-school-looking brown-haired man. He had a pasty, somewhat useless air about him, as if he had too much money and not enough drive to do anything with it. Anika held his hand in what appeared to be a pretty fierce death grip.

Jillian came prepared and knew the guy's old money thing wasn't an act. His ancestors built or invented the . . . something. She didn't care enough to remember *that* much about the guy, but she did admire his nerve. He was the first to move. He wiggled out of Anika's confining hold and put out his hand, all without wrinkling his beige linen suit. Quite an impressive feat, actually.

"I'm Harry Tolson." The rich dude name sounded even richer washed through the slight Boston elite accent.

All in all, Jillian had to give Anika credit for following the family tradition of trying to marry into piles of money. With private investigators and background checks, that sort of find-a-wealthy-spouse-and-bilk-'em planning was getting harder and harder to pull off these days.

"I'm Jillian Moorewood."

His smile froze. His arm froze. Pretty much all of him froze except for his eyes, which widened. "Oh."

"Yes, *that* cousin."

"I heard about . . ." Harry wore a very serious look now. "I'm sorry."

Someone better tell her what supposedly had happened soon or they'd all be tripping over the lie. "I'm fine, by the way."

"Okay, then. That's enough chatter." Uncle Jay wrapped an arm around Jillian's waist. "We should go inside." As he talked, he ushered them toward the grand three-story house, with its wall of French doors across the back lower level. "Family business and all that."

Ah, yes. The fear of an audience. Not that her family didn't enjoy a good performance. They'd perfected those, but they had to occur when the game called for them. Not when a wayward relative wandered in without calling first.

She was tempted to grind the entire scheme—make that plural since there seemed to be more than one scam happening here—to a halt, but now wasn't the time for a screaming scene. That would come later as she peeled back her relatives' lives layer by layer. For now, she would shake them up a bit. Inside the house or out, either would work for what she had planned.

"Your stunt with the helicopter was over the top, even for you," Anika said through teeth as clenched as the rest of her.

The helicopter choice had been a triumph. Jillian refused to believe, deep down, the family didn't appreciate the drama.

"Well, I'm thrilled you're back." Astrid slipped up to the side of Jillian not occupied by her father and slid her arm through Jillian's. "I missed you."

Huh . . . "Really?"

Astrid's big, toothy smile, complete with straight, unnaturally white teeth, slipped a bit. "Of course."

Jay picked up the pace. "That's enough talking for now. Hold it in."

The group practically sprinted across the lawn and up the stone steps to the house. As soon as they escaped inside, Jay's arm dropped from Jillian's back, and he started shooing party stragglers out of the massive family room. A clicking sound echoed through the room as he closed each glass door to the outside and every interior door to another room.

A sort of frantic energy pulsed off him, but he never broke character as he fought for privacy. Not one drop of sweat or piece of clothing dared to move out of place by the time he turned around to face the small group gathered in front of him.

"There." Then Jay's satisfied expression flatlined. "Oh, Harry. You're still with us."

"Anyone care to explain Morocco?" Jillian asked, not caring what Harry heard or didn't hear. He was not her problem. The rest of them were.

Before anyone could respond to Jillian's sarcastic question, poor-but-not-really Harry held up a hand, which somehow stopped the manic swirl of conversation and drew everyone's attention to the very expensive watch on his wrist. "Are you saying you weren't relaxing in Morocco?"

Astrid, Anika, and Jay started talking. Jillian let them verbally trip and trample all over each other. She couldn't make out most of the excuses in the jumble of words, but it didn't matter because none of what they said would be true. Never was. That was a family trait she could count on.

Jillian waited until the fury died down then gave Harry the real answer. "Prison."

Harry looked like he'd been run over by a car . . . more than once. "Excuse me?"

"I was in prison."

CHAPTER TWO

MOOREWOOD FAMILY RULE #18: *Avoid any and all talk of incarceration because it invites trouble.*

JILLIAN NOW KNEW WHAT PANIC LOOKED LIKE, AT LEAST THE *we can't show it* kind. She just never expected it to be accompanied by so much champagne. A deafening silence fell over the room. The walls actually thumped with it as everyone sipped and hid their faces behind the expensive crystal flutes.

Harry had the good manners to swallow hard before launching into more questions. Probably came from that fancy boarding school training of his. "You were in prison in Morocco?"

Good. Lord. "No."

While he pondered his next question, Jillian walked over to the massive stone fireplace and stared at the photos lining the mantel. She recognized the people in them because she was related to most of them, but the happy *we love being with each other* expressions caused some confusion. There was even one of her laughing. She'd never seen the dress she was wearing in it. How did they pull that off?

Her gaze stopped on a strategically placed photo of Anika and Astrid with their half brother, who everyone said lacked the Moorewood gene. The lucky bastard. The painting hanging over the fireplace was of Uncle Jay, the girls, and one of Jay's wives. Looked like number three but Jillian was pretty sure number three and number four were related and had long ago given up trying to tell them apart. Jillian guessed that was better than a painting of polo ponies, but only marginally.

If the house could talk . . .

Jillian turned to face the room. They all looked a wee bit paler now. Even Uncle Jay had bits of tension pulling at the corners of his mouth and eyes. The same man who rarely showed any sign of distress, even that time he was caught by the police while holding a stolen painting. Like, *in* someone else's house, *holding* someone else's million-dollar painting while the house alarm blared in the background.

Even then, Jay schmoozed and charmed his way out of the situation. He'd convinced the FBI he'd triggered the alarm when he saw someone else sneak into the house. He was the true hero, hiding the painting from potential thief savagery. *Saving it with my life!*, he'd insisted. And damn if that hadn't worked.

Speaking of distress . . . "Thirty-nine months and now I'm out of prison. Released early for good behavior." Jillian flashed Anika a smile. "Surprise."

Looking over her uncle's shoulder to the back lawn, Jillian could see the guests wandering around on the patio. Izzy entertained a group with a story that had her hands flipping around in the air and her admirers laughing. A few of the other guests peeked in the room. All engaged in the time-honored game of whispering behind their hosts' backs. Jillian treated them to a little wave, and they all scooted away in record time.

She finally gave in and glanced at Harry, whose mouth had dropped open and hung there, making his objectively appealing face look a bit out of balance. "I'm fascinated to know how my enterprising family kept the news of my arrest quiet."

Poor Harry's skin took on a green tint.

"Because a private investigator should have found the truth about my absence. Harry, honestly, and I mean this in the most helpful way, I'm thinking your family needs to hire better people."

Jay laughed. The rich sound bounced off the walls. Sounded almost real, too, but it wasn't. "Don't mind Jillian, Harry. She has an odd sense of humor."

Harry frowned. "But I was told there was an incident."

That word kept popping up, and Jillian decided to find out why. "Which was?"

"Various family members told me that you were dating a married man, and that he stole from you. From the whole family, actually, but incriminated you." Harry winced as he spoke, which probably was a sign of good breeding when gossiping. "You couldn't report it under the circumstances, of course."

"Sure." Jillian nodded. "His sad wife and all that."

"Exactly. And as a result of all the stress you had a bit of a . . ."

"Breakdown," Astrid filled in, being her usual overeager self. "An epic breakdown."

Jillian appreciated a story with a lot of moving pieces. "Go big, I always say."

"Right." Harry glanced at Anika, who hadn't moved since the word *prison* got tossed around, then turned to Jillian again. "You felt guilty and regretted your family's loss due to you being lovesick and desperate. Then you went on a long trip to recuperate."

"Okay." *Wow.* Jillian considered clapping but decided that might be too much and could scare Harry. Someone in the family had to show a healthy regard for boundaries. But really, they'd managed to squeeze infidelity, romance, heartbreak, theft, and mental incapacity into one sorry tale about her life. Saying *prison* seemed easier.

Jillian kept her focus on Harry. If he balked and broke things off with Anika, well, that would just be the icing on what was turning out to be a pretty tasty cake. Jillian justified that ending because she'd be saving him. The chance of Anika dating for love and not as part of a con was . . . was there a value less than zero?

"You see, Harry. That's why everyone is surprised to see me."

"Because you came back early?" Harry asked as he visibly struggled to understand.

Jillian refused to say the word *prison* one more time. He'd been warned and if he chose to ignore or willfully misunderstand, so be it. "My guess is they hoped I'd never come back."

"That would have been a shame," Anika said in a voice that might have sounded genuine to those who didn't know better but reeked of sarcasm to anyone related to her.

Astrid gasped in perfect dramatic fake debutante style. "So true."

Jillian didn't spare either sister a glance.

"I don't get it. It's not like you killed someone, right?" Harry ended with an awkward chuckle.

"A smart question, Harry. I like you." Jillian didn't really care about him one way or the other, but she did like him more than anyone else in the room, so that was something. "And liking you is a good thing. Because, you see, I have some serious, decades-in-the-making issues to work out with my family. Revenge, tactical warfare, scorched earth. I'm sure you get it."

Harry nodded, looking full of compassion. "We all have issues with our families."

He didn't get what she was *not* saying, but Jillian could tell from the rapt attention of her family that they did. "At its essence, we're talking about family rules, or rather, breaking them and what happens when you do."

For a solid three minutes after she dropped her verbal bomb the room exploded into controlled chaos. People shifted around. More champagne appeared. All of them tried to laugh off her comments and reassure Harry. Finally, Anika shoved Harry toward one of the doors to the back-yard party, promising she'd join him soon on the patio after they'd ironed out some *unexpected family distress.*

Jillian had a front row seat to all of it, or she did until Jay ushered them all further into the house, away from those big windows and curious eyes. After a few minutes of bicker-ing, every manner of Moorewood present for this shindig shuffled into the connecting dining room. Correction, the family dining room. Not to be confused with the ballroom, which sat one floor up on the other side of the grand stair-case.

Jillian stood with her hands resting on the inlaid wood along the back of a chair. Something about this group made her want to be on her feet and ready to spar. Her sister, Emma, slipped in and sat down without ever looking at Jillian or say-ing a word to anyone. She'd perfected the spoiled, whiny baby sister act long ago.

Only a few seconds ticked by before Jay let out one of his I'm-not-happy sighs. "Jillian, I understand you've had a dif-ficult few months, but we have family rules and—"

Nope. "Three years and you're not really going to lecture me about the rules, are you?"

Jay made that condescending *tsk-tsk*ing sound he enjoyed so much. "You seem angry."

"Really?" She clenched the chair, ignoring how the antique creaked beneath her fingers. "Do you think that's because I've been in prison?"

Anika sighed this time. "Jillian, you must know the tip-off to the FBI didn't come from any of us."

Jillian had no idea how her cousin got that denial out without laughing. "Of course not. I just happened to be the only family member arrested while the rest of you ran free and pretended not to know me. Makes perfect sense."

Emma's head shot up. "You weren't the only one arrested."

"Right." Jillian snapped her fingers, showing a lightness she didn't feel. Nothing about her father filled her with peace or calm. "Our dear ol' dad. How could I forget? We were both dragged in for questioning."

Only one of them came home.

This time Uncle Jay took offense. He pointed at Jillian down the length of the table. "Your father was a good man."

She had a limit on how much nonsense she'd tolerate, and Jay's defense of his brother slammed her into it. "We all know Dad was many things and *good* was not one of them."

Jay started to say something, but Anika cut him off. "Okay, enough. Thanks to you, Harry is locked out there. So is Izzy. Please explain how this is helpful, Jillian."

"I'm happy to see you, but you really are jeopardizing a lot of hard work," Astrid added.

"We need to wrap this chat up so I can start damage control." Anika let out a little huff that probably worked better on unsuspecting men she was in the middle of conning.

"I have no idea how I'm going to fix the prison talk you started."

Jay shook his head. "Do you have any idea what we've had to do to keep that under control?"

The family full-court press. They clearly wanted her to feel guilty. Jillian didn't, but she was curious about how they'd pulled all of this off. Her criminal record was public, after all. "You poor things. Please tell me about your hard work that didn't involve being locked up."

"I handled the social media and the computer trail," Emma said. "Planted some fake news articles. Buried your prison record with the help of targeted malware in the federal penitentiary computer system. No one has found it or tried to fix it. When they do, I'll know."

Jillian admired her little sister's computer prowess. She just wished Emma had aimed all that skill *against* Jay and his misfit children, not in furtherance of their cons.

After Jillian's mother died seven years ago a clear break emerged within the family. Jillian had forced her father, Clive, to move ahead on his promise to Mom to stop the grift. Retire the cons. Jay and his offspring disagreed. The two sides had been battling ever since . . . though it sounded like Emma had spent some time in the enemy camp recently.

"What do you want, Jillian?" Anika asked. "Tell us before you ruin everything we've worked so hard on these last few months."

Ah, yes. Jillian predicted this would happen. They'd reached the victimhood part of the afternoon. Every family member would now launch into an explanation about how her shortened prison sentence was a burden on *them*.

Jay thumped the tip of his finger against the table. "You need to let your disappointment go, Jillian. This sort of thing can eat at you, and I'd hate to see that. For you."

"Exactly." Anika shot out of her seat. "You flew in, making a big scene. We get it. You want us to be as miserable as you are."

"Sit down." Jillian waited for Anika to obey before continuing. When the seconds stretched into minutes Jillian wondered if she'd overestimated Anika's smarts, but then the blonde's knees buckled and down she went. So, Jillian started again. "Believe it or not, Anika, my return home isn't about you."

Abandoned. The word probably wasn't fair, but that's the sensation that twisted inside of Jillian. Clive, Jay's brother and her dad, died of a heart attack the minute the FBI brought him in for questioning. He'd checked out of her life from the beginning, being more excited by the lure of the con than home life. Needing the adrenaline rush. More impressed with her money-hiding abilities than with her.

She'd mourned him in her way. His death drove her to her knees in her locked cell and kept her there. She hated him most for that, but she was over all the anguish . . . or she vowed to be over it.

But, among the living Moorewoods, nothing had changed. Jillian knew the deflecting would rage on for days unless she brought it to a close. She did, mostly because she wanted to unpack and take a shower. "Did any of you apologize to me yet?"

"What happened to you was . . ." Anika looked at the ceiling as if the right word might be stuck up there. "Unexpected."

Unbelievable. "That's the word you picked?"

"It's time to move forward," Uncle Jay said.

"So, no actual apology, then." No surprise there.

"There's a very easy solution here." Anika shifted back into fake-smile mode before looking at Jillian again. "We'll find you a nice, quiet house. Maybe on one of those islands near Seattle. We can set up a fund for you. You'll be secure and—"

"And out of the way." Jillian had to give them credit. They really did not disappoint. Nothing had changed. They only knew one speed—whichever one saved their own asses. "One question, Anika. Are you more attracted to Harry's stock portfolio or the eighty-thousand-dollar watch he wears?"

"No, you're too high." Jay shook his head. "That Patek Philippe is closer to seventy."

"His Rolex is much nicer but is only worth about half that," Astrid added.

"It's rumored Harry's mother owns one of those Jacob & Co. Billionaire watches." Anika shook her head. "It's in a vault. I've never seen it."

Jay whistled. "For fifteen million it should be locked away."

"More like eighteen, and what a waste." Astrid shrugged. "What good is owning something so stunning, so rare, if no one knows you have it? Imagine what we could do with that money."

"Anyway . . . the bottom line is that we are a family," Jay said, and managed to do it with a straight face.

Jillian doubted he even knew what the term meant. He probably read it in a book once and thought it sounded good. "Of con artists."

Every single one of them looked around the room as if she'd divulged some great secret they worried would leak out. Jay was the first to scold. "Keep your voice down."

Jillian refused to acknowledge their nonsense. "We had one steadfast rule—no one snitches. If one of us gets caught, we back each other up and regroup." And boy had they abandoned that rule as soon as fingers pointed in her direction. "Someone set me up."

"We would never," Uncle Jay said in a firm voice. "But, for the record, why are you here now? Are you thinking about some form of revenge? Because I assure you that's not necessary."

Before Jillian could point out that they'd made a deal when she went to prison for them, a click echoed through the room. She saw movement at the double doors right before they opened.

"Excuse me?" First, the deep voice, so confident and in control. Then came the face. Perfect, with a slight tan and hair ruffled by a nonexistent wind.

Gregory Alexander Paul. The one person Jillian didn't expect to see today or ever again. The one person she specifically would have banned from the estate if she'd known that sort of thing was necessary.

Never trust a guy with that many first names.

"Jillian, is that you?" The smile looked genuine as he moved inside and closed the doors behind him.

She knew better. Gregory calculated every step and every word for maximum impact. That smooth affect hid a murky underlayer. He was the type of guy who lured women in with his big bank account and pretty eyes . . . then he screwed them. And not in the good way.

Seeing him standing there, in her house, with that hide-your-valuables-because-I'm-taking-them expression, shifted her priorities. Revenge, first. That hadn't changed. But now she had an additional target . . . and this one knew how to fight back.

CHAPTER THREE

MOOREWOOD FAMILY RULE #6: *Do not get attached to your target.*

THE DAY HAD TAKEN A REFRESHING TURN. ANIKA THOUGHT there might be hope for them all yet. Not the party. No, Jillian being Jillian she'd ruined that. She ruined a lot of things. Anika had not missed her cousin's face or personality one bit. Frankly, Jillian going to prison had been a bit of relief in some ways.

There. She said it. Not out loud but letting herself think it felt good.

Anika wasn't one bit sorry either. Jillian brought the destruction on all by herself. She handled the family's finances and investments. She got charged with theft, fraud, wire fraud, tax evasion, and a host of other crimes. Her mistakes. Therefore, her fault.

The one small piece of luck was that she didn't take them

all down with her. Just her and Uncle Clive, may he rest in peace. The rest of them coasted, relying on their wits and the money Jillian had stockpiled.

Not that Jillian's behavior didn't wreak havoc in other ways. It surely did. It had taken all of them spinning the *Jillian got duped by a man* story and months of working it before the excuse finally stuck. Reporters had to be paid to bury the articles. Search engines scrubbed. Not counting the months of lying low and staying in. Hiding. Being . . . regular. The one thing Anika had been trained to avoid and warned never to be.

They'd finally found firm footing and—bam!—*she* reappeared.

Now Anika had some leverage. Until five seconds ago Jillian seemed to be enjoying her big return home display and all those cryptic, taunting threats. Locking eyes on Gregory changed that. It was as if the air ran out of Jillian in that moment.

Very interesting. Anika rushed over to her new best friend. She threaded her arm under his elbow . . . and slipped his wallet out of his pocket and into hers.

"Gregory, hello!" Even Anika thought her voice rose a bit too much on the fake greeting. "Do come in and join us."

Dragging him toward the center of the room didn't prove to be all that hard. He stared at Jillian and appeared more than willing to walk right into a showdown with her. *Good.* Anika decided they could suck up each other's attention while she got started on damage control.

Anika extended a hand in her unwanted cousin's general direction. "You remember Jillian, don't you, Gregory?"

Jillian spared him a nod. "Greg."

He let out a laugh in response to Jillian's non-welcome. "I see you haven't changed."

Yes, that appeared to be the headline. Jillian returned as difficult as ever. Lucky them.

Gregory's father had been a supposed financial genius. Jay had dug around, stolen documents, and paid off a few people for intel to figure out the man was more Madoff than Gates, skimming money from clients to pay for his family's extravagant lifestyle. In other words, Gregory was a road to nowhere, which was fine because Anika'd found Harry.

Harry!

She had to get back to him and settle his fears before they spilled over to his very rich and very intolerant family members. They already doubted her because no one was good enough for Harry in their eyes. Harry's aunt and godmother ignored her until she showed up for brunch wearing an heirloom necklace—not her family's, of course, but one stolen just for such an occasion.

Jillian ruined the moment by finally choking out a greeting of sorts. "Why are you here, Greg?"

"Still Gregory." He smiled at her as if he were having fun playing with her. "When did you get out?"

"A few days ago." Jillian flicked a gaze around the spellbound room. "And I rushed right home to my loving uncle and cousins."

A little much on the sarcasm scale, but Anika remained hopeful this little talk would escalate. She needed the Jillian-Gregory battle to lead to somewhere uncomfortable for Jillian and make her scurry away again. Preferably to another country . . . one without phone access.

Gregory nodded, suddenly looking and sounding very serious. "As you probably know, I lost my father while you were gone."

Jillian's head tilted to the side. "He's missing? Have you checked the local bars and massage parlors?"

The tension ratcheted up with each verbal volley. And that voice. Jillian's carried a hint of *screw you* in every word even though her expression remained blank. Anika admired the pretend indifference skill. She made a mental note to copy the cool-but-crapping-on-you tone. It could come in handy on days like this.

"He's dead." Gregory dropped the information. Didn't sound sad or grief-stricken. More like ticked off.

Jillian hummed. "Oh, I see." No apology. No condolences. No fumbling for her ill-placed comment. Just humming.

"What's happening right now?" Astrid blinked a few times as she asked the question.

Jay waved her off. "Let them talk."

Okay, this was amusing. Even Anika could admit that. Her everybody-look-at-me relatives seemed riveted and fine with not hogging this particular spotlight. Jillian had left for prison full of that *we must be better people* crap. A true enjoyment killer. Now she commanded a room.

After a few seconds of tense silence, Jillian moved but only to cross her arms in front of her. Her focus hadn't left Gregory. It was as if she worried that if she did he might steal something.

Knowing his family, not impossible.

"Last I checked you weren't welcome in this house." Jillian fired the shot and people started shifting around. The whishing sound of silk and linen filled the room.

Emma sighed as she stood up and went to Gregory's side. "That's not true."

Ugh. Leave it to ridiculous cousin Emma to deflate the fun. Why Jay hadn't cut Clive—rest his soul—and his feral pack loose decades ago was a mystery to Anika.

Jillian looked at her baby sister and her eyes narrowed. "You should stay out of this."

"I'm in it."

Emma's tone had Anika changing her mind. Forget her earlier reservations. Emma jumping in made the whole scene better.

Emma's chin lifted a bit. She even shifted forward, as if to step in front of Gregory. "I invited him here today."

Anika liked the defiant streak. Not aimed at her, of course. She refused to battle Emma, but Emma was free to unload on Jillian all day. That almost made the ruined get-together worth it—again, *almost.*

"You invited him?" Jillian waited until her sister nodded. "Did Jay and Anika need someone to park cars?"

Astrid gasped. Anika thought that reaction was too much.

The conversation bordered more on entertaining than shock and awe.

"It's fine." Gregory put a hand on Emma's elbow and gently pulled her back to his side. "Your sister and I understand each other."

Jillian's expression looked as if she'd eaten rotten meat. "We do?"

They did? Anika was dying to know what that meant.

"We've known each other for a long time." A small smile appeared on Gregory's face as he slowed down, giving emphasis to each word. "We've been through some difficult times together."

Well, now. Anika needed more information on that, too. This time she abandoned her pretend disinterest. "Like what?"

"Isn't your boyfriend waiting by the pool?" Jillian's voice took on that sickening singsongy quality, which meant she'd moved into full sarcasm mode. "I'd hate for Harry to leave and take his money with him."

After a lifetime of being boxed in and used as a weapon, fired in this direction and that direction on Jay's behalf, Anika had grown weary of the game. Harry didn't know it yet, but she intended to marry him and have a normal, albeit wealthy, life. A rich, boring one. A life centered on keeping watch over her manipulative future mother-in-law, who would likely go all *you need a prenup* to Harry the second he bought a ring.

With the marriage done, she'd dedicate her life to running through his money and supporting charitable pursuits.

She had no idea what that last part meant but it seemed like a thing rich people did, and she wanted to fit in.

The only people on earth who could screw up her dream—her one-way ticket out—were in this room. And she was related to almost all of them.

Before she could give a little speech about the importance of her reputation remaining pristine, Jillian spoke up. "I decide."

She sounded pretty sure of herself, which had Anika's stomach bouncing around in panic. "What are you talking about?"

Jillian took her time picking up a glass of champagne and taking a sip. "I own this house. I decide what happens in it, including who gets to live here."

Anika admired the fierce delivery. "Okay, no. You *did* own it." Nice try, though. "When you went to prison it was transferred into a family trust."

Jillian's smile grew wider. "I'm not sure why you'd think that's the case."

"Anika, this isn't the time." Jay shot a quick glance toward Gregory as if to say *not in front of company*.

Anika knew that frantic tone. That look. The *I'm sure I mentioned it* Jay Moorewood disaster plan. The man could not turn off the con gene and didn't think twice about unleashing it against his family.

Forget the audience and the worries about Harry likely lurking by the door. Hell, even forget Jillian's smug face. All of Anika's attention zipped to the man she barely viewed as a father. "What did you do?"

Gregory whistled. "Uh-oh."

"Maybe we should . . ." Emma didn't finish the sentence out loud. She put her fingers over her mouth and whispered something that made Gregory's smile widen.

"This is not the time." Jay's voice rose in stern reproach. "There are outsiders present."

"I'm fine with Greg knowing this particular piece of dirty laundry since it reflects poorly on you, not me." Jillian looked at Gregory. "You okay with that, Greg?"

Sure, now they were all big friends. Anika couldn't imagine this day going worse.

Gregory shrugged. "I'll even answer to Greg this one time without balking."

Anika was two seconds away from taking that ugly blue vase Jay stole from that house in the Hamptons and crashing it over his head. "You promised us the asset ownership issue had been settled while Jillian was away."

Jay frowned. "I don't appreciate your tone."

Jillian lifted one finger off her glass. "This time—and this one time only—I agree with Anika. You should talk, Jay."

Anika ignored the assist. "What don't we know about the house?"

Not just a house. They were talking about much more than that. An estate. Acres of prime real estate. A mansion. Guesthouses. Land. Stockpiled resources. Rental properties.

Commercial real estate. A sizable portfolio but bigger than that. Prestige. Access to everything.

No one spoke for a few minutes. The heavy clock ticked on the mantel, counting down the time to the verbal punch Anika could feel coming. When the tension pressed in on her, strangling her and pummeling her chest in a steady bang, she gave in. "Well?"

Jay gestured toward the other end of the long table. "Jillian owns it. The house and everything tied to it."

Jillian could not . . . but then Anika caught her cousin's satisfied smile and knew the truth. She *could* and she *did*.

This. Could. Not. Be. Happening.

"So, that means—and I want to be very clear about this—you all being here, holding your party here, sleeping in a room on this estate?" Jillian's eyebrow inched up as she wound up for the blow. "That's happening because I've been gracious. I decide when that stops. You're here, in my house and on these grounds, because I'm allowing it."

Bile rushed up Anika's throat. She hoped the very expensive rug was vomit proof.

Gregory started laughing. "I was wrong. You have changed. Welcome home, Jillian."

CHAPTER FOUR

MOOREWOOD FAMILY RULE #3: *The family's wealth is to be shared among family . . . within reason.*

SONYA FINLAY MOOREWOOD SPENT YEARS LECTURING HER children about the need for sunscreen and the importance of family responsibility. If she were still alive today, she'd detest this scene. She'd scold Jillian for her cold behavior. Jillian felt a twinge of guilt over that but, mostly, she enjoyed the energy buzzing around the room as control tilted back in her direction.

She owned the house and the accounts because of her mom. All—the legitimate part, anyway—came from Mom's side of the family. Mom inherited it . . . and then Dad wandered along and tried to con her out of it.

Clive Moorewood, with his handsome face and sweet-talking ways, breezed into town decades ago and the wooing began. His original goal had been to steal a few jewels, maybe a painting or two, then disappear, not caring how broken he left Sonya. Instead, they got married and had two daughters, Jillian being the eldest.

Mom shifted from a stifling life filled with rules and loneliness under her religiously brutal parents to the wild chaos of being married to a con artist and pretending not to notice. She excused his criminal behavior and every lie because her family pummeled her growing up with the belief that marriage was forever and if she'd made a mistake then she was stuck with it.

Over time, Mom cleaned up their meet-cute for company. When she talked about the whirlwind courtship, she painted Dad as being a bit immature and looking for fun, as if them dating constituted a coming together of opposites instead of the potential start of a marry-then-murder-the-heiress story that luckily never came to fruition.

Her mother put up with a lot from Dad and Jay. In the end, she demanded the grifting stop, but it took years for her to impose that bold line. She died soon after they pretended to agree, leaving Jillian in the role of enforcer.

Jillian ached to make her mother proud, and she vowed to get there. She just had to wade through this messiness first.

Astrid's mouth, which had dropped open almost ten minutes ago, finally closed. "You can't own the house if you went to prison."

"Exactly." Anika nodded, clearly wanting to grab on to any hope she could. "You had to retitle everything so the government didn't take it." She looked around the room. "There were fines associated with your crimes . . . right?"

"I, or rather my attorneys, reached a deal with the government that spared the assets inherited from Mom or tied to that inheritance," Jillian said, laying out a very abbreviated version of what happened. "It's part of the reason I took a plea deal rather than risk going to trial. I saved assets but— and this is the part you won't enjoy—I worked hard to make sure all the inheritance could be traced to one trust."

Her dad had comingled the grifter assets and the inheritance long before Jillian took over the finances. She spent a lot of time re-creating paperwork, making up invoices and sales receipts, to create a false paper trail for stolen and allegedly unexplained assets and to separate all of that out from the inherited money.

Now for the best part. "When it was time to pay the never-paid taxes and my agreed-upon court fine, I made sure the money came out of the separate grifter assets, not the inheritance."

That wasn't even the biggest move she'd pulled off. No, that reveal would wait. Despite all the time that had passed and how much she wanted to see their faces when she spilled the worst, she wasn't ready to fess up to all her sins just yet . . . not until she knew the full extent of theirs. Not until she knew if there was any hope for them to change their ways.

Anika's mouth still hadn't closed. She sputtered a bit before talking. "You took our money without telling us?"

That's not the way Jillian would describe it. "Is *our* the right word?"

"How could you?" Anika asked in a harsh whisper.

"Easily, actually." Jillian viewed the advanced money moving as a restitution of sorts. She thought one day, once her family went totally legitimate as promised, she could try to unravel a lifetime of schemes and repay the victims who should be repaid.

Time for a reality check . . . the first of many Jillian hoped to deliver over the next few days. "You're free to sue me and then try to explain to the court where the money you say is missing came from and why I went to prison instead of you all."

They were back to the point in the conversation before *he* walked in. The *he* with whom she had a past, which she didn't want to talk about. The same *he* who played an unsuspecting role in the criminal activities that landed her in prison, which she couldn't talk about. The *he* who also seemed to be taking quick peeks at her baby sister, which needed to stop right now.

Gregory . . . the same *he* who looked very amused and about to jump into the conversation.

"One question." Gregory touched his nose, barely hiding the smile that lurked under his hand. "Why would your mother invest all that power in one person, namely you?"

He was a gigantic pain. Nothing new there, but still. Jillian decided to answer him anyway. "She trusted me."

That really was the answer. Mom didn't want Emma pressured by Dad and Jay or forced into difficult positions over money disbursements. Jillian tried not to dwell on the part where Mom was fine with *her* being pressured and having all the stress of being in charge.

"She gave you the power, assuming you wouldn't be spiteful or vindictive or use the estate as a weapon against the rest of us." Anika said the words in a rush, interrupting and losing the last of her calm as she fidgeted and raised her voice.

Probably true, but Jillian shook her head. "That requirement was not in the will. I would have remembered those words."

Jay clearly had sold his kids a huge pile of garbage. No surprise there. The guy's whole life was garbage.

"You can't possibly intend to throw us out." Astrid's voice hit its most whiny notes as she pointed at Emma. "What about your sister?"

"I'd think she'd be upset for having been cut out of her mother's will in the first place. There are ways to contest these things, you know," Anika said, adding her usual screeching attempt to launch more trouble into the mix.

Jillian decided to bring this to a close before the party guests knocked down the doors. "Whatever plans are twirling in your head, forget them. Jay contested the bequest to me years ago and it didn't work. When I went to prison, he tried to change ownership and get a court order letting him take over, and that also failed."

"That's not completely accurate." Jay puffed out his chest, which was one of his many tells before he told a whopping lie. "I asked a few questions about the estate, which you managed, and I did that in light of your prison sentence for fraud and—"

"The plea agreement was for tax evasion only." Jillian had been very careful about the fraud charges, knowing Jay would try to use them to argue she wasn't fit to handle the family's money. "To be technically correct, I got in trouble for not paying taxes on the assets you all stole and pretended to earn and own."

"*Stole* is a loaded word." Jay shook his head. "But going back to my point, I was worried about the money going to waste in your absence. I was stepping in and taking responsibility. I considered it my duty as the head of the family."

"Doesn't matter because it's over." It wasn't. Not by a long shot. Most of the people in this room had a lot to answer for and trying to steal the house out from under her while she was in prison definitely was on that list. "The house is mine. There's nothing else to argue about on that topic. The end."

Gregory's smile never wavered. "That sounds convenient for you."

"Why are you here?" Jillian was pretty sure she'd asked that already and he'd ignored her . . . and if he didn't put a few more inches between his arm and her sister's he'd end up in the fireplace.

"Emma invited me." Gregory shrugged and somehow managed to make the gesture look self-assured and confident.

The door that was supposed to be locked opened. Tenn—Tennessee Micah Moorewood, to be exact—Jay's son and the only person on that side Jillian truly liked, stepped inside. "Why are you all in here when the guests are out there?"

With his dark hair and near-black eyes, Tenn was far more attractive than the average Joe. He was also the non-scheming, ignored child from an affair that turned into Jay's second marriage.

"It would appear I've ruined everyone's day by showing up unannounced. Or at all." Which was the point. Jillian had aimed for chaos and from a brief scan of the room she'd achieved it. "But I am home for good, and there will be some changes around here, which we will discuss at another time."

"Is this payback?" Astrid asked.

Jillian knew she could dance around it, make it sound pretty . . . lead them on. She decided to go with the truth. Not the whys and what fors, but a simple response. "Yes."

Jillian walked over to Tenn. "I'm sure there's shrimp out there. Care to join me?"

The corner of his mouth kicked up in a smile. "I thought you'd never ask."

"One more thing." Jillian stopped right before leaving the room. "Anika, give Greg his wallet back."

CHAPTER FIVE

MOOREWOOD FAMILY RULE #12: *Never keep (accurate) written records.*

HOURS AFTER THE EXCITEMENT HAD DIED DOWN AND THE crowd started to disperse, Jillian looked around the house. Not all of it because she could only imagine what or who she'd stumble over, but she ventured into the rooms that always meant something to her, like the library with the two-story balcony lined with shelves. She spent a few minutes in there, relieved the family hadn't sold the books or furniture while she was gone.

With champagne in hand, she walked upstairs and into her old office. She'd spent long days hidden in here, trying to make things better for the family and accidentally sealing her own fate. When the FBI descended, they'd found her at her desk, but she refused to let that one horrible moment taint one of the few places on the estate where she'd always found peace.

She stared at what looked like an electronic keypad outside the door before turning the knob. She half expected the room to be locked and suspended in time as a testament to her poor judgment in trusting the fellow members of her gene pool, but it opened.

She stopped, frozen in place at the threshold.

"What the hell?" She scanned the room, not fully understanding what she was seeing. The familiar desk lamp cast the rest of the room in shadows, but she saw enough to know someone had taken over her precious space.

She turned on the overhead light and forced her legs to move, coming into the room and shutting the door behind her. The binders lining the bookshelves on the one wall looked familiar. Those contained the records the government had pored over, all created to tie estate assets to real accounts and sales. All fake and backed up with more false information. Some of her best work, really.

But that wall behind her desk. She imagined NORAD had a board like this. A commanding computer screen replaced the oversized whiteboard that used to hang there. The massive interactive map of the world took up most of the wall. There were colored lights sprinkled throughout the display, with most being centered on what looked like Rhode Island. Then there were little flags spread throughout the countries, with most right here in the United States. Along the right side was what looked like a spreadsheet, but she couldn't read it from this far away.

Did they try to conquer New Hampshire while she was gone?

"Jillian."

"What the—" She jumped, spilling champagne over her hand. Her gaze shot to the corner of the room and the petite figure folded up and lounging in the leather chair with the window open and a still smoking cigarette sitting on the sill. "Aunt Patricia?"

To the outside world, a charity-event-attending, opera-loving former debutante. In reality, a smoking, grifting, beer-drinking watcher of baseball. Hours and hours of baseball.

"Of course, dear." She used that older woman tone with a bit of a wobble on the end. Also fake. In reality, she had a husky, dockworker voice.

Patricia Moorewood was Jillian's great-aunt, her paternal grandfather's sister. The only person in the family from that generation still alive. A woman thoroughly devoted to planning and pulling off *superior cons*—her term. Over the decades she'd changed her name and pretended to be different people. Her biggest skill came in collecting other people's jewels. She stole them, bargained for them . . . found them.

Her real name: Agnes, which she hated. She dropped the name about the same time she dropped her husband. *Literally* dropped, as in her husband was shot by his mistress's husband and while in the hospital recuperating mysteriously choked on his pillow, got up from his bed disoriented, and fell out a window.

For some reason, likely due to Patricia's ability to charm and cry on cue, doctors and law enforcement believed that was an actual way for a human being to die. She declared men useless the day after she buried her cheating spouse.

None of that explained why she was here, in this house. Right now.

"You're back." Patricia's voice changed to her actual one as her gaze roamed over Jillian. "You look good. I worried you'd have that haunted expression that sometimes comes with confinement."

"It was only thirty-nine months." Jillian didn't mention that she'd been out of prison for a week. She would have stayed with friends, but she didn't have many of those. Needing to lie about every aspect of her life and upbringing made inviting other people in and building trust difficult. So, she'd stayed at a hotel in Boston while she reacclimated and stoked her anger for her big return.

She'd slept in the hotel bathroom every night because the suite she'd booked felt too large and too quiet. Without the background white noise of arguing and shuffling, she couldn't drift off. She hoped her unwanted connection to strict rules and threats, limited space, and lots of people milling around would go away quickly. She knew the slight rumble of fear that followed her like footsteps at all times would linger for years.

"Any time inside sounds hideous to me." Patricia wore an emerald-green pantsuit. Every piece the same color, all matching her jewelry and highlighting her white hair, which she'd pulled up in a bun.

Family lore said she was in her mid to late eighties, but Jillian knew that was one of her longest cons. Patricia married young and became a mother not that many months after. She fudged dates, including that of her son's birth, to cover the then-frowned-upon sex-before-marriage problem. She was barely eighty and could pass for a good ten years younger. She moved with ease except when it benefited her to go slower or pretend an illness or injury.

Having stolen a ridiculous amount of jewelry during her lifetime and fenced all of it, she moved to Florida years ago to, in her words, *enjoy the water and look at pool boys*. Jillian hadn't expected to find her here, in the house, let alone in this room. "Are you visiting for a few days?"

"I live here now." Patricia took a last drag from her cigarette before stubbing it out and leaving the lipstick-stained end balancing in the open window. "I knew you wouldn't mind."

No attempt at asking. Just a statement, per the usual Moorewood belief that everything belonged to them. Jillian remembered her father once boasting that he never asked for permission. Clearly, that sort of thing passed down through her family's paternal bloodline.

Jillian didn't even bother to contradict her aunt about housing arrangements. She wasn't about to kick out the older woman, and this sly older woman knew it. Still, Jillian needed a few details so that she was prepared for whatever fallout might strike her later. "What happened in Florida?"

"It's a long story, involving a museum charity auction and Interpol." The light caught on Patricia's diamond ring and danced as she continued to wave her hand in the air like royalty. "These things happen."

So much for the theory that she'd retired. Jillian had known that wouldn't stick. Patricia wasn't the lounge-around type. "The point is whatever happened made you move back here. To this house. Apparently, permanently."

"It's good to be near family at the end."

End? "You make it sound like you're dying, which I don't believe for a second." The woman ran on spit and nosiness. She'd outlive them all.

Patricia smiled. "You always were the smartest Moorewood of your generation."

"That's probably Tenn." Jillian knew Patricia aimed that sort of false flattery at her targets. That's part of what made Jillian's family so successful—research. They stole from people with something to hide or from people who would be too embarrassed to launch accusations. They picked their targets carefully . . . usually.

Patricia sighed, ratcheting up the drama. "Tenn and that beautiful face? The things he could do with it. He's wasted in education."

Jillian refused to debate that topic . . . again. "Uh-huh."

The door opened and Jay peeked in. He quickly slipped

inside and locked the door behind him and walked up to Jillian. "I wondered if you were still here."

"I live here."

"Yes, you've made your ownership claim perfectly clear." Jay's frown morphed into a wide grin as he turned to his aunt and immediately frowned again. "Patricia, really. You're smoking in here? I've asked you not to."

"Yes, really." Patricia continued on before Jay could answer. "Where's your new girlie?"

Jay sighed. "Her name is Izzy. Please stop referring to her as anything else."

"First, you said I couldn't call her your chippy. Now you don't like girlie." Patricia sighed right back at him. "Dumb as a lamp, that one."

"You're not an Izzy fan?" Jillian didn't want to show any interest, but she didn't have a choice after that comment.

"She yells when she talks to me. The assumption that all older people are deaf is maddening. I could take her in a fight, and the whole house knows it." Patricia stood up—all five-foot-one of her—and brushed a hand over her silk pantsuit.

Jay looked like he wanted to respond. Instead, he turned to Jillian. "Do you like what we've done to our little room?"

"You mean, *my* office?" Jillian vowed to train this crowd to understand the house and property were hers and she wasn't about to be conned, cajoled, or convinced out of any of it.

Heaven knew she'd tried. She'd made an honest deal with them more than three years ago. They all had ignored the terms. Now, if they wanted any money, they would listen. They didn't know that yet, but those were her new terms. Cash for compliance.

"Your timing is good. What with outsiders coming in and out of the house, we installed the keypad lock on the door." Jay leaned in closer to Jillian. "Need to hook it up. Just in case."

She had so many questions. She went with the most obvious one. "We?"

"Emma. This room is her baby." Jay walked over to the map. "The lights represent family members. Setting it up like this, we know where everyone is and what they're working on."

"You mean scams." A grifter map. *Great.*

Patricia snapped her fingers at Jillian. "Work, darling. Don't belittle our craft."

"The flags show where we've . . ." Jay smiled. "Worked. Previous jobs so that we don't double up by accident."

Jillian couldn't figure out if this was the most ingenious thing she'd ever seen or the most terrifying. "Who is the green dot way over there?"

Jay groaned. "Cousin Doug."

"Poor Doug." Patricia shook her head. "I fear my grandson is in a bit of trouble."

Doug's father, Patricia's only child, got stinking drunk,

fell off a yacht he'd stolen, and got sucked under it. So, as far as Jillian was concerned, Doug started off with a pretty serious gene pool deficit. "What did he do this time?"

"He failed to do his homework. Stole from the wrong family." Jay winced. "Romanced a lovely young woman who happened to be the favored niece of the owner of a private black ops company. The uncle was not impressed when his niece gave Doug her car."

"What kind?" Jillian regretted the question the second after she asked. It was such a Moorewood line of inquiry, and it made Patricia's and Jay's faces light up with excitement.

Jay's smile was almost feral. "Bugatti Chiron."

"A lovely blue color," Patricia said in a dreamy voice.

"Yes indeed." Jay nodded. "Three million dollars, and it goes three hundred miles per hour. It was quite the get by Doug, even though the uncle viewed it as a steal and not a gift."

"Right, because it was." Jillian rushed forward, trying to prevent any more vehicle talk. "But why is he in Belgium with this totally useful car?"

"He's hiding there," Jay explained. "We're not sure why."

"So, and I just want to make sure I'm clear here"—Jillian held her hand in front of the map—"this is a scoreboard of crimes committed by our family, past and present. Like, this dot in Rhode Island is . . . yes." Jillian got a bit closer to test it and, yes, it was a touchscreen. She read the description. "Anika targeting Harry."

"A lovely man," Jay said, brimming with misplaced pride.

Patricia made a face. "Boring but easy to manipulate."

Jillian actually felt sorry for Harry. "How romantic."

"Bah!" Patricia stopped the conversation with her favorite nonword sound. "Romance is overrated. If you learn nothing else from me, learn that."

Jillian leaned against the bookcase, swirling the last of the champagne in her glass. "See, I thought the teaching was over because I thought we had an agreement. No more cons."

Dead silence.

Jillian tried again. "I went to prison and in return, the family went legitimate. Does any of this sound familiar?"

Jay glanced at Patricia before speaking again. "Technically, you requested that arrangement, but no one actually agreed to it. In writing."

"Interesting loophole." She should have known Jay would find one.

"They've learned," Patricia said without providing an antecedent or any explanation for the blank comment.

"Really? If law enforcement came in here they'd have a road map to everything." Jillian tapped on a flag and a small explanation came up under Anika's name. It went into some detail about a scam eleven months ago at an art gallery and changing out an exhibition for forgeries.

Patricia frowned. "Why would they come here?"

"Hence the need for the lock on the door," Jay said at the same time.

"Yeah, no one can break those." Jillian tried to ignore her

impending headache. "Patricia can crack safes. So can Astrid." Apparently Jay thought a keypad lock would be harder.

"Emma and I have special watches. One touch and the screen and all its information disappears. There's also a button in the top desk drawer." He demonstrated his handy watch button. Now the wall looked like a large, blank television monitor. "In case of a dire emergency, we can blow up the system so there is nothing to find. Only Emma knows where the backup is kept, though I'm sure she'll share that with you."

Emma, her baby sister. One of the main reasons Jillian willingly went to prison, made deals, and bathed in generational filth. She wanted her sibling to have a reset and her cousins to go legitimate. For Emma to find a different life. Instead, Jillian going to prison had plunged Emma even deeper into the muck.

Jillian had no idea how to fix that particular mess or the family's newfound love of spycraft, but she was sure threats about cutting off the money would help eventually.

"Now, this nonsense about you being in charge of everything," Jay said.

"Jayson. You know better." Patricia patted his arm. "Jillian only has the family's best interests at heart." As soon as she started what might be perceived as a loving gesture by anyone else, she stopped. "Now, where did you say your girlie got to?"

"Kitchen. With all the excitement she forgot to eat dinner."

"She lives here?" Jillian asked because she had no interest in sharing the house or stepping over her family's victims. The urge to call them all out right now—make an ugly but impressive splash—tugged at her.

"Calm down. No. We need to keep outsiders' access to the house to a minimum. You know that." Jay frowned as if to show his disappointment in having to give the droning explanation. "Izzy is in town visiting a sick friend. That's how we met. She lives in Boston. The party today was an informal way of introducing her to some of the people in the area and help her be comfortable with us as a couple."

"Basically, you're loosening her up while you check out her assets and prepare to travel back to Boston and steal them. Got it. So, what's the payoff here?" Jillian didn't bother to read the map or the spreadsheet. "Oil and gas?"

"Don't be so negative. My feelings are genuine, I assure you."

He sounded like a bad greeting card, and Jillian wasn't buying it. "Uh-huh."

"Her grandfather owned a bank. Her father parlayed that into a string of banks, which he sold to a financial giant." Jay whispered the name of the bank.

Jillian tried not to show a reaction. "Serious old money."

"Money is money. Who cares about the age of it? It all spends the same." Before anyone could respond to that, Patricia slipped her hand through Jay's arm and guided him to the door. "Go see to Izzy before she wanders around and causes trouble, hmm?"

She shoved him out of the room while he grumbled about needing answers. Jillian admired the skill, or she did until she became the sole focus of Patricia's attention.

"Yes?" Jillian waited, expecting a lecture about not threatening the family or withholding money. She didn't have a response prepared but hoped something would come to her before her little spark plug of an aunt went off.

"Hire a bodyguard."

Not at all what Jillian was expecting. "What?"

"Trust no one."

CHAPTER SIX

MOOREWOOD FAMILY RULE #26: *Stay connected to family. Force reconnection, if necessary.*

AFTER A FULL DAY OF GENE-POOL-RELATED BULLSHIT, JILLIAN was ready for bed, or at least for a few hours of uninterrupted alone time. She'd suffered through enough talking, whispering, and death stares from Anika for a lifetime.

Jillian hadn't told her kin all her plans for them, mostly because she wanted to string them along, see how much they would twist and bunch at the idea of having to wait, of not getting the immediate satisfaction they thrived on. Also because a tiny part of her had hoped they'd changed . . . a little . . . maybe. But that didn't happen. If anything, they'd dug deeper into the world of screwing people out of their stuff, proving she was the most naive person in the house despite the years away.

If history was any indication, the more anxious they became, the worse her life would be, which would give her the excuse she needed to cut them loose and not feel an ounce of guilt. But she planned to be ready.

"You're staring at the steps. Are you okay?"

The sound of Tenn's even voice stopped Jillian at the base of the staircase. She found the energy to smile as she turned to face him. "Exhausted by the constant lies and never-ending scheming of your blood relatives."

"*Our* relatives, but nice try." He laughed. "And I'm surprised you didn't have them evicted before you returned home."

She'd been tempted. But seeing their faces, making them admit what they did, had won out. "I'm rethinking all of my life choices right now."

"Spending time with my sisters will do that to a person." Technically, they were half-siblings, the kind of thing Tenn likely wouldn't have cared about except Astrid and Anika pointed it out whenever possible, as if to suggest not sharing their entire bloodline was a negative.

Full or half, they hovered, always *right there*, listening. Surrounding her. "They wouldn't leave me alone."

"While they didn't confide in me, because we're not that kind of siblings, I'm guessing they were trying to figure out if you were going to spike their running cons now or later."

"Is Astrid running a play right now?" Jillian had listened, trying to figure out what was up with Astrid and her *I missed you* routine, but dear cousin's skills had improved. She no longer got bored and flitted off after a few minutes of a con she didn't find worthy or fun, unable to maintain her focus.

Tenn shrugged. "Isn't she always? It's not as if she has another job outside of this family."

An excellent point that Jillian couldn't refute in any way. "How are you related to them and yet nothing like them?"

"Again, we both are." He stared at her for a second before continuing. "I'd credit my mother's superior genes, but she wasn't exactly innocent in Jay's activities. That's her word, by the way. *Activities*, as if Jay hangs out at the club because he actually has real friends there."

For the hundredth time, Jillian wondered how Tenn ever made it out of this household unscathed. She'd helped . . . a little. After watching Jay take turns ignoring his unwanted son some weeks and climbing all over him at other times, demanding he join the family business, Jillian had stepped in. Quietly and behind the scenes, but she'd made it clear the family trust would fund as many degrees as he wanted if it meant he stayed away and didn't become a full-time target for Jay's disappointment.

Jay had denied Tenn's parentage at first but then decided he liked the idea of a male heir to follow in his footsteps. An attractive, flirty second-in-command whose smile could make women drop their wallets even faster than their ball gowns.

Tenn, quiet, smart, bookish, and gay, didn't play along, thus setting off a lifetime of fireworks. But he flourished the minute he moved out of the house. A relocation he pulled off at sixteen thanks to his brilliance when he left for college two years early.

Now, just shy of twenty-seven, he'd snagged a job as an assistant professor of applied mathematics at Amherst College, which was just about the least Moorewood career possible. And Jillian loved that for him.

She blocked out the day and the annoyance that lay ahead and focused on Tenn because someone in this trainwreck of a family should. "What's been happening with you these days?"

They'd actually never been out of contact. He visited her in prison. They wrote to each other. She knew she could call him if she needed to talk. He was that guy. Dependable and caring. She'd fought for him when he was younger, trying to give him breathing room and independence. He grew up and returned the favor. When she needed him, he showed up.

"Actually, I did decide on a rental house in Amherst. Picked the two-bedroom I told you about. Just have to sign the papers." His smile fell and he took a step back as he watched her. "I know that look. Are you going to hug me?"

"Maybe." Man, she really wanted to. Pride overwhelmed her when she thought about all he'd achieved and how hard he'd fought to forge his own path.

"I'm not five."

"You act like your actual age matters to me."

The rustling of silk and the patter of footsteps cut off the rest of the conversation. "There you are!"

Jillian winced at the sound of Astrid's high-pitched voice. "Shit."

Astrid flew into the grand foyer from the left. Shot out of a room, unclear which, dress billowing behind her as if she had a permanent fan aimed at her body. Without losing a step, she draped herself over the banister, directly in front of Jillian.

The move blocked Jillian's speedy exit up the stairs.

"Where are you going?" Astrid's smile faltered a little when she focused on Tenn. "Oh, hi. I didn't know you were still here. I thought you went back to campus."

Jillian gave in to an eye roll. "He's a professor, not a student living in a dorm."

"And good evening to you, dear sister." Tenn almost bowed as he spoke.

The formal greeting made Jillian laugh. Only Astrid seemed to miss that Tenn was joking with her.

Astrid frowned at her brother before focusing on Jillian again. "You should be outside. Partying. The guests have left but we have champagne." Astrid looped her arm through Jillian's and toasted her with an imaginary glass. "We could get a little tipsy then chat and gossip like we used to."

Jillian wasn't clear what fantasy former relationship Astrid had created in her head. They'd never been close, and Jillian refused to be anything but completely sober around this crowd. "I'm used to a strict bedtime."

Astrid threw back her head and laughed.

Jillian half wondered if her cousin was practicing some bizarre new flirting technique. "Okay, yeah. I should go to bed."

Astrid squeezed her arm tighter. "Not yet."

Tenn sighed. "Sis, I think we should give Jillian a break. It's been a long day."

Astrid lifted her arm and glanced at her watch. "It's not late."

Jillian noticed the bracelet. The same one Izzy had been wearing earlier. "I see you helped yourself to some new jewelry."

Astrid's unnaturally bright smile dimmed a bit. "Huh?"

Jillian pointed at her cousin's wrist. "Jay will be upset you snagged Izzy's bracelet before he could."

"Oh, no." Astrid fingered the tiny diamonds. "This is mine."

"Right." Tenn nodded. "Totally believable."

"Return it tomorrow," Jillian said at the same time.

"Tenn's right. You need rest." Astrid gave Jillian a quick hug. "I'll see you in the morning."

Tenn and Jillian watched her go, breezing out as strangely as she'd blown in. Jillian was the first to state the obvious. "Izzy's never going to see that bracelet again."

"Not a chance."

The stealing almost covered up the other notable part of that unhinged little visit. But Jillian could admit that she might be a bit paranoid where fellow Moorewoods were concerned. It had been years since they'd interacted. Maybe she saw schemes where none existed. "Her greeting was weird, right?"

Tenn continued to stare in the direction of where Astrid

ran off. "How can you tell weird from *not* weird where Astrid is concerned?"

Some things never changed. He was still the smartest person she knew. "Good point."

"They're jumpy. All of them, and more than usual." Tenn looked at her again. "Are you still planning to banish anyone who refuses to toe the line? Your line."

"Is that your way of saying you disagree with my plan?"

"I totally support you but trying to change them could backfire on you."

Jillian thought about the last three years. "Already did, but this time I'm smarter."

CHAPTER SEVEN

MOOREWOOD FAMILY RULE #10: *Listen to your elders . . . unless they're breaking another rule.*

A FEW HOURS LATER, JILLIAN FELL ACROSS THE DOUBLE BED she'd slept in as a teenager. The fluffy comforter puffed around her, making a soft nest. She thought about everything that had happened during the long day and the fifteen wardrobe changes she'd survived before finding the right revenge outfit to wear for her big *I'm home* reveal.

She'd been so tightly wound tonight, so desperate to hold in her simmering emotions and deliver a killing blow to the people who deserved it. She'd been running on adrenaline and little else. That energy sputtered to a stall now and her muscles ached when she moved even an inch.

She opened her eyes and stared at the ceiling. A quick scan of the room showed nothing had changed from the last time she'd slept here. It had always been a no-frills, too-grown-up space, but it had been hers. The medium blue walls that teenage her believed would help her sleep. The antique roll-top desk her mom passed down from her great-grandfather. The thick drapes that shut out the morning sunlight from the floor-to-ceiling windows because she used to fight off draining migraines.

The flashy wealth of the house had never been a comfortable fit for her. She'd moved back home after college at her mother's request to straighten out the business. Her mom also knew she had cancer at that point, but she kept that a secret for a long time, until the wreckage the treatments caused forced her to confess.

A knock on the door had her lifting her head. "Come in," she said, assuming Tenn had stopped to check on her. No one else was really talking to her at the moment.

The door opened and Kelby McAllister stepped inside. His unreadable expression didn't give anything away. "Is Anika in here? I thought I saw her open your door."

"Anika?"

"I swear I saw her. Maybe she just knocked on the door?"

"Not while I was in here." Jillian would remember an unwanted visit.

"Let me go find—"

"Wait." *Unwanted visit.* That was the answer. Jillian jack-knifed into a sitting position with a finger covering her lips. "I know what this is."

They wouldn't . . . would they? Who was she kidding? Of course they would. It would certainly explain Astrid's stair-blocking maneuver earlier. They were working together, and Astrid put on a show to give Anika time.

Kelby frowned. "Uh, Jillian?"

She ignored his confused tone and jumped off the bed, landing on legs that barely held her. With a newfound determination, she wandered around the room, tracing her fingertips under every edge of furniture and up and around every lamp. She listened for buzzing but couldn't pick up a sound. Then she found it. A small square at the back of the base of the light by her bed.

She held up the listening device and watched Kelby's eyes grow wide.

"Try harder, losers," she yelled directly into the bug before smashing it into pieces with the clock on her nightstand. "There."

"A listening device. How did you know?"

The bigger question was why she'd been naive and not automatically assumed. "Spying on each other is an old Moorewood trick. Back when Jay realized Mom was working on Dad to give up a life of thievery, Jay resorted to spying to listen in." Jillian glanced around the room wondering if she'd missed one . . . or ten. "I found one in my office right before the FBI showed up. Jay plants the bugs when he gets nervous about being out of the loop. I'm sure he taught the girls the same trick."

"You've only been home for a few hours."

As if time mattered to panicking Moorewoods. "Not knowing how I'm going to screw them on the money is bound to bring out a lot of old tricks."

"I guess nothing should surprise me with this crew." Kelby swore under his breath. "Well, welcome home."

Kelby, the family's business manager. The same financial genius hired by Jillian's mom to help the family go legitimate and to guide Jillian in making it happen. Back when he stepped in he knew only that he'd have to untangle a mess. He had no idea about the scamming or the full extent of the damage. Then he met the family.

He had to train Jillian, fight off Jay's worst nature, say no to her father's unreasonable demands for more money, shift the family's financial focus into real investments, and ignore the lack of a real paper trail for some assets. He performed all those tasks, and a few others, while various Moorewood relatives tried to go around him.

He had the world's most thankless job.

"You forgot to fill me in on everything during our prison visits. I asked you if they were still pulling cons and I believe you said . . . now that I think about it, you ignored me." She silently congratulated him on that maneuver.

"If I had told you the family was back to their full-time grifting you would have broken out of prison and killed them."

She wasn't in the mood for common sense. "It would have been worth it."

"Wrong," he said in a firm dad voice. "This way you got

out and had at least a few days to cool off before seeing them in action again."

He would have made a great dad. Jillian had discovered his ability to protect and guide almost immediately. The traits formed the backbone of who he was.

He'd admitted to Jillian recently that he'd almost walked a bunch of times over the years, including the first day. He'd been absolutely clear he'd sell them all out in a second because he had no intention of ever going to prison. But his connection to her mom convinced him to stay.

Mom proved to be his biggest weakness. The reason he put up with everything else. He'd never said it out loud, but he loved her. Seemingly unspoken and unrequited, and Jillian had never gotten up the nerve to directly ask because *did you sleep with my mom* doesn't just roll off the tongue in casual lunchtime conversation.

Kelby had been around for almost a decade. Solid, dependable, and not a blood relative, which Jay brought up whenever possible. But no one messed with Kelby because he knew all the family's secrets. He was collegiate basketball tall. Fiftysomething now with hair graying at the temples, but he'd played at North Carolina once. A black man who pivoted from sports to finance. A soft Southern accent still floated through his voice.

Since he'd picked Jillian up from prison a few days ago, her presence in town was not exactly a surprise to him. Years ago, he fought her, trying to get her to shift the blame to where it deserved to be before she went to prison. During her last month there he begged her to sell the house and move away. Start over.

Let it go. Those were his actual words.

Not a chance.

"We missed you at the party." She could have used the support.

"I heard Jay intended to show off a new girlfriend, and that can only mean one thing—a new target has been acquired. Some days distance is the only way I refrain from punching him."

"Wise. Just know that there's a high likelihood *I'll* punch him at some point."

"I worry he'll strike first." Kelby pointed at the smashed pieces on the nightstand. "They're already deploying listening devices. His side of the family is unpredictable and you're threatening what matters to them. The money."

"Don't care." She shrugged even though she felt anything but nonchalant. "Blame prison."

"I blame your father."

"Which is why we get along because I blame him for almost every crappy thing that's ever happened, too." His death didn't absolve him of the wave of destruction he'd crashed over their family.

The man never grew up. Never took responsibility. He got married and didn't have to be *that* person anymore. He could have settled down, taken a job, or even lived off Mom's money, been a father. But no. The pull of the next big scam never let go of him.

His duplicity slowly killed her mother. She loved him and paid for that weakness over and over. That's how Jillian saw it. He lied to her mom from the start. Played on her belief in *until death do us part* and extinguished the spark inside her. Stole her dreams and contentment. He let her die.

Clive Moorewood never deserved his wife, his children, or the life he had. When faced with the chance to do the right thing, to step up when the FBI came knocking and take responsibility, he fell on the floor—literally and figuratively—and looked to Jillian to fix everything.

Her rubbery legs forced her to lean against the edge of the mattress again. "Don't ask me to be nice to them."

Kelby snorted as he sat down next to her. "I'm pretty much done protecting Moorewoods. Emma is a worry, but I'm hopeful she jumped into the business of family administration and started doing Jay's bidding only because you weren't here. Now, she can jump back out."

"I'll drag her out." By the hair during a full-on tantrum, if necessary. The idea that Emma took orders from Jay, or worse, willingly helped him, sent Jillian's enthusiasm for revenge spiking.

"That brings me to my current worry," Kelby said. "You."

"Me?" Defensiveness jolted through her. "I'm the most dependable member of the entire family. I mean, did you hear that Doug is in Belgium? He's an impulsive mess. He'll blow a million dollars on chocolate."

"We're talking about your stability, which is questionable at the moment."

"Oh, come on." She was not the problem. She was fine. A felon, but fine.

"This taunting you're doing to Jay's side of the family is dangerous. It's not like you to invite trouble." Kelby shifted, his body length and broad shoulders taking up most of the room on the edge of the mattress. "I'm going to ask you to listen to me one last time and end it now. Tell them the truth so they know they are out of options."

"Last time? Where are you going?" She could not handle more retirement talk from him. She'd been out only a week and seeing Astrid and Anika for a few hours made her head pound. Trying to wrestle back control of everything from their greedy little manicured hands—even though it was all hers—might put her in a coma.

He stared at her. "I'm serious, Jillian."

So was she.

He put his hands on his lap. Rubbed his thumb along the inside of his other palm. "If you're going to threaten their money supply—"

"I already did, I just didn't tell them how yet."

He sighed at her again. "If you're really going to do this, you need protection."

She'd spent a lot of time practicing kickboxing in her white-collar prison, but that was more about a release from boredom than survival. "You mean like a gun? I don't think I can—"

"Of course not." Kelby gave her the same disgruntled look he used whenever he thought she was daydreaming and not listening to him. "A bodyguard."

That didn't . . . no. "You're the second person to suggest that today."

"Because your aunt and I have already discussed this and agreed." His smile was infectious. "Patricia came over to my house using a cane and looking all worried. When I didn't immediately jump up and agree with her, she lifted the cane and threatened to smack me with it."

Jay might dislike Kelby, but Aunt Patricia loved him. Like, tried to baby him and feed him. He towered over her, but she loved to boss him around . . . and he tolerated it. He once said he viewed Aunt Patricia as a pseudo grandmother. A vicious, conniving, cheese-stick-eating grandmother.

"She'll outlive all of us," Jillian said and meant it.

"No doubt." He shot her one of those *nice try* looks he did so well. "But don't ignore my point. "You're getting a bodyguard."

She bit back the automatic no. It had been a long time since anyone gave a crap about her or her safety. Mom used to hold that role. Losing her had killed any thought Jillian had of anyone genuinely caring about her well-being as separate from her ability to manage and hand out money. She should have known Kelby would step up, all gruff and insistent.

Patricia? Jillian didn't know her angle. It would be interesting when that became clear. So, she gave in. Capitulated without a fight. She treated him to a dramatic exhale. "Okay."

He blinked. "Really?"

It made her grumbly to concede and now he was making

her say it more than once. "Yes. If you want me to have a bodyguard, I'll find one."

"No need. I have one for you."

"Of course you do." She pretended to look around the room. "Is he hiding in the room right now?"

"He'll be here tomorrow morning." He stood up but didn't move away from the bed. "I'm happy you're back."

"You still living next door?"

Kelby smiled. "Being your neighbor annoys the shit out of Jay, so yes."

When Mom died she left the strip of land next to the Moorewood estate—prime oceanfront property—to Kelby. Jillian liked to think it was Mom's way of telling Kelby she loved him and was sorry they could never be together.

Jay, of course, kicked up an unholy fuss. He tried to fight the transfer. He really was the most consistent pain in the ass ever. Unfortunately for him, Mom had tied up the property and a chunk of money and put it in Kelby's hands, out of Jay's reach.

Jillian waited until Kelby was almost at the door. "I'm not going to rescue them again. Jay and his brood, I mean." She refused to be swayed or listen to reason. Guilt pricked at her, but she didn't let it penetrate her hard outer shell. The one she built brick by painful brick in prison. "They had their chance to honor their deal, and they didn't."

Now it was her turn to get even.

Kelby nodded. "Then let the battle begin."

CHAPTER EIGHT

MOOREWOOD FAMILY RULE #9: *Take every opportunity to size up your target.*

"EXCUSE ME, BUT—"

Jillian was too busy screaming at the intrusion and jumping out of her fluffy new slippers to immediately answer.

A woman should be able to come out of a bathroom and step into her bedroom—with a closed door—and not be greeted by guests. That was the civilized version of the thoughts running through Jillian's head. The real-time screeching version went more like *What the hell is wrong with you?*

She inhaled, trying to tamp down the temptation to throw Jay's new girlfriend out the second-floor window. Jillian's heart hammered in her chest. Her fingers refused to unclench from where they'd balled her robe in her fist at her throat.

"What are you doing in here?" Jillian could hear the shake in her voice.

Izzy let out a little *oh*. "I didn't mean to scare you."

Every part of Jillian remained wound tight, but she forced words out somehow. "Then why are you in my room uninvited at eight in the morning?"

Blame prison or maybe it was just the expectation of common courtesy, but Jillian coveted privacy. She'd survived years of keeping her back to walls, being careful, and not letting her guard down for a second. She'd slept in small sprints and dreamed of getting out and savoring some alone time.

All of that and she'd had it easy. She'd done her time in a minimum-security federal prison camp. The nickname Camp Cupcake didn't fit, but she knew she'd been lucky even as she'd clawed through a suffocating blanket of despair and loneliness, panic and anger. She could wander the grounds during certain hours, but every advantage came with rules and violating those cost her.

She'd met women inside who had run into bad luck or had limited choices or, like her, screwed up. Some of the crimes were horrible, desperate. Judging didn't help her one bit in there, and after a while the innate tendency to make those distinctions stopped.

To get through, to survive, many women shared their skills and taught classes in subjects from knitting to yoga. But it was still prison. A scary lockdown where many women needed treatment and support. Calling a cellblock a cottage didn't fix those issues.

Izzy had the good sense to wince at the scolding. "I wasn't thinking."

Obviously. "Oh, really?"

"I should have knocked."

"Or you could have stayed out of my room completely." Jillian relaxed her circulation-strangling hold on the robe but didn't totally let go of the terry cloth material.

"Yesterday got a little convoluted, what with your arrival. Jay invited me over today. I think he wanted to make sure I was okay since our little party got . . . well, I didn't mean to startle you." She sighed. "I should go."

Too damn late now. "What did you come in here for, Izzy? This room, specifically."

"Just to make sure you knew it was time for breakfast." Izzy bit on her lower lip. "Or it will be. Soon."

Nah, not buying it. This felt like snooping. Possibly a *what does a former prisoner own* thing. Not clear. "I live here, Izzy."

"Yes, of course." The older woman started fidgeting. Shifting her weight around and not quite meeting Jillian's gaze.

Still not buying it. Jillian did a quick visual inventory of the room. Someone, likely Astrid or Anika, had cleared out most of her personal possessions. Jillian had brought exactly one bag home with her. Kelby had bought some clothes for her and all of those looked to be hanging in the closet where he put them. But something was off.

Jillian kept talking because it gave her an opportunity to watch and assess Izzy. "We tend to fend for ourselves around here. The kitchen is always open and—"

"No." Izzy winced. "Excuse me for interrupting, but Jay

said there were set mealtimes because that level of precision made service easier on the staff."

What staff? They'd always had a cook and a housekeeper. An older couple who asked to stay on when Jillian's mother took over the estate from her parents. Two no-nonsense, we-don't-want-to-know-what-goes-on-here people who lived in a small condo over on Mary Street that they bought with the money Mom left them.

Fran and Stan, names that always made Jillian smile . . . but not this morning. The idea that Jay may have taken advantage of them made her temperature spike. They'd given years of loyal service. They didn't need Jay's mess.

"Exactly two people work here." Jillian thought about the grounds and the pool. "Well, and the landscaping and pool guys come through, but—"

Izzy snorted. "Don't be ridiculous."

"Excuse me?" Jillian made sure to use her best *what the fuck* tone when she asked the question.

Izzy waved a hand in front of her face. "Please forgive me for just blurting out like that, but your uncle clearly has an appropriate staff. This house is far too grand to piecemeal the work it must require to keep it pristine."

Jillian tried to imagine Jay paying people to do anything for him . . . nope. "Uh-huh."

Izzy's gestures seemed to become more exaggerated the more excited she was about a topic. She was practically dancing now. "But I must say, the staff does an impressive job of staying out of sight. I've never seen any of them."

Because they didn't exist. They were part of Jay's fake story about owning the house, running it, and supervising people. He did none of that. Kelby took care of paying Fran and Stan. Jillian knew because Kelby had provided her with financial status reports during the months she was gone.

"The staff are very well trained, which isn't a surprise. Jay clearly has a knack for handling business affairs," Izzy continued.

If she said *staff* one more time Jillian was going to lose it.

Jay sure knew how to pick them. The woman sounded like quite the humanitarian. And that jewelry. Today she wore diamonds. A blingy diamond ring that practically begged to be stolen and would be seen as a challenge by at least three people in the house.

Diamond bracelet. Diamond studs. Diamond-studded watch. Apparently she thought she was having breakfast with the queen.

"Who do you think owns this house?" Jillian asked, knowing Izzy wouldn't provide the right answer. Why should she be different from anyone else on the property?

Izzy looked seriously confused. "Jayson, of course."

Uncle Jay was not one to tell a small tale, and this appeared to be no exception. Jillian planned to make his life miserable, so why not start now. "Actually—"

"Izzy, dear." Jay swooped in from the hallway and wrapped an arm around Izzy's waist. "I've been looking for you."

By skulking around, sneaking, and listening in. "Were you eavesdropping, Uncle Jay?"

He chuckled in that uncomfortable way people did when a lying response got stuck in their brain and refused to pop out. "Of course not."

So, yes.

He wore khakis and a navy blazer. The crisp white shirt underneath matched his perfect teeth.

"We were talking about the house." Jillian dropped the comment knowing Jay wouldn't show an outward reaction but on the inside he'd be scrambling.

More laughter from Jay. "Real estate. How incredibly boring."

"Not for you," Izzy said. "You're an expert."

That explained it. This was some form of Jay's old favorite, the millionaire-property-developer scam. This scheme fed Jay's ego. In it, he basically built most of the buildings in New England but was too embarrassed to talk about his amazing accomplishments.

Jillian needed caffeine to survive this conversation.

"I am a little confused. See, Jillian suggested . . ." Izzy frowned. "Actually, what were you suggesting about the estate, Jillian?"

Before she could answer, Jay jumped in. He leaned down with his head resting against Izzy's, half whispering to her. "Honey, this is Jillian's first morning home in more than three years. She's had a terrible experience. I'm sure she's feeling . . . things."

"Oh, I definitely am." Jillian was two seconds away from describing exactly how she felt.

"My goodness." Izzy let out what sounded like a very practiced gasp. "I'm not being considerate at all. You need time to refocus and relax." Izzy's saccharine smile slipped a bit. "You know, to get your priorities straight."

She was talking slowly, as if she had to emphasize each word in order for Jillian to understand them.

Well, wasn't that annoying.

Jay must have picked up on the tension or saw Jillian winding up because his eyes widened ever so slightly. "We unfortunately can't stay. We have a reservation at the club."

The club in this case being his private supper club that, lucky for him, also served breakfast. The Marksman was an invitation-only, old-school, rich-people institution. So, of course, Jay was a member.

"Of course." Izzy stepped away from Jay and showed off her long black sheath and matching blue-and-black jacket. "Should I change? Is this too informal?"

Jillian guessed the outfit cost at least a thousand dollars and Izzy referred to it like most people did to yoga pants.

"You look divine, as always." Jay actually leaned down and kissed Izzy's hand.

Jillian managed not to make a gagging sound. That had been her go-to move as a kid . . . and her mother had not approved.

"Let me find my purse." Izzy smiled, then turned and walked down the hallway.

Jillian watched the other woman go. She couldn't help but

feel Izzy was making this scam too easy on Jay. She seemed to lap up every lying word. "You have her fooled."

Jay leaned in and whispered, "Do not blow this."

They'd finally arrived at the threat portion of the family welcome home. Jillian issued one of her own. "I thoroughly intend to. End it now."

"Jillian, really." He sent her a dismissive look. "You know how these things work."

"*Did* work. No more scams. Fix your mess or I will."

"How dare—"

"You've been warned."

CHAPTER NINE

MOOREWOOD FAMILY RULE #22: *Hire outside help sparingly and only after securing their loyalty.*

BREAKFAST. HER FAVORITE MEAL . . . EVERY DAY BUT TODAY.
Jillian dreaded going downstairs and being greeted by a chorus of whining Moorewoods. Dreaded having to be on her game and ready to defend whatever preposterous thing the twins said before she had a chance to recover from Izzy's visit or down even one cup of coffee.

Basically, she dreaded seeing anyone biologically related to her. So, maybe it wasn't that unusual a day after all.

She threw on a light and flowy dress. Blue with small white flowers. Pretty, but not her usual style. One of the items Kelby had bought her until she could shop or find clothes or steal some from her sister. The dress had the dual positives of being clean and matching her white sneakers, so it won the day.

She barely made it into the hall before she saw Kelby coming up the stairs and heading right for her. "Did they already kill each other over orange juice?" she asked. "And note the hopeful tone of my voice before you answer no."

He snorted. "As if your family members would limit themselves to juice with breakfast."

"Good point." She shut the bedroom door and eyed him up, trying to assess what damage had been done before nine in the morning. "What's going on?"

"Jay and his newest left for the club." Kelby made a strangled sound.

"You can't grift if you don't pretend to be rich." That wasn't a family rule but it could be.

Kelby shook his head. "Jay refuses to change."

"Oh, he'll change."

"On a different topic, the female members of the family have assembled in the dining room." Kelby winced. "All but your sister."

"Is she with Greg, because . . ." *Ugh.*

What to say next? That guy. Them. The thing she did. The threat he made. There was a lot to untangle.

Kelby sighed. "I believe she is, yes. Would you like me to shoot him for you?"

"Is that a real question? Because yes."

He sighed at her again, the same way he'd been doing for years. Beating her into submission with disappointed exhales. "Emma is an adult, so maybe you should let her make her own dating decisions."

Mistakes. He meant mistakes. And Jillian refused to even entertain the word *dating*. "I don't care for that answer."

"You could tell Emma the truth about why you don't want Gregory near her, or you, or the property." Kelby leaned in with a finger behind his ear. "No? Didn't think so."

He was the only person Jillian completely trusted with her secrets and this was a big one. "I hate that guy."

"I'm aware. I believe he's aware." Before she could launch into a list of Greg's failings, Kelby moved on. "Since he won't be at the table, we can find another subject."

She let Kelby verbally pivot because she didn't have the bandwidth this morning to take on a new project like *How to Destroy Gregory Alexander Paul in Two Days*. That planning would need to wait until she had caffeine and screamed at a few assorted relatives first.

"Your bodyguard is here," Kelby said.

She thought back to last night and groaned. "That was a joke."

"It was a promise and, unlike some members of the family, you honor yours."

The slick move impressed her. Only Kelby and her mother had ever held the power of guilt over her. Still, she glared at him to let him know she didn't like the trick. "Look at you bringing out the heavy artillery."

He shrugged. "You learn some things by hanging around Moorewoods."

She needed him to stay and keep her from smothering one of those beloved family members with an expensive silk pillow or throwing one down the winding staircase. Both dramatic solutions sounded good in her head, but she wasn't looking to head back to prison, so the blood relatives were safe. For now . . . "Fine. You win."

"I won yesterday."

He was the only person in this house who could go head-to-head against her in a verbal battle and potentially win. "Where is this muscle man of yours hiding?"

Kelby motioned for her to walk down the hallway with him. "He's not the hiding type."

"Is he the type who will help me bury a body? Because I might need that." She let out a little hum as she mentally ran through what that plan would look like. "Hypothetically, of course."

Kelby pinned her with the same side-eye her mother had perfected. A testament to how much time Mom and Kelby had spent together . . . though it hadn't been enough to save her. "I know you're kidding, Jillian."

Well, she was *mostly* kidding.

He cleared his throat. "And yes. Actually, he probably would."

She stumbled to a halt at the top of the stairs as she tried to remember what he was responding to, then she did. The burying thing. "Wait . . . really?"

Now he had her attention. Her family liked to pretend they were smart, educated, wealthy, and so entertaining. They barely cleared the bar for tolerable, but this bodyguard guy sounded like he really could be interesting.

Kelby kept walking, his tall frame marching down the steps in front of her as he carried on the conversation. "He is not going to kill anyone for you."

Well, that was disappointing.

Kelby made a sharp right turn at the bottom of the staircase, avoiding the dining room and opening the door to the library. She hadn't spent enough time in there yet. Last night's scare-the-family tactics had drained her. She'd expected to feel invigorated and ready to burn through their nonsense only to be left with an ever-increasing pile of anger and the faint whiff of sadness.

Now, she followed Kelby inside the dark-paneled room and shut the door behind them. For a second, she let her gaze wander over the rows of books she'd collected and stored here among the dusty, barely ever opened ones that came with the house. Nonfiction. Her mysteries and romance. She loved getting lost in the pages, dreaming of being in any family other than the one her parents insisted she'd been born into. A fact she still disputed.

An oversized antique desk supposedly passed down from her father's father and smuggled over in pieces from Austria— or whatever ridiculous family lore her father invented—sat in the middle of the room. There was nothing on the desktop but a fancy chandelier dangled over it.

All she saw was the big dude sitting behind it.

She wouldn't describe him as handsome because that seemed unfair to handsome people. But compelling. He had a gruff, could-wrestle-a-bear-and-win look about him. A scowling mass of muscles. Black pants. Black hair and an expression that bordered on menacing. Most people would see that angular face and do a double take and then, maybe . . . probably, run.

He looked even less excited about being in the house than she was. She had no idea how that was possible.

Kelby took a step forward and gestured toward their guest. "Jillian, this is Beck Romer."

Good Lord, no. "Is that your actual name?"

He stood up. All six-foot, crap-he's-tall of him. "Beckett Gabriel Romer, but Beck is fine."

He sounded sure, so it must be real. But she wasn't quite ready to let the topic go. "That name is a lot."

He snorted. "No kidding."

A few short sentences and he didn't break into a smile during any of them. She wasn't convinced he could. But, to his credit, he didn't go into jerk mode either. Between the wow-he's-big gawking she couldn't seem to stop and her poking at his name, she probably deserved moodiness and he'd refrained, so they were off to a decent start.

"How do you two know each other?" She pointed between Kelby and this Beck guy.

"I would joke and say prison, but that might be a sensitive subject for you," Beck said without missing a beat.

She glared at Kelby to let him know what she thought about that knowledge imbalance. "Sounds like Kelby has been chatty."

"I investigated you," Beck said as if it were a perfectly normal thing to say to someone.

A voice in her head started screaming *what the hell* because Beck's honest response suggested Kelby's bodyguard plan had been in the works for longer than one night. She hated that, too. "It seems unfair I can't say the same thing to you."

"For the record, the prison sentence doesn't matter to me."

That grabbed her attention. Everyone else in the house cared. The FBI had sure cared. Some folks at the police station likely still cared. She even cared a little. "It doesn't make you curious that I've been incarcerated?"

"No."

He sounded sincere, or as sincere as someone with a voice that deep could. Which led to her most pressing question. "Have you been in prison?"

"No."

Huh. She thought for sure they'd have that in common. He looked like a guy who attracted trouble. "Is that because you've never committed a crime or because you've never been caught?"

Kelby let out a long, loud exhale. "Jillian."

Beck stayed quiet.

She liked a guy who didn't flinch.

"Yeah, you'll be fine." She shifted and started to leave but turned back to face him again when a rule—a major one—popped into her head. "One thing, Beck."

"I doubt there will be only *one thing* where you're concerned but go ahead."

The guy had a back-talk problem they'd need to discuss, but he wasn't dumb. She liked smart people. Not necessarily book-smart-only people because they tended to be useless in real life. No, she liked savvy. Wise. People who knew how to fight back if you screwed them.

"You answer to me and only me." When Beck glanced at Kelby she made a *nuh-uh* sound. "Me, not him."

"It might be good for you to have backup," Kelby said.

She never broke eye contact with Beck as she answered Kelby. She needed the big guy to get this point. "You're too nice for what's about to happen. Beck here, I'm guessing, isn't."

Beck frowned. "Thank you?"

"Since when am I the nice one?" Kelby asked.

"One question." Beck's deep voice broke through the relative quiet of the room. "Who's paying me?"

A practical man. Jillian liked that, too. "Me."

Beck nodded. "Then you're the boss."

Yeah, they'd do fine together. "We should have breakfast."

Beck shrugged, looking confused yet somehow still like he could punch through a wall without trying very hard. "Sounds boring but not dangerous."

"Oh, you poor deluded man." She motioned for the new guy to follow her out the door and into the great unknown. "You'll see."

CHAPTER TEN

MOOREWOOD FAMILY RULE #7: *Meals are a time to discuss family business. Plan accordingly.*

THEY WOULD STRAIGHTEN THINGS OUT THIS MORNING. ANIKA mentally repeated that phrase for the four hundredth time and was no closer to believing it now than she had been in the shower an hour ago.

She said it out loud only once. To Harry last night. He believed her story about *shading the truth* to protect Jillian's privacy and reputation. He vowed his support. He even squawked about disavowing his inheritance if his mother got upset about Jillian's *pedigree*. Yeah, he used that word.

The whole discussion made Anika wonder if he should ask for a refund for that fancy Harvard education of his because *wow*. One did not walk away from a quarter of a billion dollars. She certainly didn't plan on giving up one nickel of Harry's money without a fight.

Not that the climb into his family's good graces—
something she hadn't quite achieved even before Jillian blew
into town—would be easy. She guessed that at this very
minute his mother and aunt were huddled together under
the gaudy dining room chandelier with an investigator and a
feral pack of lawyers, trying to figure out how to ban Harry
from dating her.

Anika assumed so because when she met the woman who
would one day be her mother-in-law, whether she liked it or
not, the older woman, weighed down by diamonds and an
overinflated ego, mumbled, *This is not going to happen.*

Harry didn't get it yet. He didn't understand the measures
his family would use to remove her from his life if they grew
too close, but she did. Hatchet. Flamethrower. Lies. Tricks.
They'd pummel poor Harry until he cracked. She just had to
keep him on the line, which meant outmaneuvering Jillian.

It sounded like her overzealous father overplayed his hand
while Jillian was in prison. He'd promised to syphon off as
many assets as possible while Jillian was away, and put them
out of her control and Kelby's reach. Neither of which had
happened and Anika still didn't understand why.

That was one of the many problems with having a con
man for a father. The conning never stopped. He used fake
charm to get what he wanted, even with family. When that
failed, he lied and cheated, two things he excelled at.

She'd long ago stopped thinking about him as a parent, or as
being responsible, or as someone who would step in and save
her. She'd separated from him in her mind. To her, he was Jay,

the man her mother married. The man *a lot* of women married. Her mom retired to St. John years ago after Jay bought her a fancy villa. The distance kept her far away from Jay . . . and equally distant from anything resembling motherhood.

Anika wanted more, or at least different. Harry offered her an out from under the nasty pile of tainted Moorewood family garbage. She vowed to be a good wife to him . . . once she figured out what that meant.

But before she went to find Harry today, she had to survive breakfast. Jillian picked that moment to walk into the breakfast room. The man with her stopped a few steps inside the doorway. A man Anika had never seen before. Tall, bulky with a bit of a lopsided nose that Anika guessed came from being punched one too many times.

The overall effect was tough to describe. Not attractive, certainly not traditionally so. He'd probably look ridiculous in a suit, but she couldn't stop staring. There was something about him that commanded attention.

Ugly Hot. That's the description that swept through Anika's head and it fit.

"Good morning," Jillian said in a voice that sounded far too happy for the sullen mood of the room.

She carried her coffee mug to the table and pulled out a chair but didn't sit down. She nodded to Ugly Hot to stand next to her. Together they formed a solid wall between Anika and Astrid on one side of the table and the door to the hall on the other.

Anika had hoped to get a clearer picture of whatever annoying drivel Jillian had planned now that she'd reappeared. Those thoughts withered and died when the unknown guy showed up. *No more arguing in front of company.* That was Jay's last order before shuffling off to breakfast with Izzy.

Anika was about to say something smug when Aunt Patricia bounded into the room. Her red cheeks and quick stride suggested fury.

Great.

Patricia slipped around Jillian and slammed something on the table. "Who did it?"

Ugly Hot leaned in and took a closer look. "Is that string cheese?" He whispered the question to Jillian, but his voice carried. He wasn't the type who could sneak.

"Explain." Patricia made the demand, abandoning all pretense of being infirm today.

Astrid groaned.

The dude with Jillian looked totally confused.

No one owned up to the cheese theft.

Patricia picked up the opened plastic bag containing the individually wrapped sticks. "This package was brand-new and now two are gone, which means someone put their dirty fingers on my cheese without permission."

"And good morning to you," Jillian said into the quiet room.

Patricia glanced around and looked at Jillian . . . then at Ugly Hot. Patricia's expression immediately morphed from outraged accuser to sweet grandmother in two seconds. How that woman could pull off sweet was a mystery. She steamrolled over anyone in her way and could wrestle property away from even the most savvy businessman.

"Jillian, dear." Patricia took Jillian's hand in hers. "I thought you'd sleep in."

"I've lost the ability to sleep."

"It will get better." Patricia patted Jillian's hand this time before sneaking another peek at Ugly Hot. "Who is this?"

Astrid snorted, which earned her a quick glare from Patricia that carried a hint of *shut up now* before her expression reverted to concerned grandmother status.

"Someone stole your cheese?" he asked.

Patricia waved her hand in the air. "No worries, dear. I'm not blaming you."

"Consider yourself lucky. Her cheese sticks are sacred," Jillian explained. "My guess is Izzy did it when she was rummaging around in the kitchen last night. She probably doesn't know the cheese stick rule."

Patricia's fake smile slipped. "That woman is not worth the effort."

"The good news is Dad insists he's not going to marry her," Astrid said.

Anika didn't buy that for a second. "But he's so good at marrying."

Ugly Hot glanced at Jillian. "Is breakfast always like this?"

She smiled up at him. "There's usually more yelling and grumbling, so this is a good day."

Well, wasn't this intimate and totally disconcerting. Jillian with a man. Some unknown man. Jillian *who had been in prison until ten seconds ago* had a guy. A thought hit Anika—maybe he was a prison guard.

But Astrid—all nervous and fidgety this morning—refused to wait for any sort of proper greeting. "Aunt Patricia asked, now I'll try. Who are you?"

Ugly Hot stared at her but didn't respond.

As standoffs went, this one was hard to take seriously. Astrid, with her pressed light pink linen dress, looked like she'd stepped out of a country club dining room to take a call. Ugly Hot was all tall, dark, and I-could-kick-your-head-in.

The flat line of Jillian's mouth and the way her one eyebrow lifted said it all. This was not going to be a good conversation. Anika didn't need the fancy college education she pretended to have to understand that.

Jillian traced her finger around the top of her mug. She didn't count out loud, but a silent countdown vibrated through the room.

The quiet must have gotten through because Astrid rushed to clean up her mess. "I didn't mean to sound cold, but there are things going on at the house right now." Astrid tiptoed through her words. "We need to talk about those things, though I'm sure you'd prefer to pick up your life and . . . do whatever with this man."

"Maybe stop talking," Anika said.

Anika thought she should win an award for patience right now. She needed to be with Harry. That was the thing about jobs based on romance. You couldn't let up for a second. If you looked the other way for too long—boom!—some other bitch moved in. Yet here she was, showing infinite control, not causing trouble. Toeing the line at breakfast because Jay wanted her to be here *just in case*.

She really hated this family.

Kelby picked that moment to slip into the room. He didn't sneak because he *never* snuck. He grabbed a coffee and some fruit and sat at the far end of the table, away from the fray.

Aunt Patricia dug out one of her cheese sticks and peeled the plastic off. "Well?"

"He traveled from Finland to Belgium. I have no idea when or why," Kelby said between sips of coffee. "Probably switched countries for a few days of drinking."

"Doug . . ." Jillian's voice trailed off, then her eyes widened. "He's moving around? How?"

There was only one answer as far as Anika was concerned. "Car money."

"Oh, no." Astrid groaned. "He sold that beautiful car?"

Jillian shook her head. "He needs to stay in one place. He's—"

"Asking for it." Anika rarely agreed with Jillian, but yes. Doug needed to get on a boat to nowhere and stay on it. Take a new name. Catch fish or whatever would be the best cover. Not flash money around and attract attention.

Ugly Hot cleared his throat. "Is this Doug guy wearing a tracker or something?"

"Yes." Kelby, Patricia, and Anika all answered at the same time.

"A special watch," Astrid explained.

All respect to Patricia, but her grandson was a huge problem. If you needed someone to deal with logistics and set up the framework of a job—yes, use Doug. He had the skills and the beautiful face needed to pull off an elaborate heist, but he was lazy when it came to picking targets.

It's not like this was even hard. Don't steal from crime families. Don't steal from people who could kill and dismember you and still be on time for dinner. And never, ever borrow a rare, prized car worth millions and expect people not to notice.

Anika thought they'd wandered a bit too far off topic and tried to pull them back. "Jillian, you were about to introduce your guest."

"Right. This is Beck. He's my bodyguard." Jillian dropped the comment without any other explanation. A simple *I hired a dude with a gun* in general breakfast conversation.

None of it made sense to Anika. "Did you say—"

Jillian kept on talking, like Jillian generally did. Talked and talked and talked. "For the record, he works for me. Only for me. He answers to me and only me."

Ugly Hot nodded. "Seems clear."

Jillian rolled her eyes. "You'd think, but they'll try to shove and push and generally order you around. You have my permission to ignore them."

Ugly Hot scoffed. "Done."

"Let's go back for a second." Anika spoke louder, trying to get everyone else to be quiet for ten seconds. "You hired a bodyguard to protect you from . . . who?"

Jillian glanced around the room. "All of you."

That was a tad insulting. Anika refused to believe a simple little listening device had Jillian this wound up. A lot of families used those sorts of tools . . . probably. "A bodyguard to keep you safe from your own family?"

Ugly Hot physically turned to face Jillian this time. "These people are your *family*?"

"I know, right?" Jillian managed to combine a snort and an eye roll that time. Then she pointed around the table. "Beck, meet my cousins, Astrid and Anika. This is Aunt Patricia and Kelby, of course."

"It's lovely to meet you, dear." Patricia held out her hand and Ugly Hot shook it.

Jillian continued her seemingly private conversation with Ugly Hot. "There are more of us lurking about somewhere, but you get the idea. It's pretty much always like this but sometimes without food."

"Huh." Ugly Hot looked completely unimpressed by the chaos raging around him.

"Does he know you've been in prison?"

They all stared at Astrid. She'd managed to ratchet up the tension with one question, as was her way. She'd sit quietly, so still that most people would think she'd nodded off, then she'd come out with some zinger that launched the whole room into an uproar. It was her superpower.

But Jillian being Jillian and generally unreadable didn't take the bait. "Yes."

Ugly Hot shrugged. "It happens."

Maybe Jillian hiring the bodyguard was a smart move after all.

But that didn't change the fact that Jillian had to be stopped. She'd found the listening device in record time, which meant they needed a new way to collect intel and defuse her. Anika didn't want her hurt . . . not exactly. But her dear, bookish, always-huddled-in-the-office-running-figures cousin needed to understand they would fight back, play dirty. Jay didn't have many boundaries and Anika had no interest in a lifetime of begging Jillian for pennies.

"We have a lot to talk through, and we need trust for that." Anika didn't believe in any of that, but it sounded sort of right.

"Exactly." Astrid gestured around the table. "We would never hurt you."

Jillian set her coffee cup down. "You all continue to play this game as if you have a winning hand."

Okay. New tactic. Anika always had a spare, just in case. "Jillian. You know that Astrid and I are very fond of you. I'd go as far as to say you're our favorite cousin."

Jillian made an odd noise. "Is that something that happened in the last sixty seconds?"

Anika decided to ignore that. "The point is we should enjoy each other's company and ease our way into deeper conversations about bigger topics later."

"The one part I agree with is timing. Now isn't appropriate." Jillian shook her head. "Give me a day or two to get adjusted to being back, and then we'll have a family meeting. Those always go so well. After that, I'll set a deadline."

Wait . . . "Deadline? Did you not hear what I said about the fondness thing?"

"I heard and I'm ignoring what you want." Jillian smiled. "You have only yourselves to blame. I learned that trick from you all."

CHAPTER ELEVEN

MOOREWOOD FAMILY RULE #30: *Stop to enjoy the benefits of your hard work.*

THE ROOM CLEARED OUT AFTER THAT. AMAZING HOW THE TALK of money and hints about taking it away could throw a spike into the middle of good breakfast conversation. Even Kelby excused himself. He said it was to do some paperwork, but Jillian sensed he felt the need to spy on the others and make sure they didn't burn down the house with all of them in it.

That left Jillian and Beck alone on either side of the table. He sipped coffee. She ate a stack of bacon as big as her head.

"They seem nice," he said as he watched her butter her toast and make a bacon sandwich.

"They already tried to eavesdrop on me in my room. I hadn't even been here one full day and they'd deployed their usual stunts." She held up a finger but not the one they deserved. "I figured it out because I'm smarter and they suck."

He froze mid-sip. "What are you talking about?"

"Last night." She munched away. "A listening device."

"Not the usual welcome-home greeting."

"Exactly, but that's nothing. Years ago, after I told them the family was going to clean up its act, the brakes went out in my car. I only stopped before hitting water because I slammed into a Jersey barrier." She tried to keep her voice light even though nothing about the experience was funny.

"What the fuck?" He set his mug down with a thunk. "That's true crime television stuff."

"The mechanic said the brakes were worn, but the timing of the accident was a bit too convenient." She swallowed and went in for another bite, pretending the incident hadn't kept her out of a car for months. "The mechanic also had a crush on Astrid, so I'm skeptical of his opinion."

"I know I should ask for more information, but do I want to?"

"My cousins are determined."

"They sound like psychopaths."

Jillian enjoyed a brief rush of relief at being believed. No questions. She said it, and he supported her, swearing where appropriate.

"They would eat their young if they thought they could make money doing it." Jillian thought about what he'd heard at the breakfast table and figured they might as well make a few things clear in case he wanted to run now. And he should. "My family is . . ."

"A menace."

She was going to say criminal, but okay. "They make their living—"

"As con artists." He nodded. "Yeah, it's obvious."

"Really? Most people don't see it. They've gotten away with it for generations."

"They need to rein it in and leave you alone from here forward. As you've pointed out, you're my priority."

That sounded close to right, so she didn't fight the words he picked, just the concept. "How is it possible you don't care that you're working for—"

"Thieves?"

She played with a piece of crispy bacon. "They would dispute that word, but you technically don't work for them. You work for me. Not a thief, though the FBI would say otherwise."

"Honestly, Kelby filled me in on who your relatives are to the public versus who they really are." Beck winked. "My work is confidential, and I needed to know, but that's as far as the judgment goes."

"Oh, please. You're judging. Hell, I judge them."

"Silent judging, maybe. Tampering with your brakes suggests a bigger problem. Desperation." His eyes narrowed. "You're really related to these people?"

"That's a very popular question. My parents said yes, but . . ." She snorted because there was just no way.

"And that's why I'm here? The possibility of violence or is it something else?"

The chewing sounded so loud in her head that she had to

stop to hear him. That's what happened after going *literally* years without decent food. To maintain some sense of dignity, she had to force her fingers not to shovel the bacon in her mouth.

But she still didn't understand the reason for his question. "Why are you confused?"

"You clearly can handle this crowd. You're not afraid, and I'd guess you could beat the crap out of Anita—"

"Anika." But she wanted to see her cousin's face when he mispronounced it.

"Right."

The conversation hit a lull. She assumed he thought it was her turn to talk. Never mind that she was the boss and should be able to inhale bacon in peace. "First, Kelby hired you, not me."

"To do what?"

She stopped mid-thought. For a supposed quiet, sullen bodyguard he sure had a lot of questions. Not that she could blame him. That breakfast scene showed the household thrived on chaos.

"I had a longer list to my explanation. Which is why I said *first* before I started talking." But his insolence fascinated her. She admired his ability to cut through bullshit. More than once during the verbal volleying at breakfast she'd heard him swear under his breath. And not the easy, normally used ones. No, he strung impressive lines of profanity together. Though she did think calling Anika a shit stain might have been too much.

He shrugged. "I get that, but—"

"Do you usually ask questions of the people who hire you?"

"I'm retired."

Uh . . . her mind blanked out on her right as she was going to launch into a nice little speech about how his interruptions made her head explode. He sidelined her with that piece of information. He was forty, not much more. Whatever the number, it seemed low for retirement.

That left one reasonable explanation. "Does *retired* mean something else in the bodyguard world?"

"I own the company but don't actually go out on cases these days." He eyed a piece of bacon resting on the edge of her plate as if he thought it might be okay to reach over and take it.

It wasn't.

If he did, he might get fired.

His fingers twitched. She sensed that he was on the verge of making a career-shattering mistake and she pulled the plate in closer toward her stomach. "Don't even think about it."

"You have eleven pieces."

"There's a whole tray on the buffet. No touching my plate." But that wasn't what she wanted to talk about. Him, his business, whatever he was trying to say, had her locked in confusion. "So, retired. Was everyone else sick at your company when Kelby called and asked for help?"

"He specifically asked for me to protect you."

The words screeched in her brain. She didn't like the way

that phrase sounded at all. "You mean to watch over things at the estate."

She was the protector. That was her position in the family. Fix things. Watch over things. Handle things. Bury things. Save things. Basically, all of the guarding and the cleanup fell on her.

Thanks, Mom.

Beck just stared at her. "Not sure why you're making a word salad here. The point is Kelby called in a favor."

Not good enough. She trusted Kelby with her life, with everything really. She would have been on the sidelines, cheering, had Kelby stolen Mom away from Dad and given her the life she deserved. But that was Kelby. Her relationship with him grew over time. It was earned.

"How do you know Kelby?" she asked.

No part of Beck moved. He didn't even blink. "I'll let him tell you."

How annoyingly evasive of him. "I'm asking you."

"And I answered."

She couldn't fault the response. She'd likely give the same type in his position. She valued privacy. She kept things close, knowing that if she spilled even an ounce of real emotion, the vultures in her family would swarm.

Still, she was supposed to be in charge. "You're a smartass."

He cracked his first smile of the morning. "As my father used to say, *Better a smartass than a dumbass.*"

"I think I'd like your dad."

"You really wouldn't." Beck shook his head. "He was a gigantic ass."

This guy got more interesting the longer they sat there. Not *sexy* interesting. Interesting like . . . well, she didn't know. It had been years since she'd sat and talked with a man. Before prison there had been Greg, and that had been a disaster. Which snapped her back to reality. "I know the type. Of man, I mean."

"That's a shame because a woman with your energy deserves to be with someone who knows how to help her work that off and appreciate her while doing it." He picked up his mug and took a long, slow drink this time.

If this was flirting, and she had no idea what that even looked like anymore, it needed to stop. She cleared her throat. "Let's stay on topic, shall we?"

He leaned back in his chair as he listened and seemingly dissected every word she said. "Right. Returning to my original question. If you're so quick on your feet, why the need for a bodyguard?"

"They've had a lot of time to refine their skills since the thing with the brakes. Their boundaries, as weak as they were, could be gone now."

He nodded. "People under pressure tend to do stupid shit."

She considered that observation to be the informal Moorewood family motto. "I really hope so."

His eyebrow inched up. "So, you're looking for trouble."

"Satisfaction." An end to the grifting madness, which she'd thought she'd guaranteed by going to prison for all of them.

"So, revenge."

She'd been wrong. That smart dude thing he had going on really was sexy. "That is the right way to put it, yes."

He stared at her, watching with a suffocating closeness. "You let them attack. I stop it. Then they go to prison."

She decided to call that Plan B. "Where were you the last few years while I plotted my revenge?"

"Not in fancy Rhode Island."

"Yeah, it's a lot but it's not really me." She stammered a bit because this topic made her uncomfortable. Always had. She loved the house because her mother had loved it.

The property was this tenuous thread that bound them together. Walking in the halls, sitting on the back patio, Jillian could almost smell her mother's shampoo and the lotion she used after she'd been in the sun. Picked up the scent of fresh lemon bars—Mom's favorite—floating in from the kitchen.

"The cousins sounded like they think the money issue is open for discussion," he said.

"They're wrong. They'll figure that out sooner or later."

After a few seconds of quiet, he nodded. "This week should be interesting."

Jillian certainly hoped so. "That's the plan."

CHAPTER TWELVE

MOOREWOOD FAMILY RULE #28: *Never let your guard down.*

AFTER THE DAUNTING MORNING OF BLOOD-RELATION SHE-nanigans and bacon eating, followed by a tour of the grounds with Beck, Jillian headed back to her room. It was tempting to hide in there for the rest of the day, but she had a specific goal in mind: find her phone before her privacy-challenged cousins did.

She hadn't seen them in over two hours. Letting her feral cousins roam free without supervision meant anything could happen.

Jillian jogged up the steps and slipped into her room. After making her bed and double-checking for stray Moorewoods, she retrieved the cell off her nightstand and turned . . . and ran right into a rather impressive chest attached to a very angry face.

Beck. *Did he get bigger after breakfast?* "Are you unclear on the concept of personal space?"

Beck's eyes widened but he stayed silent.

She tried again. "Are you still upset I wouldn't share my bacon?"

"You can't just run off."

He sounded so serious she almost laughed. "Not to state the obvious, but I walked upstairs, leaving you for approximately one minute, and—"

He held up his hand before she could say more. "You've been up here for ten."

Jillian chalked the comment up to bodyguard embellishment because she refused to believe she'd lost track of time. Of course, every minute had been so regimented and spelled out for her for the past few years that maybe not having anyone watching, waiting for her to mess up, did make her move slower.

Still, the grumpy face and how-dare-you tone seemed over the top. "Do you think, maybe, you're blowing my short detour out of proportion?"

"If you wanted me to think this was an easy job where I don't need to be concerned, you shouldn't have told me about what they did to your brakes."

Right. That. In hindsight, that might not be the type of thing you shared with a dude you wanted to be ready to beat people up on your behalf but not be so close as to smother you with protection. "Clearly, I miscalculated, but I thought it was better to err on the side of more information."

"It is, but I can guarantee your safety only if I can see you."

The whole barking orders thing was not her favorite, but he had his hands on his hips and for some reason her attention got stuck on that. Her brain sputtered a bit, but she forced out some words that sounded sort of reasonable. "There will be times—"

"No."

He really had a thing for interrupting. "No?"

"You're going to try to carve out exceptions to my ground rules. The answer is no. You don't run off. Period."

He wasn't wrong about being concerned for her safety, but that wasn't the point. She was the one with a point. "I thought I was the boss."

"Not about this."

If he wanted a verbal battle, fine. "Bathroom."

He stilled. "What?"

"I'll want privacy in the bathroom."

He sighed at her, and not a little sigh. One of those *oh my God* sighs. "Sure."

"And when I change my clothes," she continued.

A nerve in his cheek ticked. "Of course."

She was starting to like this game. "And when I shower."

"Yes, that's not a question." He frowned at her. "You know I meant—"

"Nuh-uh." This time she held up a hand to stop him from talking over her. "I'm not done."

"Lucky me."

"In bed."

A slow smile spread across his mouth. "If you insist."

Well, that backfired. Her stomach performed a mighty tumble. She possessed all the self-control of a teen on prom night and about the same level of finesse. She even made herself cringe.

In an attempt to wrestle control back to her side, she cleared her throat. "I am now going to the top of the stairs. From there I will walk down the steps. All of them. One at a time. No skipping or running because that's dangerous and I've learned my lesson."

He stared at her but didn't say anything. She took that as an invitation to be obnoxious.

"After that I will walk across the hall, probably through the great room because that's the faster route. I can't promise I won't stop to look at something, but I guess we can handle that horrifying possibility when we get there."

His expression didn't change. "You aren't going to win this argument by annoying me."

"Oh, you underestimate me, sir." She kept going, leaving him no room to interrupt this time. "Then I'll go outside because it's a sunny day and I like sun. It's likely I will sit on a lounger. I'm not sure which one, but I can advise you once we get there so that you know in advance and aren't left wondering where my butt will land."

"Jillian."

She shot him her best eat-me grin. "Are those directions about my day specific enough for you?"

"Perfect, actually."

She feared he meant that. Rather than fight or stare or do any other embarrassing thing, she pushed past him and headed for the staircase. "I'm not great with taking orders."

When she didn't hear him thundering right behind her, she kept going. She rested a hand on the balcony railing for balance. It wobbled. Like, a full-scale whoosh back and forth, and she fell forward. Her weight shifted, and her upper body kept going. All she could hear was the sound of the impending *splat* in her mind.

"Whoa."

She heard him that time but couldn't see him because she'd closed her eyes, convinced this was the way she'd die. Killed in the act of being a giant smartass.

Big hands grabbed her, and her body switched directions mid-flight. One minute she was careening toward the floor—not really, but it felt that way—and the next Beck lifted her off her feet and into his arms. She stopped screaming the second her back slammed against his solid front. His arms wrapped around her as she fought to breathe again.

"You're okay. I've got you."

His harsh whisper blew over her ear and echoed in her head. When she finally opened her eyes again, she saw Astrid and Anika standing in the foyer below. Dainty mouths open. Perfect blond hair perfectly in place.

Holy shit, they tried to kill me.

The thought tumbled over and over in Jillian's mind as she fought to come up with the right words. Kick them out now, leaving them pathetic and penniless? That option sure sounded good.

"What happened?" Astrid squealed the question.

"You could have been really hurt," Anika said, stating the obvious.

Beck loosened his hold.

Jillian clutched him tighter.

"Now do you get it?" he asked in a tone probably meant only for her, but it rang out loud enough to bounce off the walls.

She managed to nod her head. "I'm not leaving your side."

"Right answer."

CHAPTER THIRTEEN

MOOREWOOD FAMILY RULE #29: *Rest when you can but never on a job.*

A FEW HOURS LATER JILLIAN SAT IN AN UNLADYLIKE SPRAWL on a lounge chair facing the ocean. The position would have earned a glare from her always appropriate mother, but Jillian needed to spread out after her near-death swan dive off the upstairs balcony.

The moment would forever be known in her head as *the grab that saved my life*. The second after it happened, Beck demanded answers from her cousins, wanting to know about the railing.

Astrid and Anika insisted they had no idea. Neither of their rooms was at that end of the hallway. It was an old house and things failed or needed to be repaired all the time . . . blah, blah, blah.

"We're switching rooms," Beck said out of nowhere.

This time Jillian didn't balk at the order. Unlike the rest of the family, she learned from her mistakes. "Want to tell me why?"

"I can't be sleeping on the third floor with you on the second. I need to be closer."

That sounded romantic, but she knew he really intended to boss her around and be up in her business twenty-four hours a day, which right now sounded pretty good to her. "We can move into my mother's suite. There are two rooms. One is supposed to be an office, but—"

"Fine."

"You could be nicer. I almost died today." It was an over-statement. One she'd bet Beck would use against her later, but whatever. If he hadn't come racing, she probably would have taken a good tumble down the steps, landing at her cousins' feet.

Beck checked and exactly one section of all the banisters in the entire house was loose—the one right outside her door. Jillian couldn't pretend that away as a coincidence.

It was one thing to think relatives wanted to get rid of you, and a totally different thing to have them try it on the second day you were home. She was entitled to be overly dramatic for the next few hours in response.

After the chaotic last few hours, she'd wanted to be outside, celebrating the fresh air and blocking out the memories of her confinement and her family. She'd missed the way the wind would cool her cheeks. Missed being able to move around. Missed being able to breathe without being hit with a choking mix of fury, fear, and frustration.

Beck seemed to sense that she needed a few minutes of outside recovery. Without asking, he'd dragged a chair from the pool area and set it up for her on the far edge of the green lawn. Out of the fray and away from nosy watchers, tucked behind one of the guesthouses.

Now, he stood nearby, not hovering but close, with one foot planted on the stone wall outlining this edge of the property, before the land hit the rocky beach. His gaze focused on some spot in the distance. She knew because every now and then he'd mumble about the *amazing* view. The same view she'd taken for granted for years, but not anymore.

From the time she was little, maybe six or so, Jillian could remember sitting down to dinner with no sounds but the clink of silverware and thump of plates as her mother passed and set down dishes with more than the usual amount of force. Dad would stare at Mom and try to engage in forgettable chitchat. Mom would ignore him. It was how Jillian knew when Dad had messed up. Not his usual daily mess-ups. His grand, even-hard-for-her-to-deny-his-lying infractions.

Their dysfunction, this bizarre marital relationship, turned Jillian off to romance. She knew her parents communicated and operated one way and that there were many other ways for families to move forward. She knew it but watching their daily lives play out poisoned her belief that something easier, more pleasurable, could result from being in a serious relationship.

"I really want to go in there and interrogate your cousins again and then move on to Jay," Beck said after a few minutes of quiet.

"I'm tempted to let you, but I'm going to pretend the railing could have been loose for a long time and I got lucky until that moment." A silly excuse but one that would help Jillian sleep at night. The excuse and having Beck nearby.

He said something under his breath that sounded like *bullshit*. "Or they could have loosened it while we were walking around the property earlier today."

Yes, that one. Clearly. The distance between bugging her room and setting up a fall onto a harsh marble floor struck her as considerable but she'd threatened their money. The Moorewood business model. Last time she did that she ended up in prison. Killing her might have been their Plan B.

The steady thump of crashing waves and the soft breeze rustling through nearby trees calmed her. For these few quiet moments, she abandoned thoughts of revenge and fear and let contentment fill her. Reveled in the humbling joy of her view of the vast openness spread out in front of her. The mix of blues punctuated by a smattering of white as the waves rolled and tumbled. The jutting boulders that formed a ledge just offshore.

"What the hell happened?" Tenn's voice broke through the quiet as he walked up behind her. "I left for a few hours and the house started falling apart."

"Convenient, right?"

Beck spun around, his arms up and tension snapping as he morphed into a ball of energy and action. "Who are—"

"It's okay," Jillian said, hoping to cut off the possibility of unnecessary fighting.

The stiffness across Beck's shoulders eased as he watched Tenn drop a folded blanket on her lap. Jillian recognized her mom's favorite cashmere scarf. Baby blue and so soft. Mom would carry it outside as the sun went down and the chill in the air kicked up, then throw it around her shoulders and insist on staying out long after the coolness turned to actual cold. Jillian mimicked the movements now, wrapping it around her body, stopping to hold the material to her face. Aching to smell Mom's familiar scent after years of re-creating it in her mind.

"Are you okay?" Tenn asked as his gaze flicked to Beck and back to her.

Jillian bent her knees to make room for him on the end of the lounger. "I've had a morning filled with widespread sighing, concealed threats, and really good bacon. Very crispy. Or do you mean the near-death experience?"

"Are you ignoring the question on purpose?"

"No." She caught Beck staring at her, ready to jump in. "Do not snort at me."

Tenn's eyebrow lifted. "You could introduce us."

She could, but she dreaded it. With very little warning, and without really knowing him, she'd dragged Beck right into the middle of her family squabbles instead of letting the poor guy stand there and do his bodyguard thing. Maybe it was the need for a confidant after going so many months secretly plotting from a cell. She hated to admit that since it made her sound a little pathetic.

Now that she'd let Beck in, giving him more information than she intended, stuffing him back into the bodyguard-only role seemed impossible. He was not exactly the easy-to-push-around type.

Both men stared at her and Beck stayed silent, as if challenging her to handle the basic stuff.

Men . . .

"Beck Romer, this is my baby cousin, the one we like, Tenn."

"Who is no longer a baby, so it's fine to call me Tenn without the descriptive." Tenn lifted up into what looked like an uncomfortable, not-quite-standing crouch and held out his hand. "Hey."

Beck met Tenn halfway for the handshake. "Hey."

"Hey?" she asked, testing the limits of the newfound male bond.

Beck exhaled loud enough for the entire estate to hear it. "Was the greeting offensive to you?"

"It's very . . . guttural."

"Are you using fancy words because he's a professor?" Beck shrugged when she stared at him. "This isn't my first assignment. I investigated the entire extended family."

He had the upper hand and she still needed to grumble at Kelby about that. "I hate it when you say stuff like that."

"We've known each other for less than six hours."

Tenn smiled. "I like him."

"He's my bodyguard." When Tenn's smile grew bigger, Jillian rushed to clarify. "He's the one who caught me when the railing slipped."

"After being tampered with. I'm betting one or both of your sisters did the deed," Beck said to Tenn.

Tenn nodded. "No question. Thanks for catching Jillian. Can I help at all?"

"Are you two best friends now?" She really didn't need Tenn and Beck teaming up. She could handle each one's concerns separately. As a united front of bossiness and testosterone? *Ugh.*

Beck stared at her for a second with an undecipherable expression that might have been a now-you're-going-to-get-it promise before looking at Tenn. "She made it clear to them that she was in charge of the money and now this."

She'd lost control of the topic. They obviously needed to review the who-is-in-charge discussion from earlier. She sent Beck the warning she knew he'd ignore. "Don't tattle."

Beck snorted at her, as was becoming his habit.

"My original thought was to string them along, make them suffer, but it might be quicker and less dangerous if I just tell them the bottom line," she said. "Give them the ultimatum and boom."

"No."

Jillian glanced at Beck. "Do you just like saying the word?"

"I like the idea of ending the suspense, but we need leverage. What's to stop them from coming after you once you tell them whatever you have to say? I'm assuming they aren't going to like it."

"Oh, they'll hate it." This time they didn't get a say on making a money deal with her. She had no desire to make their lives easier.

Beck nodded. "So, maybe wait. Let me gather some information."

"What kind?" Tenn asked.

"The kind that will make them have to choose between going to prison or leaving Jillian alone."

"You mean blackmail." She liked the sound of that except for one thing. "Tenn, maybe you should head back to Amherst where it's safe?"

"No."

Wrong. She liked his confidence, but it had been easier to convince him to do what she wanted back when he was a kid and thought he had to listen to her. "That was a rhetorical question. Sorry I wasn't clear."

"Jillian." Tenn slid a little closer and rested his hand on her calf.

Uh-oh. She could hear the big guns being rolled in.

"You know I'm not a kid, right?"

"Irrelevant. But handling this kind of thing was easier for me when you were a perpetual student. You couldn't be here."

"You prefer that time because you like being the one who handles everything."

Okay, that stung a bit. It was also true. How dare he point that out. "I just don't want you to get pulled into your sisters' mess."

"It's *Moorewood* mess and we've both been nailed by that collateral damage." His smile came back. "Thanks to you, I've come through mostly unscathed."

Battle lost. Time to back down and preserve a bit of dignity. "Why do you have to be decent?"

"I thought I'd try to be a different type of Moorewood man."

Five minutes after Tenn left in search of food, Beck sat down on the stone wall. This time facing her. He didn't say anything but the stare telegraphed his intention to talk.

She decided to stop the lecture before he started it. "What?"

Beck didn't flinch at her snotty tone. "He seems like a smart kid."

"As he just pointed out, he's a grown man. I don't like that, by the way."

"So, he's right? You preferred when he was younger and you could manipulate him."

Wasn't everyone insightful today? She shifted them to another, semi-related topic. "How old are you anyway?"

"A hundred and seven."

"You look good." For some reason he got better looking the more time she spent with him, which was going to be a problem.

"Thank you for noticing." He stretched his legs out in front of him, crossing one ankle over the other. "But I'm serious. Whatever happened in this house or wherever he lived, he turned out pretty good."

"He's so smart. Like, painfully so. He has a monster IQ."

"I wasn't commenting on the size of his brain. A man's money, where he went to college—that's all fancy outside bullshit that says nothing about a person's character."

That kind of talk would get him kicked out of the yacht club. "Agree . . . until I see where you're going with this. I reserve the right to disagree later if your point backfires on me."

"Noted." He nodded before verbally plowing forward. "What I'm saying is, Tenn seems pretty grounded. Normal. Loyal, even-tempered. Nothing like his father."

She had to fight back a huge grin since she really didn't get to take credit for how Tenn turned out. "Yeah, Tenn might be adopted, too."

"Or, maybe"—Beck held up a finger as if he were conducting a class on the Moorewoods—"just maybe, not every family member is as bad as you think they are."

"I was smart to reserve my right to disagree with you. Sounds like you've already forgotten about the railing."

"I assure you I haven't."

She settled deeper into the lounger-shawl cocoon she'd made. "Just stick close."

He winked at her. "Oh, I definitely intend to."

CHAPTER FOURTEEN

MOOREWOOD FAMILY RULE #16: *Reassess and revise before abandoning any job.*

TODAY PROVED ONE THING TO ANIKA—THEY NEEDED A BETTER plan to deal with Jillian. Hoping she'd be ashamed and stay away failed. Appealing to her sense of family loyalty might get them all kicked out of the house.

And the railing thing? Amateur move. It tipped their hand and fired up Ugly Hot on Jillian's behalf.

To prevent more mess, Anika rallied the troops. Except Tenn. Tenn was not part of the troops—ever—by order of Jay, and she'd recalled Jay from the club, which resulted in a lot of grumbling about messing up his work with Izzy. Astrid was in attendance because where else would she be?

They'd gathered in the small sitting room off the kitchen where Jillian's mother used to work on seating charts and invitations for charity events held at the estate. The room

Jillian was the least likely to enter without warning. Probably had something to do with memories of her mother. Anika didn't understand the sentiment but even she missed Aunt Sonya.

"Who messed with the railing?" Anika asked. "Jillian could have been hurt."

"None of us." Jay made a humming sound. "But, just so we're clear, who benefits if something does happen to Jillian? Which it won't. Of course."

Astrid answered. "Emma."

They'd spent most of Jillian's incarceration trying to win Emma over. Sweet, insulated, relatively carefree, and easy-to-trick Emma. They just needed to weaponize Emma in the *right* way.

Astrid made a strangled sound. "I think we should—"

"No one asked you, Astrid." There was a reason her younger-by-minutes sister was considered an assistant on jobs. Anika doubted Astrid had *it*, and Doug and his overseas disaster already proved *it* could not be taught.

One knock, then Emma opened the door. She walked in wearing tights and what looked like an oversized shirt. Maybe it was a dress. The short raincoat hanging open down the front of her made it hard to tell. "What's with the mysterious text? Why did I need to come home?"

"Did you forget your pants?" Astrid asked.

Not the best start to a secret meeting, but Anika didn't panic. Not yet. "We have something we'd like to talk with you about."

"Where have you been?" Jay asked from his seat at the desk. It was a small piece of furniture. Rather dainty. Likely only his perfect posture, something he considered a necessary skill, prevented him from lounging all over it.

Emma didn't look impressed with the show of force. "Out."

Anika decided to appeal to her screwing-all-night-long side. "You and Gregory . . ."

"That must be difficult for Jillian," Astrid said, stomping all over the delicate touch.

Emma leaned against the doorframe. "Why?"

Some conversations called for tact. This one called for devious maneuvering and careful tiptoeing. Astrid possessed neither skill, so Anika took over. She gently pried Emma from the entrance and brought her into the room, steering her toward a chair that sat too low to the floor, making it harder to escape without some flailing.

Anika sat on the edge of the ottoman in front of her. "Well, they clearly have a past." Emma's expression stayed blank. Anika had no idea what to do with that, so she tried again. "You didn't know?"

"Is this really why you texted me and told me to run home for a clandestine meeting?" Emma put her hands on the armrests and started to push up.

Astrid joined Anika on the ottoman. "No one said—"

Anika rushed in because who knew what Astrid might say next. "No, no. Your personal life is—"

"Not your business." Emma's eyebrow lifted as if waiting for agreement.

Anika nodded. "Sure."

Jay let out a long, loud exhale. "Jillian is insisting on a family meeting. She clearly believes she's in charge."

Astrid gasped.

Enough. Anika was getting sick of her sister's dramatic noises. Astrid followed Jay around like a puppy and was almost sickly eager to take on more responsibility. Anika and Jay had talked about that over-the-top enthusiasm and decided it proved Astrid was not ready for the family role she wanted to assume.

Anika put her hand on Emma's knee. "This is a delicate situation."

Emma frowned. "What is?"

Anika refused to believe her cute but annoying cousin was this clueless at twenty . . . something. Anika actually had no idea how old Emma was, but the point was the same. "You know what we're talking about, Emma."

"I do?"

Jay got up, letting the chair screech across the inlaid wood floor. "Your sister is walking into a stable, thriving situation and trying to blow it up. Blow us up when we've been doing fine together."

"A month ago you charged almost nine thousand dollars on my credit card," Emma said.

Well, of course he did. Anika didn't think there was a pill big enough to combat her growing headache.

"That was a misunderstanding." Jay poured on the Jay

charm, sounding all reasonable and not a bit contrite. "We have the same credit card company. When the envelope came, I saw the card and used it."

Emma frowned. "It was in my name and you somehow activated it."

"It was a secondary card on your account." Jay shook his head. "Blame the company for its lax security."

Emma sighed. "The credit card company said—"

"Emma, please." Astrid jumped back in with her soothing voice and sweet smile. "The point is that we've thrived and things have gone smoothly."

"Until Jillian's unexpected return," Jay said. "She's trying to drive a wedge between us, get us fighting with each other. Test our trust."

Anika didn't care about that. They had a bigger problem. "Jay and I are in the middle of delicate work. Izzy could go back to Boston without him. Harry could balk at proposing."

"What exactly did Jillian say while I was gone that has you all so rattled?" Emma asked.

Not enough. Too much. To Anika, typical Jillian bullshit. "She's made it pretty clear she intends to impose new rules, likely disrupt our plans by imposing ridiculous deadlines. The work you have put into getting our . . ."

Emma finished the sentence. "Command Center."

Anika refused to use that term, so she breezed right over it. "Technical and strategic side of the operation. Those, your babies, would be in jeopardy."

"She's making changes and pretending she has all the power when, in reality, she should be thanking us," Jay said, going too far. As usual.

Emma's flat affect broke and she smiled. "I would love to see you explain that to her."

Jay shrugged. "Her choices impacted other people. Your father, for instance."

Uncle Clive had a heart attack before he entered his cell. Anika could still remember the look on her father's face when he found out. Jay was an imperfect man, but he loved his brother. Maybe *only* his brother. Anika realized that truth that day.

"Without proper medical care and not being at home, Clive was vulnerable. If Jillian had been more diligent . . . let's just say it's the one thing I can't forgive." With that, Jay brought his speech to a thunderous close.

Anika took over. "Emma, listen. A woman doesn't swoop in on a helicopter if she's trying to be subtle and settle quietly into her former life."

The buzz of energy and emotion died out, leaving only silence. Emma sat there, watching. Her gaze moved from one cousin to the other before she spoke. "What exactly do you want from me?"

Gotcha! Interest. Curiosity. Anika could work with either of those. "Your assistance."

"Loyalty," Astrid added.

Emma rubbed the side of her head and closed her eyes.

When she opened them again she looked just as annoyed as before. "Could you be more specific?"

"Jillian wants a family meeting. That's fine. We should clear the air, but family meetings mean family votes." Jay crouched down, looking at Emma with pride . . . basically, playing the role of his life. "You could, maybe, provide intel. Let us know what she's planning."

"Vote with us, not her." Astrid patted Emma's leg.

"Wow." Emma stood up. Didn't fumble or shift. Got right up and out of the trap chair. She maneuvered around Astrid and Jay and didn't talk again until the chair stood between her and them. "It's almost as if you all rehearsed this."

Anika tried to salvage what she could. "Our preference, of course, is that Jillian have a fresh start."

"And not run afoul of her probation restrictions," Astrid said.

Emma's eyes narrowed at that not-so-subtle threat. "How would she—"

"She's always been protective of you." Anika fell back on family loyalty. That phrase meant nothing to her side of the family, but it did mean something to Emma's side. "Jillian has no reason to doubt you. She wants a relationship, and you can give her one."

"Voting against her could actually save her," Astrid explained, as if what she said made any sense.

Unbelievable. Anika wondered if her headache would ever go away.

Emma whistled as her arms dropped to her sides. "That is quite a proposal."

The tone sounded sarcastic. Anika let Emma's response roll around in her mind a few more times. Yeah, definitely not a full-throated support of the plan. Anika plowed ahead anyway. "One tiny thing. There is a bit of a time crunch."

Emma didn't seem impressed. "I need to think about your proposal."

"Sure." Anika tried to tamp down the anxiety boiling inside her, but it wasn't working. "Quickly, but sure."

"Good." Jay took on a now-that-it's-settled tone that probably didn't fit here. "In the meantime, be careful of the bodyguard. After Jillian's near fall, he could be a problem."

"What fall?" Emma stilled. "What bodyguard?"

TWENTY MINUTES LATER Anika was alone with her sister and Jay in the den.

"The trick is to let Emma think that she needs to defy Jillian." Anika hadn't totally worked out how yet but was hoping to be struck by a shot of brilliance.

"Emma seems like she'd be easy to lead around but every now and then she has this flare of will. It's annoying." Astrid shifted until she sat in the chair Emma had abandoned. "And never forget they are sisters."

The sisterly bond talk always confused Anika. She didn't feel it. Sense it. Crave it. And she definitely didn't trust it. Not in this family. "Meaning?"

An odd look came and went on Astrid's face. "Despite

whatever is happening with Gregory and Jillian's feelings about that, Emma, underneath it all, feels some tug of loyalty and compassion toward Jillian."

"You're putting too much emphasis on the sibling relationship." Anika was ready to find another topic.

Astrid frowned. "How can you say—"

"Gregory might be the answer," Anika said.

A month after Jillian got picked up, the FBI came snooping again and Gregory's dad disappeared. Then he was dead. It was a whole thing and no one ever provided a good explanation for that fatal car chase. Not even the press, and Anika knew because she'd researched the subject thoroughly back then.

Jay sat forward on the desk chair, fully engaged now. "You're saying Gregory blames Jillian for his dad's death?"

Anika hoped so. "I'm saying if he doesn't, maybe we help him get there."

CHAPTER FIFTEEN

MOOREWOOD FAMILY RULE #8: *There is a family hierarchy. Follow it.*

BY THE MIDDLE OF THE NEXT DAY, JILLIAN WAS IN A NEW SUITE of rooms as Beck had insisted. Astrid had a fit about Jillian getting the *big* room. Apparently, Astrid had been intending to update it and move in. Without asking, but when had that stopped Astrid?

After hours of unsubtle family whispering about her, Jillian went to her new room and stayed there. If someone used the word *hid* to describe her actions, they would be correct. She needed a few minutes to breathe. Being in a new suite didn't ease the tension that had a grip on her down to her bones.

The rooms were large with high ceilings and an expansive view of the water. A lavish bathroom and closet bigger than some city apartments sat on one side of the bedroom. The other side led to a sitting room, likely used as a nursery in earlier generations.

Size and style really didn't matter because she thought of this suite as her mom's. Her parents slept there all during Jillian's childhood. At some point Dad moved down the hall, and Jillian never asked why because she just assumed Mom wanted to spend as little time with him as possible.

Dad was not an easy man, not ever. His connection to Jay and the nonstop need to earn Jay's praise far surpassed Dad's loyalty to his wife and kids. It was your basic unhealthy brother relationship where the dominant personality ruled, and Dad was not the dominant one.

With or without Dad, no one had occupied the suite since Mom's death. Jillian never redecorated through all those years because she'd never been ready to let go of that last tie to her mother. For so long it smelled like her.

Sitting in there now Jillian didn't know how her mother, the perfect mix of sunshine and grace, tolerated the old-fashioned décor. Purplish-gray walls and brocade curtains. Dark furniture, complete with a recliner chair set up to block the window seat. The room had a wall safe tucked behind a painting of a random countryside, once filled with paperwork like birth certificates and passports but now empty. There was a false wooden plank under the bed that hid a steel box. Grandma used to put her jewelry there.

The suite swallowed up the far end of the second floor.

The matching suite at the other end of the hall had belonged to Jay. Jillian didn't want anything to do with the rooms behind that particular set of double doors.

In the hours since Beck's musical rooms pronouncement, the suite had been cleaned and refreshed. Mattresses had been switched. Jillian's new clothes hung in the closets and filled the drawers. Tomorrow Jillian would think about redecorating and letting this part of the house move on from the past. She'd make the space hers and comfortable . . . for however long she stayed.

That was an open question. One she couldn't answer yet. She'd made a promise to herself not to dive into any choice out of anger, depression, or frustration. That meant living at the estate and concentrating on who she wanted to be outside of this family.

For the next fifteen minutes she managed to busy herself with rearranging her shampoo and the five outfits she owned. At some point she'd need to ask her thieving relatives where all of her old clothing went. Honestly, they'd steal and sell anything not nailed down.

"You okay?" Beck's voice floated through the quiet room.

She smiled even though she didn't feel much happiness at the moment. "How do you like your temporary bedroom?"

The sitting room had become his room. He traveled with a duffel bag and a hard case that she assumed carried weapons or was where he hid the bodies or something equally intriguing.

His eyes narrowed. "We're ignoring my question about you?"

"For now." Because she was not okay. Being in this room, so close to her mother yet so far away, brought all those conflicted feelings back. Her mom's life, quiet and a little sad. How sick she was at the end, and the choices she'd made that locked them all into a lifetime of infighting.

Almost as if he sensed the need to move on to another topic, Beck nodded and started a slow walking tour around the room. He dragged his fingers over the jewelry roll where Jillian kept her mother's simple gold wedding band and the necklace, a thin gold *S* on a fragile chain, that Mom had always worn.

He stopped in front of the window bench and stared at her with an unreadable expression. "I didn't expect to be sleeping in the room next to yours."

"Did you think you'd be on the balcony or in your car or—"

"Adjoining rooms is not the norm."

"How do you know?"

Beck frowned. "What?"

"You're retired. Maybe adjoining rooms are the norm now."

The start of a smile twitched at the corner of his mouth. "I do actually talk with my employees."

But now that he mentioned it . . . "Look, if you don't want—"

"I said it was unusual, but it's not a problem."

Huh. "Okay."

He shrugged. "Okay."

The energy bouncing around the room slammed into her.

Suddenly, she felt like she was treading water and gasping for air. She swallowed a few times, trying to draw in enough breath to talk. "Were you trying to make things awkward between us?"

"That was an unexpected result." He seemed to shake it off and plunge ahead. "What's wrong? You seem upset, though in this house I'm tempted to use the word *melancholy*. It's like a gothic novel in here."

There was sharing and then there was oversharing. "You don't need to be my friend."

"Really? Because you seem like you need one."

The rising tension eased. They again fell into a back-and-forth banter that she enjoyed more than she would ever admit. "Are you saying I'm unlikable?"

"I'm saying that other than Tenn and Kelby—neither of whom live in this house—you don't appear to have many allies under this roof. You have seen your sister only in passing, so I can't comment on her."

"What if I told you that not everything is what it seems?" Jillian debated opening up and explaining how they all got to this point. But those topics invited questions, and she was looking to downsize in that area.

He put his hands on his hips and got all I'm-about-to-lecture-you. "If I thought you'd listen I'd tell you not to hide things from the man tasked with protecting you."

"I'm fine." She'd repeated the words so often in the short time since getting out of prison that even she thought they rang hollow. No one in her position could be *fine*.

His eyes narrowed. "We're not going to debate your state of mind right now."

"Meaning?"

"Nothing is fine here, Jillian. Or do you actually trust your cousins not to set fire to you in your sleep?"

"Hell no. Though, to be fair, it's not as if they had much of a chance at decency with Jay as their moral compass." Now she was making excuses for their behavior, just as her mom had done.

In prison she'd been scared and lonely. Spent hours day-dreaming about revenge and nights unable to sleep through the constant clanking noise and mumbling of voices. Fear combined with a lack of control. No privacy and no choices, but no family nonsense either.

"Your uncle is . . . I can't really think of the right word to use."

Beck's comment didn't immediately register in her brain. Once it did, she glanced at him. Took in the relaxed way he hovered in front of the window, all calm and sure, and wondered if it was all a facade.

She'd made a quick introduction between Jay and Beck, mostly as a warning to Jay that she had backup. But Jay was a schmoozer. He thought he could win anyone over by getting them alone and saying the right things. Strangely enough, that tactic usually worked. The smooth tone. The concerned expression. He knew just enough about a huge number of topics to carry a conversation and build trust.

"Did Jay say something snide to you?" she asked.

This time Beck didn't hide his smile. "Will you beat him up if he did?"

"I'd be happy to." She didn't need another person to protect, but why not?

"He cornered me while you and Tenn were having coffee this morning, all carefree and pretending not to be the target of potential familial murderous attacks."

"You're not funny." Okay, he was.

"I'm hysterical." Beck went back to sizing up the room, looking at every inch of wall and floor space. "What type of name is Tenn?"

"Ridiculous."

His gaze shifted back to her. "Is his mom from the South?"

"She's from Costa Rica." Jillian didn't remember much about her except that she gifted her good genes to Tenn. "In case you want to keep score, Jay has four ex-wives. One from Norway. One from Costa Rica. Two from England, who are related. Half sisters, I think."

"Talk about keeping it in the family."

"Exactly. Then there was a brief fifth marriage with a woman from New Jersey, but she annulled it. Very different women but all compelling and with some skill or access Jay needed at the time." She realized he must know all of this since he'd performed background research on her misfit family, but she finished her thought anyway. "They could all do much better than Jay and hopefully have."

"New Jersey sounds like an outlier."

"She was my favorite. She lasted three weeks. Seems going in she didn't know she was wife number five. When she found out she took a mulligan on the marriage and left."

Beck nodded. "Smart woman."

"Very. The whole thing took Jay by surprise. He was usually the dumper, not the dumpee. He didn't even have a chance to selectively steal pieces of her inheritance, which I remember being substantial." Jillian tried to call up the right answer then decided she didn't care. "Transportation or shipping money."

"So, none of these women shared Jay's love of—"

"Stealing? Some." She thought back on the women over the years. There had been several Jay never married, usually those who just had assets he wanted but not enough to be offered a ring, proving he did have some boundaries. "Astrid and Anika's mom had a gift for languages and for seducing. She enjoyed her role at Jay's side until she had children, according to my mom. Watching out for Jay was one thing. Watching out for three people, two of them under the age of four, was too much."

Beck winced. "Damn."

"Tenn's mom worked at a huge art auction house and sometimes passed important private intel to Jay. She had a really romanticized view of what life would be like with him, in this house, going to fancy parties."

"Then reality kicked her ass."

"Understatement. Jay treated her more as a nanny to the girls. She left when Jay floated the idea of more children, dumping the girls and Tenn on Jay."

"The other two wives?"

The talking took her mind off the pulling sadness of missing her mom, so she continued. "Daughters of a European financial guru. Jay used them for information. The oldest got bored with being in her wealthy family's disfavor due to the marriage and agreed to a divorce in which the family paid off her and Jay. The youngest, most think out of spite and misplaced competitiveness, married Jay but then realized the day-to-day version of him actually wasn't much fun and quickly bailed."

Beck whistled. "Wow."

She remembered Beck talking about his dad, and not favorably, but she had to believe he had a more stable upbringing than the kind anyone in this house had experienced. "I'm guessing you were raised with both parents and enjoyed weekday dinners together."

"My parents died in a car accident when I was twenty."

The air rushed out of her. "I'm so sorry."

"So am I." Some of the color had left his face. "It was a long time ago. Even though my dad and I had issues, it's not a thing you ever get over."

"I can understand that."

He nodded. "You grieve, and at some point the good memories push forward, but the pain is always there. Waiting."

Relief washed through her. The kind that came from a mutual understanding. That's how she felt about her mom. Grieving but still conflicted. Loving her so much then losing her without ever understanding her choices, like why her loyalty to a destructive marriage battled so hard against her sense of self-preservation. The pressure. The disappointment and resulting guilt from that disappointment. The sense she could have fought harder to save her children from their father and Jay.

The pain was always there . . . waiting.

She took a step toward Beck but stopped when she heard a knock on the door. "Come in."

"Don't do that." Beck swore under his breath as he stalked around her and across the large bedroom to the door in three steps. He got there in time for the door to narrowly miss smashing him in the head. Kelby stepped inside and jerked back when he came face-to-face with Beck.

"See? It's Kelby." No harm done except for a near miss of a big guy pileup.

Beck spun around to face her. There was nothing blank about his expression now. "The person at the door could have been anyone."

"What am I supposed to do?" She thought he was blowing this a wee bit out of proportion. They were inside her house, after all. "Have a secret knock?"

Beck's mouth dropped open. It took a few seconds for him to close it and rev up for his usual lecturing. "You wait for me to check."

Kelby cleared his throat in the least subtle bid for attention ever. "Am I disturbing something?"

She rolled her eyes because, really, this was an eye-rolling moment. "A lecture on how to open a door."

"I wanted to make sure . . . uh, things are okay in here." Kelby's gaze traveled from Jillian to Beck. "With you two. Together."

"Is that your real question?" Beck asked in a deadly soft tone.

"I didn't think through the sleeping arrangements," Kelby said as he glanced at her mattress.

That snapped her out of her head and back into the present. "What's with the sudden concern about beds? Beck was whining about the same thing a few minutes ago."

"I do not whine."

"Right." She snorted. "Okay."

Kelby's attention stayed locked on the mattress. "If this sleeping arrangement violates your privacy . . ."

"Kelby." She wiggled her fingers in front of his face to break the spell. "What exactly are you saying?"

"Yeah, Kelby. What are you saying?" Beck asked in a singsongy voice.

For a few seconds Kelby didn't seem to be able to say anything. Then he shook his head, as if bringing his mind back to the topic from whatever mental tangent it had been on. "I didn't come in here for this discussion."

That sounded . . . not good. She'd known him for more than a decade and that sentence was code for trouble. "What's going on?"

"Emma will be here for dinner tonight."

Nothing radical or awful about that. Unless . . . "Alone?"

"She's not bringing Gregory, if that's the question."

"Who?" Beck asked, because clearly a bodyguard should be in the middle of this topic.

"A loser who will destroy her." Jillian had a longer, meaner description but she held it in because it would only invite questions.

Kelby barely let her finish before he added his comment. "Gregory is the man Emma is dating."

Emma and Gregory. Jillian's nightmare. He was . . . the worst. Really, just the worst. "I refuse to believe that's true. She has better taste. At least I hope she does."

Beck did that annoying humming thing he did. It was a sort of tell for him. When he was about to come out with some big wallop of a statement, he hummed. "Why do we hate him?"

"Excellent question." Kelby's eyebrow lifted. "Jillian, you want to take this one?"

"He's walking pestilence." Again, still nicer words than he deserved.

Beck nodded. "So, you've slept together."

"I didn't say that." They had, but still. She wasn't in the mood to talk about it.

"I don't want to know about this." Kelby closed his eyes as if shutting them would block out the words.

Beck kept right on nodding. "I kind of do."

So much for her idea of being alone and relaxing for a few minutes. "You are the nosiest bodyguard in the world."

That stopped him. "Have you had a bodyguard before?"

"No."

"Then which one of us is the bodyguard expert?"

Jillian didn't realize she'd closed the gap between her and Beck until Kelby stepped between them. "Is something going on between you two, or is there some sort of problem I should know about?"

Beck was obnoxious and annoying and intrusive and a bit too easy to get used to having around. So, yes. Big freaking problem. "He thinks I need friends."

"Well, he's not wrong about that," Kelby said.

"I should fire both of you."

Kelby shook his head. "Not going to happen."

"Don't make promises you can't keep," Beck said at the same time.

Jillian gave up in the hope of salvaging some sort of dignity from this discussion. "So, about Emma?"

"Jay and the girls trapped her in the den for over an hour."

"This information makes you smile?" Beck asked.

She couldn't help it. They never strayed from their usual schemes and evil plotting. "Dinner should be fun."

"I'm eating out," Kelby said.

Beck hummed again. "Me too."

Men. "Cowards."

CHAPTER SIXTEEN

MOOREWOOD FAMILY RULE #13: *Always work every angle of a potential job.*

HOURS LATER JILLIAN AND BECK WERE BACK IN THE BEDROOM suite after a walk around the grounds and several safety quizzes from Beck. She now knew to lock doors and never open one without an assistant. Got it.

Her biggest problem was trying to figure out where she put her one sneaker. She kicked it off in a dramatic *we're done for today* show post-walk. Now she couldn't find it.

She was about to beg Beck to crawl under the bed for her when the door opened. Beck shifted to high alert. His shoulders tensed and his body stilled. One hand looked like it was reaching for a weapon. He pulled back from jumping into combat mode just in time when Emma whizzed inside and quietly shut the door behind her.

She stood there, leaning and staring.

"What the hell are you doing?" Beck asked, clearly still locked in an adrenaline haze.

Emma smiled. "Visiting my sister."

"I have to ask, and don't get all grumbly, but what is the point of safety drills if *you* don't lock the door?" Jillian asked. When Beck glared in response, Jillian turned to Emma. May as well get all of the lectures out of the way. "Your being in here is risky."

Emma winced. "The door isn't his fault. We were practicing lockpicking a year ago and figured out how to open these with a paperclip. It's not hard."

Beck's glare didn't lessen but it did shift position to aim at Emma. "Excuse me?"

"You were what?" Jillian asked at the same time.

"They're old and easy to pick. And if anyone asks me about being up here, I'll say we were arguing. Problem solved." Emma pushed away from the door and met Jillian in the middle of the room for a hug.

It was awkward, but not because of a lack of genuine sisterly love. Rather, because Jillian had a sneaker dangling from her fingertips and Beck still hadn't moved.

"Someone want to fill me in on what's happening?" Beck asked.

Jillian sighed, knowing she needed to step in since no one seemed to care that she'd lost her sneaker. They'd moved on from her crisis. "Remember how I told you things weren't exactly how they looked around here?"

"No."

Come on. She was pretty sure she'd dropped a big hint. "I said it."

"Still no."

"Anyway . . ." Emma sat on the edge of Jillian's bed. "You forgot to mention this—him, you two, the hot flirty thing—in our texts about having an unwanted bodyguard."

Okay, no. "We're not going there."

"Unwanted?" Beck asked.

He wore an unreadable expression as he let out a *you're killing me* sigh of exasperation. Jillian had heard that more than once already. She had a feeling she was about to hear it a lot more.

"Okay, what's happening right now? With you two." He pointed at them. "Spill."

Emma laughed. "Just tell him. He won't say anything . . ." Her amusement faded. "Will you?"

"I don't know what I'd say."

Jillian took pity on him. "Emma knows everything. She's an undercover ally."

The fighting and sniping had all been an act. Admittedly, Emma was good at it because as the baby sister of the family she'd been born to play the role of spoiled brat. She'd literally spent years perfecting it.

"That's kind of sparse on details." Emma snorted then kept talking, taking up most of the explaining. "We knew Jay's side of the family would line up against her. Well, except Tenn. He's not like the rest of them."

"The rest of them are problem enough." Jillian thought

that might be her greatest understatement of the day, but then the day wasn't over yet.

"About that. They lured me in and did their usual *let's win Emma over because she's not smart enough to know she's being played* thing. Totally annoying, by the way." Emma stopped just long enough to sigh. "They tried to be coy but . . . expect another attack. I sense it's coming."

"I'm going to drown your uncle in one of those pools out there." Beck sounded completely ready to go make that happen.

Emma smiled. "Aw, that's sweet."

Jillian loved that Beck rushed to her defense. Sure, he was paid to, but no one had ever really dropped everything to support her. She did the dropping and the protecting and the fixing.

"No need to commit homicide, no matter how tempting. We know they're locked and loaded, and we're ready for whatever they do." Jillian tried to make her voice sound firm, as if she actually believed the nonsense she was spewing.

Emma shifted until she faced Beck. "You're going to watch out for her, right?"

"Emma."

"Jillian," Emma said back in the mimicking tone younger siblings throughout time have perfected to annoy their older siblings.

"I get Anika's angle. And Jay . . . is Jay." Jillian tried to reason her way through what might happen next. "What's Astrid doing?"

"Following Jay around, being overly friendly in an attempt to hide her underlying evil ways. She's been pretty involved in getting information to Doug."

"Are Astrid and Doug close?" Beck asked.

Emma grimaced. "Define *close*."

Poor Beck looked lost. "I don't know how to answer that."

"I think Emma is referring to the fact that Astrid isn't particularly close to anyone. Not even Anika." It felt odd to be talking about her cousins in the abstract, but Jillian did it anyway. "Astrid is always out for Astrid. She thinks no one appreciates her skills and that Anika gets all the attention."

More Beck humming. "Is this just weird sister stuff or is it something bigger?"

"Sister stuff?" Jillian asked.

"Bigger. Astrid is a wild card. Hard to read. Impulsive." Emma made a face. "Greedy, vicious, and mean."

"My cousins are just lovely creatures," Jillian said.

"I'll keep up the spying." Emma leaned down and pulled the missing shoe out from under the bed. "Infiltrating the enemy camp and all that."

That sounded like trouble. Not that Jillian thought Emma was in danger. More like she feared Emma was getting sucked into shiny parts of grifting, like strategy and gameplay. "You're enjoying this too much."

"Until I hear some details and get an idea of what their plan is, I'll keep my distance from you in public." Emma then pointed between Beck and Jillian. "You keep him with you."

Beck nodded. "I'm not going anywhere."

Emma bounced off the bed. She'd always been this ball of energy and getting a little bit older hadn't curbed that. She bolted across the room but slowed down when she got to the door. She opened it and peeked into the hall. A few seconds later she shut the door again and turned to face them.

Beck had never really relaxed with Emma in the room and was now back to his rigid stance. "What is it?"

Emma looked at Jillian. "Astrid is coming out of your old bedroom and going into your old office."

"What would she be doing in there?" Beck asked.

"She could be using the office to check on Doug." Jillian thought that option made the most sense.

"I provide the intel. It's up to you two to figure out what it all means." Emma shot them another smile and opened the door again. "See you at dinner."

This time she didn't come back.

Beck stared at the closed door for a few seconds. "That was a surprise."

"You'll find the Moorewood family is full of those."

Beck shook his head. "Again, the man who is assigned to protect you shouldn't be taken off guard."

"Then you're working for the wrong family."

"I need to get into that office and have a look around." He glanced at the practical black watch he wore. "Maybe I can figure out what Astrid's doing."

"Be forewarned. This isn't the usual office." Jillian had no idea how to explain the elaborate setup her family had created while she was gone.

"Of course not."

She could tell he wasn't fully understanding the breadth of the problem here. "It's what I imagine CIA headquarters looks like."

"Your family is pretty messed up."

"Thank you. Yes." Vindication and very satisfying. "That's what I keep saying."

CHAPTER SEVENTEEN

MOOREWOOD FAMILY RULE #25: *Clear the air now and then. Communication is key.*

JILLIAN WORE A DIFFERENT DRESS AND HER SNEAKERS TO THE family dinner. A nap helped her focus. Uninterrupted sleep was a luxury she no longer took for granted. She drifted off while Beck stood by, or walked around, or stared at her, or whatever he did. She just knew he was there, and no one could touch her.

One thing she did get used to at those large group prison meals was noise. The low hum of voices mixed with blasts of laughter or yelling. The silence at the family dinner table tonight unnerved her. No one had spoken in more than five minutes. Silverware clanked and everyone ate, except Beck, who insisted on staying on his feet and just inside the door, watching them, while they shoveled pan-fried sole and green beans into their faces.

She sat at one end of the table; Jay, the other. The families had basically divided and sat on opposite sides. Kelby, for all his talk about not wanting to be there, showed up right before the food hit the table.

Izzy wasn't in attendance. She'd begged off, claiming to have plans with a friend in the area. Jillian knew Jay would blame her for that.

Thinking non-family topics might be the safest in a sea of unsafe ones, Jillian tried her knack at conversation. She looked at Anika. "Have you talked with Harry?"

"I actually thought he'd be here tonight," Emma said, clearly taking a more delicate route to the same conversation topic. "He's been here most nights lately."

"He insisted on telling his family about Jillian." Anika dropped her fork on the good china with an ear-piercing clink as she looked up. "About her time in prison."

Jillian wasn't sure what the expected response was to that. "How nice of him?"

"He told them and then his mother insisted they have dinner this evening. Just the two of them, so they could talk. She also had a beautiful diamond necklace and embarrassingly expensive diamond-encrusted watch that she kept at her house sent to her safety-deposit box, *just in case*. Those were her actual words: *just in case*."

Hiding expensive jewelry from this family struck Jillian as very wise. But . . . "How do you know about the safety-deposit box?"

"I just do."

Jillian tried to place the emotion moving through Anika's voice. Heaps of anger and frustration, sure. But a note of something else. The exact emotional undertone was hard to assess through the sarcasm, but Jillian still picked up on the strain.

That raised more questions than it answered. Anika had spent her entire life worrying about only herself, so Jillian couldn't imagine her prying open the space to make room for Harry. More likely, she was annoyed about getting so close to snagging a rich husband and potentially losing him before he bought a ring.

Jillian never entertained the idea of either female cousin having a genuine emotion. They'd learned from the *King of Deception* how to pretend to care. How to fake cry. Rising above that level of human disconnection would be a herculean task for anyone, and Jay hadn't exactly given them a lot of interpersonal tools to work with.

Jay slowly lowered his silverware before looking at Jillian down the long table. "I suppose you're happy with yourself."

She stabbed her fork into a green bean. "I'm not unhappy."

"You single-handedly turned this household upside down." Jay folded his linen napkin with a great flourish. "All our hard work—three years of it—is now in peril."

"Wait, you want *me* to apologize for losing those years?" He had to be joking.

"Izzy isn't here tonight because she thought we needed family time. And it's not just my work." Jay rambled on, clearly enjoying the role of martyr. "Harry, who has barely left Anika's side, is now spending more time away. That does not suggest an engagement is imminent, as we'd hoped."

"Save your breath. Jillian doesn't care about what she's done," Anika mumbled.

"Jillian, no one begrudges you being out." Astrid shook her head. "But your presence here, at the estate, is causing problems."

"All of you stop," Aunt Patricia scolded. "Jillian is home and we're grateful."

Jillian didn't have to take a poll on that topic to know the comment was an exaggeration.

"We're having dinner like civilized people." Patricia picked up an unlit cigarette then set it down next to her knife again. "You've all been taught how to behave, now do it."

Tenn sighed. "I agree with Aunt Patricia. Is the bickering necessary? There's enough money to go around, right?"

Jillian gave Tenn points for hitting the real issue head-on.

Anika stared at Tenn. "How would you know what there is or isn't?"

"Yeah, I thought you didn't care about the money," Astrid said in her usual rush not to be left out.

"Your sisters are correct. This discussion and our frustration over Jillian's antics are not your concern, Tenn." Jay's attention stayed on the son he'd spent a lifetime ignoring. "You made the choice not to live here or engage in the family business."

"Enough." Jillian was done with this part of the never-ending *Jay Show*. There was a limit to how much pretend drama she could take. "Don't speak to Tenn that way."

"It's okay." Tenn brushed off the concern as he had done his whole life.

"You've done everything possible to taint Tenn's opinion of us. Pushed him to give up his birthright." Jay leaned back in his chair as if he were about to impart some great knowledge. "Yours is not the only vote here. This is a family. We do things, make decisions, as a family."

Jillian rested her elbow on the table and her chin in her hand. "Please share more about this fantasy family world of yours."

"Jillian." The warning was clear in Patricia's voice, but she stopped there.

"We should clear the room and discuss this." Jay's eyebrow lifted. "That's what you want, right? To have it out?"

"Yes, of course." Astrid cleared her throat. "The help should leave."

"What is wrong with you?" Emma asked. "*The help?*"

Jillian wasn't in the mood for her family, and she certainly wasn't in the mood for their entitled bullshit. "Do you mean Kelby, the man who keeps the estate running and made sure you didn't sell the silverware while I was gone?" She turned, lifted her hand, and gestured behind her. "Or are you talking about Beck being in the room? The same man who is single-handedly keeping me from kicking your sorry asses."

Patricia tut-tutted. "Language, dear."

"Listen to your great-aunt. You should be more respect-ful." Jay sat up, his elbows on the table, and leaned in. "Do you understand how much jeopardy you put all of us in when you tangled with the FBI?"

An explosion went off in Jillian's head. "Me being hauled off by the FBI saved this family."

Astrid's eyes narrowed. "What?"

"How?" Anika asked.

From their perspectives, fair questions. Jillian could admit that. They all had a hand in building the massive wall of heat and anger between the two sides of the family, her included. No one showed an interest in tearing it down. Jillian liked the security of having it there, a dividing line between *them* and *us*.

There was so much they didn't know about what had hap-pened before, during, and after her arrest. So much Jillian wasn't ready to share . . . yet.

Jay sighed. "Honestly, Jillian, you're as difficult as your mother."

Jillian ignored Astrid's gasp and the stunned expressions of everyone else around the table. All of her attention—every last inch of her rage—focused on Jay. He touched on the one subject, plan or not, Jillian refused to ignore. "What did you say?"

Astrid's hand shook as she waved it in front of her. "Let's just eat."

Tenn blew out a long breath. "Jesus, Dad."

Jay ignored all of it. "I appreciate everything Sonya did

for this family, including the way she stepped up for my kids. You know I loved your mother."

"Obviously." Jillian filled the delivery of the word with as much sarcasm as possible.

Patricia picked up that cigarette again. She twirled it in one hand and rested the other on Jay's arm. "Jayson, you should probably stop talking now."

But he didn't. "The reality is hard, and we made a pact not to dwell on this, but it's time everyone deals with what we know to be true. You all know Clive loved Sonya. But no matter what he did and what he sacrificed, it was never good enough for her." Jay stopped looking around the table and faced Jillian. "Your mother wore him down."

They were in it now. Forget eating and light conversation. They'd passed into the stage of family grievances and fury.

Jillian decided to air a few of her own. "What marriage were you watching? He only started dating her as part of a con."

Patricia pushed her chair back. "I think we should find a new topic."

Yeah, sure, but Jillian had one more point to make. "Like how he killed her?"

All of the color drained from Astrid's already pale face. "That's not true!"

Emma made an odd noise. "Jillian, don't."

"Listen to your sister." Kelby stared at Jillian, concern obvious in his eyes. "Be careful."

Nope. Too late. Jillian held on to her fork. Tightened her fingers until the metal dug into the fleshy part of her palm. "Day by day. Inch by inch. Dad chipped away at her stability and self-esteem. Both of you did, Jay. You and Dad. You both had her rattled and frail at the end."

"That is not true." Jay's gaze skipped over the table as he spoke. Landed everywhere else before finally resting on Jillian. "We softened the blow for the press, but you know the truth. You were here when we lost your mom."

Jillian hadn't planned on airing this now, but when they started talking about family grievances this one floated to the top. All that grief and anger she'd buried and ignored bubbled up and demanded attention. The pain of knowing her mom had to make terrible decisions to save all of them . . . then turned around and asked her to do the same by taking over everything. Jillian couldn't deny that Mom inadvertently made her the target and that the demand of loyalty landed her in jail.

Bottom line: woman after woman on this side of the family tried to rescue the entire gene pool and failed.

"Clive never strayed. He stayed close. He tolerated being treated like your mother's employee when it came to money," Jay said. "He even conceded to you being in charge of the estate, and we know how that turned out."

Right. Her fault. Always her fault. "I put Dad on an allowance because without that limit we'd all be living in a car."

Jillian hated Jay but he at least had some boundaries. Dad had none. He craved the adrenaline high, the thrill of the chase. He lacked any sense of responsibility. He'd never had to possess any because first Jay, then Mom, shouldered that for him.

"You didn't make that financial decision about your dad alone. Sonya and I agreed with you," Kelby said. "If people want to cast blame, they need a wider net."

"Yes, Kelby. What about you?" Jay asked in a voice filled with condescension. "You slipped into Clive and Sonya's marriage and tried to destroy it."

Jillian's protective instincts rose. "Don't blame Kelby. Mom trusted him."

Those rumors of a torrid affair had raced around for years. Part of Jillian hoped they were true because that would mean Mom had at least some true happiness and romance near the end.

"If anyone has an allegation about Mom cheating, you should say it." Emma, not one to throw down a gauntlet, did so now.

Patricia shook her head. "No one is saying that, dear."

"Jay." Anika's eyes widened. It looked like she was trying to send Jay a silent message.

Jillian refused to be sidetracked. "Despite having whatever you wanted and all the money you should have needed, you refused to give up your old grifter life and go legitimate. You didn't do it when Mom asked. You didn't do it when I bargained for you to stop."

Jay shook his head. "You don't understand how the family business works."

"Which is evident because you went to prison," Anika said.

"And"—Astrid looked around the table before finishing her thought—"your mother killed herself. It sounds harsh, but that's the truth. She chose to leave us."

Emma sat up straighter in her chair. "She had cancer."

Astrid didn't back down. "Right, but she still ended it."

The pills. The shocking quiet that fell over the house as the ambulance pulled away. The sound of Jillian's father weeping as he hid in the laundry room. Jillian remembered all of it. Every last terrible, shocking second of it . . . including *why* her mother did it. The cancer. Mom's fears about what would happen if Jay or Dad contested the power of attorney she'd drawn up and went to court to become her guardian instead. If they tried to move in and take over while she lay there powerless to stop them.

"Okay." Tenn stood up, looking unsteady on his feet. "I can't do this."

Jay watched Tenn leave the room and then started again. "I know this is hard for you to hear, but Astrid is right. Sonya made the choice, and I don't blame her. None of us should. The pain had to be unbearable at that point."

Jillian despised the sound of his voice and the way he talked about Mom's death like it was a subject for debate. "You made this house and her life a chaos-filled mess. Any chance Dad had of going legitimate, of rising above how he was raised, stopped when you moved in."

"Okay, we've all done some talking." The legs of a chair squeaked as Kelby stood up. "Maybe we should take a break here."

"I thought Jillian was going to give us her list of demands," Astrid said. "Isn't that what this meal was about? Her telling us what to do."

Patricia glared at Astrid. "You just can't help yourself, can you?"

"The exact demands can wait." Jillian's voice shook with fury, but she stayed focused because she knew Beck wanted more time, and that meant stalling . . . for now. But she needed them all out of her house and soon. "But you can start by ending the plans you have for Harry and Izzy. You end them or I will."

"Ridiculous." Jay mumbled something else that sounded like it ended with *bitch* but who knows.

"Those are my easiest requirements." Jillian smiled. "I'm not going to change my mind and I'm not going anywhere, so capitulate. You have three days."

CHAPTER EIGHTEEN

MOOREWOOD FAMILY RULE #14: *Keep anyone in law enforcement or related fields at a distance.*

ENERGY SURGED THROUGH JILLIAN. THAT HORROR OF A FAM-ily dinner ended more than an hour ago. She couldn't actually eat, so Beck took her out for fast food french fries. She laughed when he suggested it. Then she ate her portion and his.

Now, back at the house, her mind started racing again. All that talk about her mother had punched her in the heart. She'd come out swinging to keep from doubling over. But as the adrenaline burned off, so did her ability to push away the memories.

Finding Mom in bed. Seeing the empty bottles next to her.

Jillian blinked as she walked around the bedroom, trying to fight off the crash of pain she heard thundering in the back of her mind. As furious as she was at Jay and Dad for driving her mom to the edge, a tiny piece of her always blamed her mom, and she felt like crap for doing so.

In the guilt game, Jillian shouldered the largest load. Her father hadn't possessed the emotional tools to deal with real life or, in Mom's case, real death. Her mother couldn't find a way out. Jillian had known better, but she didn't step in soon enough, yell loud enough, insist hard enough.

"Jillian." Beck's deep voice moved through the room.

Before turning to face him, she struggled to gain control. No tears. No weakness. That meant focusing all of that unspent energy on the other side of the family. "I know you're collecting evidence, but I should kick them all out right now. Not give any chance to stay."

"Jillian." This time, Beck reached out and touched her arm.

The hold was gentle. She could break out of it simply by moving, but she didn't want to.

"How long ago did your mother die?"

The question, so quiet and sincere, sent a million thoughts spinning in her head. She sat down on the edge of the bed. Stared at her hands. "He pushed her to—"

"I'm not debating the method right now."

Right. Think.

"Seven years ago." She meant to stop there but the memories tumbled out and she gave a voice to them. "I didn't know until near the end that she had cancer. She hid it."

He made that now familiar humming sound. "I guess she wanted everything handled while she was still alive."

"We worked overtime to move money around, take it out

of their reach. Changed the rules. Limited them to monthly spending accounts. Invested in real estate and businesses, instead of pouring the money into shiny new ways to rip people off."

Beck scoffed. "I bet Jay's side of the family loved that."

"They blamed me and secretly worked on Mom. It went on for years. They were relentless as they tried to get her to release some funds. To make calls to bankers. To sign off on paperwork that would have threatened every resource."

Beck sat down next to her. "But you had the final say."

A power she balked at when her mother first gave it to her. She didn't want the burden. She also knew being in charge tied her to the estate and the family, shutting out any option for a different life. "Kelby and I stood firm. Mom would waver, thinking if Jay and Dad had more access to money they might not be so desperate."

"They used guilt on her," he said in a quiet voice.

He got it. She didn't have to convince or baby-step him through it. She wished everyone had been so clear about what had happened. "She knew the sicker she got, the more power they'd have." Tears pushed at the edges of Jillian's eyes, but she inhaled, trying to stop them from falling. "Imagine thinking the only way to keep your family from getting into trouble and continuing their series of cons was to kill yourself and take away their power."

"She did that because you inherited upon her death?"

"While she was alive she had a husband and he had rights. If a court made him her guardian, he'd fight to be in charge, regardless of the assets mostly being inherited and not his marital property." She sighed, trying to summon up the same level of grief for her dad that she had for her mom, but she couldn't do it. "She worried he would ignore her wishes. Fire Kelby. Blow up all the strides we'd made to slough off the part of the family finances attached to cons."

"Did they give up after she died?"

"If anything, Jay took her death as a green light to push harder. He probably felt the money slipping away." She saw through every ruse to the shallow, empty man he was underneath. "And he isn't the type to leave things to chance. He found a work-around. Faked financial documents and got this guy at the bank to let things slide, insisting they had control of Mom's trust fund as her heirs, which wasn't true."

Beck shook his head. "It's amazing how guys like Jay can always find that one guy in the system without morals and work him until he breaks."

"The bulk of the estate went to me. Mom left instructions on how to use the assets I inherited to support the family and fence in Jay." Every word Jillian said felt as if it were dragged out of her. With each syllable, the immediate rush of anger slipped away. "By the time we realized Jay and Dad had made all of these promises based on lies, they were in deep again."

Beck's gaze switched from her face to her hands and back again. He didn't touch her, but he stayed close. "And you tried to fix it. Again."

"Which ended up making me look complicit." She'd played right into their schemes and didn't realize it until she was drowning and had few options to get out. "They'd faked documents. Forged my signature."

"You took a plea but the two other people who were implicated in scams—your dad and, interestingly enough, that Greg guy's dad—both died before they could even enter a plea," Beck said.

Now he was wading deep into *I don't want to talk about this* territory. Into topics she couldn't discuss. "You were busy studying before dinner."

"Am I wrong?"

"Dad had a heart attack." No deception there. "Weeks later, the FBI moved in on Greg's dad on his own financial scams. He panicked and tried to run, flipped his car, and died on impact. Avoided any responsibility to the people he bilked of their life savings and retirement accounts." That part skipped over several big details she tried not to dwell on.

Beck rubbed his hands together as he hummed. "Some would say your dad paid the ultimate price."

Not her, but others. Sure. "I guess."

Beck whistled. "That's not even half the story and it sounds exhausting."

"What do you mean by half?"

He shot her a don't-play-games side-eye. "I'm smart enough to know there's a whole lot more you're not saying about those charges, your ex's dad, your agreement, and why you got out early."

Well, damn. Of course she was lying and keeping secrets. That sort of thing had been coded into her DNA.

"Greg isn't my ex. Not exactly." But she had a much bigger problem. Her guard fell around Beck. It needed to stay up high enough not to allow him to peek around the other side. They'd talk and she'd overshare—not something she ever did but with him the words tumbled out.

"I'm not judging or asking." His shrug ended with his hands folded on his lap. "You can tell me the details on your own timeline, or not."

No pushing. No digging or trying to find facts he could twist and use for his own benefit.

He was so different from most of the men in her life. Made her believe, even for a flash, that maybe Kelby's kind of decency could be the norm.

The rest of the tension left her body. She let her shoulders relax and leaned against him. "Why are you so easy?"

He chuckled. "I have never been called that."

His breath blew over her hair and tickled her ear. "You sit there and barely say a word and I cough up all these family secrets and painful experiences."

"My guess is that happens because you need to talk."

No, too easy. He did this to her. Made her feel . . . free.

She glanced up at that face, not handsome but strong. "I'm tired of talking."

Then she pounced. Not delicate or romantic. She knocked him back on the bed and climbed on top of him. Her knees hit the mattress on either side of his hips. Her hands slid up and down his chest.

Her lips grazed his and she felt his hands . . . *Wait*. Pushing away. That was the only description. He held her away from him even as she tried to wrap her body around his.

"Jillian, no." He shifted his head to the side, away from her mouth.

She sat up, ignoring his groan. "What?"

"Give me a second."

Her mind struggled to catch up. He wasn't moving. His hands lay by his head, palms up. He was . . . recoiling from her.

Oh my God.

He was struggling to get away and she was all over him. Embarrassed and a little sick, she jumped off him and shot to her feet. Stood next to the bed, staring at him, and hoping she'd disappear.

If there was any fairness in the world, a giant sinkhole would open up and swallow one of them. Never mind that the room was on the second floor. The whole house could fall into the abyss for all she cared.

He balanced up on his elbows. "This isn't—"

"No. It's okay. I should have asked first." She needed to get out of there. "I didn't mean to do that."

He shot her a grin. "I'm kind of hoping you did."

No smiling at her!

Maybe if she threw up he'd bolt. Crying? Men hated crying, right? She could burst into tears or crawl out her window and hide on the roof. Run away. All good options and she was willing to do almost any of them, maybe more than one, to stop this conversation.

He *worked* for her. What was she thinking? "Consent matters. That was totally out of line."

The amusement left his face. "Huh?"

"Listen . . ." She should probably have something brilliant to say after that introduction, but she didn't. The poor guy wanted to do his job and she launched herself at him. She needed to apologize and promise never to do it again. As soon as her insides stopped shaking she planned to do just that. "You're my employee."

He sat up. "This isn't a human resources issue."

"I'm sorry."

"I'm not."

She swallowed what was left of her dignity. "You should go."

"Jillian." He stood up.

No, too close. She took a few steps back and rammed her hip into the side of the dresser. Tears filled her eyes, and she clamped her mouth shut to keep from yelling *Son of a bitch!*

"Really. I'm just tired." And way needier than she thought.

"Okay, look." He searched her face until she gave him reluctant eye contact. "My negative reaction was about your piss-poor timing and nothing else."

Right, timing.

"You're my bodyguard." Maybe if she repeated that a few hundred times he'd look a bit less enticing. Even now with his disheveled clothes and messy hair and . . . *ugh.* "That's all you should be."

"Because the lady of the house deserves better?" An edge moved into his voice.

"Because there's nothing left of me to give." That slipped out before she could block it. She hadn't been thinking it. Her brain hadn't been working at all, actually. He smiled at her, listened, and that's all it took. Her body downshifted into jumping mode.

His gaze softened. "Jillian, come on."

That looked a bit too much like pity to her. "I'll see you in the morning."

SLEEPING WITH BECK in the room next door proved impossible. Only a thin wall separated them. She shifted around for hours. Back to side to stomach, never a favorite position, then returned to her back. Covers on. Kicked them off. Tried the position with one leg out of the covers and the rest of her body under.

Nothing worked.

She glanced at the clock and saw it was after three.

She sat up then flopped back onto the mattress again. This was her fault. She came on to him. Crawled all over him. The whole scene, the version that kept replaying in her head, was so embarrassing. Just remembering it made her cheeks flush and her brain melt down all over again.

She stared at the ceiling and tried to think of something to count. Anything to get her mind off the chaos swirling around in there. Her uncle. Sympathy for Tenn.

The sound of footsteps threw her back into the present.

Light but deliberate. The knock on the door separating her room from Beck's came next. Not his usual banging that preceded the barging in. No, this one asked for permission.

She mentally ran through her options. Excitement hummed through her, but her mind stayed scrambled. She didn't know the right words to use and couldn't imagine going another verbal round with him. The wounds from his earlier rejection hadn't scabbed over yet.

The door opened, dragging cooler air from his room into hers. They needed to talk this out. Her apology should be bigger. There were a hundred adult ways to handle the situation.

She closed her eyes and pretended to be asleep.

Her heartbeat hammered in her ears as she heard him step into the room. Despite knowing him for only a short time, she trusted him not to pull anything. She also slept with a knife under her pillow. Thanks, prison.

At each hesitant footstep her breath stammered inside her. She tried not to gulp in breaths, but it was so hard to draw in enough air to lie there without having a coughing fit.

The covers brushed over her. With a gentle touch and barely a sound, he tucked her in. Her bare leg now fit under the blanket. She could sense that big body of his move around her bed then turn away.

"Goodnight, Jillian," he said in his normal voice before shutting the door with a click.

CHAPTER NINETEEN

MOOREWOOD FAMILY RULE #11: *Be aware of shifting alliances.*

THE NEXT MORNING, LOST IN THOUGHT, JILLIAN HEARD A noise but ignored it. A few minutes later Beck knocked on the door then walked in. An uneasy awkwardness spun around them. He didn't joke. She didn't shoot out a sarcastic one-liner. He told her Harry had showed up and was waiting for her in the library.

Harry had texted an hour earlier, asking for a private meeting. In a house of this size, privacy was pretty easy to find, but she didn't understand why he wanted it. Why he wanted anything to do with her.

A reasonable assumption was that after seeing her family in all its yelling, lying glory maybe he needed to make a run for it. And, honestly, no one would blame him. But instead of being filled with glee or even satisfaction, Jillian experienced a gnawing emptiness, a painful hollowing out at the idea of Anika getting discarded one more time.

Winning should feel better.

She walked downstairs in silence next to Beck. The stilted interactions reminded Jillian of junior high. Her least favorite time period.

She slipped into the library, once again hit by the grandeur of the room. The floor-to-ceiling shelves. The ladder that moved around the periphery on a track to help anyone trying to reach a book on a high shelf. The dark, studious formality of it all.

Harry stood by the window, staring into the verdant backyard and the ocean beyond. He spun around at the sound of the door, looking a bit pale, which really was genetic and not a statement about his panic level. But the tightness around his mouth signaled trouble.

"Thanks for agreeing to see me." He winced as he said the words. "Sorry for sounding so . . ."

Desperate. Pathetic. She went with a slightly nicer version. "Dire?"

He took a bit of time staring at the handwoven rug beneath his feet. "I can't deny it."

She sat in one of the chairs deliberately arranged for a chat. Her father once lectured her on the importance of maintaining appropriate sitting areas for private conversations. To her, two chairs and a table didn't make an area magic, but whatever.

She gestured for Harry to sit with her. "Does Anika know you're here?"

"God, no." He rushed over but stayed on his feet.

Their positions left him looming over her. She hated that.

"I'll go see her right after . . ." He put his hand on the back of the chair but still didn't drop his butt into it. "Uh, this."

"What is *this* exactly?"

"I was hoping . . ." His wincing had become a habit now. This time he shot it in Beck's direction. "Is he going to be in here the whole time we talk?"

That explained it. Harry wanted total privacy to drop whatever bombshell was coming. Not going to happen.

Beck beat her to it. "Yes, I am."

Something about him jumping in . . . yeah, not a fan. She looked over her shoulder at him, hoping her expression sent the *I'm actually the boss* message she kept failing to hold around him. After a bit of mental wrangling, she put ego aside and let Beck do his job. Even if it killed her. "He's here for my protection. Pretend he's a wall."

"I promise not to listen," Beck said.

She wasn't even facing Beck and she could hear the eye roll in his voice. "There. See? All's well. Beck promises not to listen."

"There's no use going around in circles." Harry finally sat down and leaned in, as if they were sharing some big secret. "I'm here about Anika. Our relationship."

A little dramatic in the lead-up, but okay. Anika was going to blame her for this, and that was fair. The *no more grift-ing* demand made going after Harry's money a violation. But that didn't mean Jillian wanted to be in the middle of the fake relationship implosion.

She tried to remove herself from the mess as quickly as possible. "You want to—"

"My mother."

Uh . . . "Excuse me?"

"My mother is very strong willed. She has very rigid views on what she believes constitutes appropriate family conduct."

Jillian had studied Harry's family before she ever met him and knew he was guilty of vastly underselling his mother's stringent moral code. Beverly Lanier Tolson, the matriarch of the Tolson clan and its leader ever since her overbearing, slap-everyone-on-the-shoulder husband died of a heart attack in a *business meeting*, which, according to local gossip, meant *while at his mistress's house.*

Beverly's father invented a thing that did something related to shipping and then sold the company for wads of cash and heaps of stock options that ensured Harry could cough and five members of his private staff would come running with a tissue. Basically, Bev—a name no one dared call her—came from money. She married more money. Together they made gobs of money, as money usually does.

Bev's sister, Alyce, had lots of money but not Beverly-level money. With their husbands dead and permanently removed from the corporate ladder, the women schemed to make sure none of their children—seven combined, including Harry and his brother—threatened the family's stacks of money by marrying a thoroughly unsuitable mate . . . and almost every potential life partner fell into that category.

Jillian decided to test her knowledge. "My memory is that your mother already has an issue with your brother and his wife."

Harry nodded, not stopping to question why or how Jillian would know about his family. "Mother made quite a scene about his engagement. Blew up the whole thing. He eventually defied her and eloped."

Jillian listened to the sanitized version but enjoyed the real version much more. Word had it the brother followed the family rules for most of his life. Went to the right schools. Knew the right boring people. Landed some sort of diplomatic job then married a woman who worked in a coffee shop, which the family referred to as *he had a breakdown due to work pressure.*

Call it whatever you want, the guy was off happy and sailing with his new wife . . . and failing to hold up the Tolson name as promised. Despite never having met him, Jillian liked Harry's brother.

"I'm assuming your mother feels equally indignant about not approving your relationship with Anika." It was an educated guess that Jillian knew was correct.

"That's an . . ."

"Understatement?" That seemed to be an issue in this

conversation. "And now I assume she wants you to call it off with Anika."

Jillian guessed again, but this really wasn't a hard game. People like Bev tended to play by the same rulebook forever.

"It's more like . . ." Harry stopped and visibly inhaled. "She was already a bit . . ."

Horrified? Exhausted? "Harry, this conversation is going to work a lot better if you finish a sentence. Is my past a problem for her?"

His ever-present wince took on a pained edge. "Sort of."

So, yes.

"If it helps, Anika and I aren't close." The words ran out of Jillian, tripping and flowing, and she couldn't stop them. The first chance she'd had to slam the trap shut on Anika, she defended her. Sort of. As much as she could without blurting out lies to poor Harry.

"My mother is very big on reputation and public perception."

It took all the control Jillian possessed not to make a smartass comment about the death-by-mistress thing. The dead man in question was Harry's father, after all. Some decorum was required.

"I'm not sure what I—"

"Would you talk with her?" Harry asked at the same time.

Ugh. That's not where Jillian wanted this conversation to go at all.

"I'm not sure your mother would accept news about your

relationship any better coming directly from me." And then there was the part where Jillian didn't want to get involved. No matter how tempting it might be to end Anika's relationship by launching into a detailed description of prison time for Bev over the dinner table. Jillian refused to do Anika's dirty work for her . . . unless pushed.

"Mother said she'd be willing to discuss things with you, family leader to family leader."

Jillian almost choked. Is that what she was? "My uncle would likely disagree with the assessment of me as leader."

Harry shifted in his chair. Put his elbow on the armrest then took it down again. Did the whole cycle a second time. "Jay is a solid businessman. I get that."

He wasn't, but okay.

Harry blathered on. "He's also a bit eccentric. Funny and charming. Moves in the right circles but there is one problem."

She couldn't even guess where this conversation was going at this point. "He's none of those things but continue."

"He's also been married several times."

Oh, that.

"My mother thinks of him as a playboy. Not someone who can be trusted in a discussion about long-term loyalty and marriage."

"She's a smart woman." Brilliant, actually. Jillian might have to rethink her initial impression of the other woman. "But you know I've never been married, right?"

"Absolutely. My mother wouldn't think of you as her societal equal." Harry's eyes grew wide right after he said the words. "I didn't mean that as an offense."

"Of course not. Who would be offended by that?" Jillian had fallen into a pit of sarcasm and wasn't sure how she'd ever get out.

"I was thinking about you and Aunt Patricia. Together." Harry's fidgeting reached crisis proportions. Much more and he'd break the chair he was sitting in. "Her as the matriarch. You as the businesswoman who could explain what happened and why it shouldn't stain Anika's reputation in any way."

"So, and correct me if I'm missing the point"—wow, did she hope she was missing it—"you want me to talk to your mother about prison, and for Aunt Patricia to ease her mind about Anika's sense of family loyalty?"

Jillian fumbled at the end, actually not sure what role Patricia—a woman who likely killed her husband and maybe her son . . . and possibly others—was to play in terms of a discussion on the sanctity of marriage and family.

"Anika is sweet and funny." A sappy smile filled Harry's face. "We understand each other. Have fun together. I don't like seeing her worried or in distress."

Jillian's brain sputtered a bit. She was pretty sure the *sweet* reference caused the malfunction. She turned her head and snuck a peek at Beck. Of course, he was smiling.

No help at all there.

"Harry . . ." Really, she didn't have anything else to say. Just his name.

He shifted to the front of his chair and leaned in very close. All signs of stress and concern had vanished. Now he had a glow.

Then it hit her . . . he loved Anika. Like, really loved her. The poor, misguided bastard.

"Um, Harry . . ." Still nothing. Not a single intelligent sentence popped into her head.

"I just want us to have a chance. You can understand that, right?" He reached out but didn't touch her hand. Just let his fingers dangle. "My mother has had to deal with several personal disappointments. My dad wasn't easy. My brother is doing great, but she can't accept his choices. But she is who she is, and I can't change her."

Jillian reluctantly admired Harry.

"When I saw Anika the first time . . ." His grin carried a bit of awe. So big and bursting with energy. "Everything else stopped." He shook his head. "I mean, I never thought she'd go for someone like me."

Oh, Harry.

"I just want us to have a shot at finding the kind of peace and happiness my brother has."

Jillian hadn't seen it coming but the truth smacked right into her. He was a good guy and she liked him.

Well, crap. Now she had to hope Anika didn't break him.

"We'll do it." Patricia's voice filled the room.

Jillian looked up and spied her aunt on the second level of the library. She wore a peaceful expression. Jillian didn't trust that look at all.

"I didn't know you were in here." Jillian thought that carried the right amount of surprise for Harry's benefit and *I see what you're trying to do and no* for Patricia's.

"I was reading." Patricia smiled. "I certainly didn't mean to eavesdrop."

Riiiight.

Harry stood up. It looked like he bowed, but that would be weird, so maybe not. "I should have invited you to join us, Aunt Patricia."

"It's fine, dear boy." Patricia's smile slipped a little when she looked at Jillian. "Tell him you agree."

Cornered by an old woman who hadn't read a book in this library in . . . ever. "Fine. We'll talk to your mother, but I doubt—"

Harry leaned in and hugged Jillian before she could finish the sentence. The whole gesture came off as awkward. He half lifted her off the chair until her feet only skimmed the floor. He squeezed her too hard. His social interaction skills needed some work.

She looked at Beck, silently begging for help. He winked at her instead. So did Patricia.

After a minute that felt like two hours Beck rolled his eyes and stepped in. He peeled an apologetic Harry away. Really, after that display there wasn't much to say. Jillian suggested a family lunch where they could privately chat with Beverly before or after. Harry was so eager and grateful he looked like he was going to try for a second hug, but Beck stopped him.

Ten minutes later Harry was off to search for Anika and

Jillian stood in the middle of the library—once her favorite room but now forever tainted by the memory of this very odd meeting—and tried to figure out what just happened.

Plan to destroy the cousins? Ignored. Personal promise not to get into the middle of her family's messed-up private lives? Imploded.

She glanced up at Patricia. "I'll get you for this."

"Sure you will, dear," she said as she stepped out of view.

Beck picked that moment to finally say something. "That was interesting."

"You could have stopped that hug a bit sooner."

Beck's smile grew even wider. "The poor guy seemed so grateful."

That's the part that sucked her in. She should have told him to run and find someone else, but he loved Anika. Jillian didn't know what to do with that information. "You real-ize I got roped into the role of family counselor for a family that's not even mine."

He laughed. "That was my favorite part."

"And a talk with Harry's mother?"

"Technically, you *let* yourself get roped in. With Patricia's help, of course." Beck glanced up and his eyes narrowed. "Where did she go?"

"Back into her cave," Jillian said.

"I heard that." Patricia's voice floated down from above.

Beck was smart enough to swallow his smile when he looked at Jillian. "I know you're going to get violent when I say this, but—"

"Then don't say it." Jillian wasn't in the mood for earnest.

"—is it possible, despite everything, a tiny part of you cares about what happens to this wrecking ball of a family? That you'll always rush in to save them?"

"No."

"I'm not so sure you're right." He shrugged. "But I do have to admit I was tempted to take Harry aside for a chat."

Interesting he waited until now to bring that up. "Why didn't you? You could have handled this mess and I could have spent the day anywhere else. Literally, anywhere."

Beck shook his head. "Not that kind of talk. A talk that tells him to step up."

"Is that guy code for something?"

"If I wanted to date you, your family wouldn't stop me. I wouldn't need an intermediary or any kind of help. I'd say, *She's it for me* and that would be the end of it."

Her heart jumped a little. She hoped that was heartburn or something else easily curable. "It's easy to say that hypothetically, but—"

"Nothing would stop me." His voice, so sure and confident.

"Well, we don't have to worry about that, do we?"

He snorted. "We'll see."

CHAPTER TWENTY

MOOREWOOD FAMILY RULE #21: *Don't accidentally make a simple problem complex.*

JILLIAN HAD HOPED TO SPEND THE REST OF THE DAY HIDING from her overbearing family. She wandered into the kitchen for a snack and on the way back out ran into Izzy. Jay came rushing down the hall, nipping at her heels. Unfortunately, he didn't think or talk fast enough to stop Izzy.

She stared at Jillian's mug. "Is that tea? It smells good. Could we join you on the veranda?"

Jillian didn't actually know what part of the house qualified as the veranda. She would have said no, and *really* wanted to eat her apple and drink her tea in private, but Jay stood slightly behind Izzy, motioning for Jillian to turn down the offer.

"Of course." If having tea with Izzy upset Jay, Jillian was all for it.

A few minutes later the three of them sat at the round glass table on the stone deck with Jillian facing the water. The idea of knowing she could swim away and take her chances with the ocean current, if needed, made the impromptu gathering semi-tolerable.

Izzy emptied a spoonful of sugar into her tea with a flourish then clanked the tiny spoon against the cup. "I'm so happy we could finally sit down together and talk."

That made one of them. "Sure."

"I think you can excuse your"—Izzy's gaze traveled to Beck where he stood by the doors back into the house— "man."

Okay, that made Jillian smile. "But *my man* looks good standing there."

Beck shot her a you'll-pay-for-that-later glare.

"You're so amusing, Jillian," Izzy said as she took a tiny sip of the piping hot tea.

Jillian really wanted to talk about prison, slice open the *time away* lies, and dissect them right there until Jay started squealing for mercy.

He must have picked up on the direction of her thoughts because he started talking. "Jillian has had a difficult time. We're all happy she's home and doing so well."

Izzy nodded, looking all grave and concerned. "The wrong people can derail us."

Jillian lifted her mug in an air toast. "Amen to that."

She eyed the other woman. Looked at her long blue sheath and the floral scarf tied in this extravagantly complicated knot that had to take hours to accomplish. Throwing on a cardigan would be easier, but whatever.

"I've had friends who have lost everything—homes, fortunes, children, self-esteem—due to getting entangled with the wrong men," Izzy added.

Jillian glanced at Jay. "Yeah, some men suck."

"Well, I wouldn't use that language, but yes." Izzy put her hand on Jay's knee. "That's why it's so refreshing when you find the *right* man."

"I would argue some of us don't need a man at all."

Jay barked out a laugh. "On behalf of my sex, I object."

Izzy laughed along with him. "You're not a problem, of course."

Of course. Little did Izzy know the exact type of man she should run from was the one playing with her fingers. They sat close, almost on top of each other. Nuzzling, sharing sweet looks.

Jillian tried to figure out how much damage she could do if she threw the apple at them. She went for a verbal shot instead. "If you're going to be around here, you should know the truth about this family and the estate."

Jay's jaw clenched. It was a subtle movement, but it happened. "Now, Jillian. Let's not overwhelm Izzy."

Treating women like clueless children was Jillian's least favorite thing. Her dad had done it, too. That overly schmoozy but really condescending thing they did to control the women they targeted. Whatever it was, Jillian wasn't in the mood for it. "Izzy doesn't need protecting."

Izzy threaded her fingers through Jay's. "I admit I'm old-fashioned on that score. The idea of a man taking care of things, handling everything . . . well, I'm sure you respect my choice."

Izzy threw her head back and laughed.

An odd sort of unease sent Jillian's insides squirming. Izzy seemed . . . off. Her words and age didn't always match. Sometimes she sounded much older—and richer—than how she presented, as if she'd gone to some weird finishing school that followed a rule book from the 1800s.

"Speaking of which, we should go." Jay shifted his chair back and started to stand up.

Izzy put her hand out to stop him and her thin sapphire bracelet caught the light. "But Jillian was saying something about the truth?"

"Of course, but I wanted to surprise you and have us meet a few friends at the club." Jay shook his head. "I fear we're already running late."

Knowing Jay had downshifted into panic mode but still didn't show any outward signs of the internal flailing never failed to impress. Jillian didn't know how he hid so much. Maybe he just felt so little. "Hasn't she met all your friends by now?"

"Surely we can stay a little longer." Izzy almost dropped her teacup as Jay pulled her out of the chair and hustled her to her feet. "Oh, okay . . ."

"It's fine. We can talk later." Jillian picked up her mug and took a long sip, never breaking eye contact with Jay over the rim. "Maybe when Jay's occupied with his work or club business we can sit and have a nice, long chat. Just the two of us."

Izzy smiled. "I'd love that."

Jay shuffled Izzy away from the table. Right before he followed her into the house, he turned and looked at Jillian.

She pointed to the nonexistent watch on her wrist. "Tick. Tock."

"Nicely done, dear."

Jillian jumped in her seat at the unexpected sound of the voice. It came from right over her shoulder. "Patricia? Where were you hiding?"

Patricia marched up to the table, looking like she could bench press it if she had to. "This is my house. I do not hide."

Jillian rolled her eyes. "Neither of those comments are true."

"Fine." Patricia dragged out a chair, making as much noise as possible as she did so. "I was getting some air."

"Smoking," Beck said.

Patricia turned on him. Even wagged her finger in the air. "Do not tattle, young man."

Beck's eyebrow rose, but he didn't verbally respond.

"So . . ." Patricia picked up the teacup Izzy left behind and studied it. "What do we think? Is Izzy slow, clueless, problematic, or just annoying?"

"All of the above," Beck grumbled.

Jillian agreed, but she was busy watching Patricia. She handled Izzy's cup with her fingertips, barely touching it.

The kind of thing you might do if you wanted to preserve an object for fingerprinting. "What are you thinking?"

"Something's not right with her."

"But that's why the family always does a thorough review of a target before moving in." Well, most of them. "Except Doug."

"His little dot thing on the map hasn't moved in two days." Patricia's mouth flattened into a thin line. "That's not good."

"I thought you wanted him to stay put," Beck said.

"Don't hover. Take a seat." Patricia tapped the chair next to her and waited until Beck sat down to talk again. "I love my grandson with all my heart—"

Jillian could hardly wait to see where this sentence landed. "But . . ."

Patricia seemed to ignore Jillian's comment and kept on topic. "He's a bit impulsive."

"Reckless," Jillian added.

"Don't help me." Patricia flashed Jillian a grumbly look before focusing on Beck again. "He's not the type to have a flashy car or access to a lot of cash and not . . ."

"Spend it?" Beck asked.

Patricia sighed. "Exactly. He's never been a fan of lying low, waiting things out."

Jillian didn't care about Doug's newest predicament . . . or about him much at all. He'd spent a lifetime getting into close calls only to have the family fish him out.

"Can we get back to Izzy? She's . . . too much." Too much. Too little. Too okay with Jillian showing up. Too okay with Jay's excuses. The whole package felt off to Jillian.

Patricia smacked the table. "Exactly."

Beck frowned at them. "Are you two speaking in code?"

"We're worried Izzy is not what she seems." If Jillian had to guess she'd say Izzy wasn't as super rich as she pretended but was looking to get that way by marrying Jay, which was hysterical in its own way.

"You can't even trust a target these days." Patricia shook her head. A second later, she pulled a plastic bag out of her pocket and gently placed the teacup inside. "We can check this. Look for prints to back up the in-depth investigation that supposedly already happened."

"Do you all have a science lab in this big house, too?" Beck laughed like he thought he was making a joke.

Jillian and Patricia both stared at him.

He waved a hand in front of his face. "Forget it. I don't want to know."

"Who is in charge of the target background checks these days?" Jillian silently whispered *Please don't say Emma* about four hundred times in her head.

"Astrid."

"Has she missed information before?" Beck asked.

Patricia hesitated for a few seconds before answering. "Once."

Beck sat forward in his chair. "When?"

"When Jillian dated Gregory."

Jillian really hated that guy. Just the sound of his name ticked her off, but Patricia was forgetting or purposely causing trouble—something. "Greg turned out to be an ass, but he wasn't a target."

"No, dear." Patricia winced. "As we both know, you were the target."

CHAPTER TWENTY-ONE

MOOREWOOD FAMILY RULE #27: *Remember Rule #26 and stay connected . . . even if it kills you.*

ANIKA SERIOUSLY CONSIDERED IGNORING JAY'S TEXT. HE asked her and Astrid to *assemble in the operations center*, which sounded like a pretty dramatic way of asking them to come to the den.

She couldn't blame him for being on edge. Waiting for Jillian to cause more trouble was starting to be a full-time job. The money-control issue had Anika pretty twitchy, too. Everything would be easier if she could talk to Harry face-to-face. They texted but missed seeing each other. If this dragged on for much longer, she'd go over there and wrestle him away from his mother. Put him in a plane and take his butt to Las Vegas.

Starving because she'd missed two meals thanks to chaos spinning around her, Anika stepped into the room to find

Astrid mixing drinks and Jay downing them. That was never a good sign.

Anika barely shut the door before her father launched into planning mode. "We have a new problem."

Anika bit back a groan. "I think we're full. Maybe later."

"This isn't a joke."

"This is about Jillian?" Astrid asked.

"Of course it is." Jay took a long drink, emptying the glass, then gestured to Astrid for a refill. "She was a difficult child and became an unbearable adult."

"None of that is new." And none of it rose to the level of an emergency in Anika's view.

"I sat in on a private conversation between her and Izzy." Jay put his finger and thumb less than an inch apart. "Jillian was this close to talking. She was about to spill everything about the house and prison. I could feel it."

"But you stopped her?" Anika asked.

"This time, but what happens when I'm not there?" Jay's eyes grew wide. "I can't watch her every second. Soon she's going to get Izzy alone and ruin everything. We need to defuse her. Now. Not with listening devices. We need something bigger."

"There was that issue with her brakes in the past," Astrid said.

A new admission. Anika had tried for years to get Astrid to own up to that over-the-top attack on Jillian. "Is this the same brake failure you've always denied knowing anything about?"

"Accidents happen." Astrid swooped in and removed Jay's glass, only to replace it with a new one. One with more liquor. "But the bodyguard is a problem."

Jay's expression said *no problem*. "We'll get control back and fire him."

Anika tried to imagine Jay throwing Ugly Hot out of the house. "The car. The balcony railing. Haven't you learned a thing?"

"At least I'm trying to save us," Astrid shot back.

"Stop fighting." Jay took a drink. "But your sister is right, Astrid. Fooling with the car is too risky. We need subtle."

Astrid made a *pfft* sound. "Subtle is old school. It doesn't work."

Anika did what she did best—she ignored Astrid and her insipid mumblings and painful sucking up to Jay. "We should exploit the issues between Jillian and Gregory. There's something there. Pick at it."

"Right." Jay pointed at Anika. "You're on that."

Wait . . . what? On Gregory? "I have to keep Harry and his family from balking."

Jay sighed, delivering a load of disappointment and frustration in the sound. "I've told you before. Nothing is going to happen in terms of an engagement to Harry unless and until we neutralize Jillian."

Anika glanced at Astrid . . . who said nothing helpful or supportive. "What are you doing in all of this?"

"I'm not allowed to do anything."

Jay groaned. "Girls, stop. I'm serious. That's enough."

"Has anyone heard from Tenn?" Anika asked.

Jay frowned. "He wouldn't be of help in this sort of situation."

Yeah, that wasn't the question. "I was just asking if he's okay."

He ran out of the last family dinner and Anika hadn't seen or heard from him. They weren't close, but they did check in with each other. She'd texted Tenn today and gotten an *I'm fine* in response, which usually meant he was anything but.

Jay swore under his breath. "He's useless."

In other words, Tenn wasn't part of Jay's plans, so he didn't matter. Anika had ignored Jay's slights and verbal shots at Tenn growing up. Ignored them until Harry mentioned Tenn a few weeks ago and brought up how left out he seemed to be from family events. Now she saw it in every action Jay took. Anika sensed Jillian did as well since she kept sticking up for him.

"Astrid, I need you to stay on Emma," Jay said in the middle of the silence. "Figure out what worries you about Jillian being home, turn up the volume on it, and shoot it back at Emma. Be relentless. Jump on the lack of sisterly loyalty. Anything."

"There's one other option." Astrid seemed to be playing coy, which was not her strength. "Jillian's probation. There are limits on what she can do. She can't get in trouble while on probation."

The words clunked inside Anika. "You'd do something to send her back to prison?"

"I'm talking about how she's restricted from certain activities, and we should be able to use that against her." Astrid
didn't show an ounce of shame. "But her returning to prison
would make our lives easier. Don't pretend you haven't
thought about that."

Anika could honestly say she hadn't. Being frustrated by
Jillian? Sure. Absolutely. She was a problem. She wielded a
lot of power over them now, but like it or not she was family.

Anika tried to use reason. "She's already paid a steep
price."

"She went to prison because she messed up. If she messes
up again that's on her." Astrid smiled. "There's no way she
could keep the money from us a second time. We're ready
for her."

Anika didn't like this turn at all. "Are we?"

Astrid shrugged. "I am."

CHAPTER TWENTY-TWO

MOOREWOOD FAMILY RULE #36: *Sometimes you have no choice but to sneak around.*

NOT LONG AFTER SHE'D FINALLY DRIFTED OFF TO SLEEP, JIL-lian heard a noise. Not the faint kind. A thump. Maybe a scratch. The doorknob . . . or footsteps. She'd been lost in a dream about bacon when the sound pulled her out.

She hopped out of bed, groggy and unsteady, and stared at the partially open door between her bedroom and the room where Beck slept. She skipped waking him because she wasn't in the mood for a lecture, especially since she wasn't totally sure she *really* had heard anything. The loose balcony railing had her twitchy, and she'd been triggered since she found that ridiculous listening device. Her mind might be playing tricks on her, but . . .

She quietly eased her door open. A peek into the hall supported the *dreamed it* option about the sound. She looked for lights on downstairs and under doors. Strained to pick up any sound. Nothing. Not a person in sight.

She turned, intending to slip back into bed and pretend the fog of paranoia never happened and . . . Beck. Right there, lounging in the doorway between their rooms with his arms crossed, looking hotter than he should with his hair all ruffled and his perma-frown firmly in place.

He hadn't made a sound. All those muscles and that height and nothing. Not even a pitter-patter of footsteps.

She tried to convince her heart to stop doing that terrified hammering thing. "Sweet baby Jesus. Don't sneak up on a person."

As usual, he ignored her demand. "What are you doing?"

He wore sweatpants that just sort of balanced on his hips. Like clung there. His broad chest and tight stomach made his slim white T-shirt basically obsolete. "I'm sure they have bigger sizes."

His frown somehow deepened. "What?"

She forced her gaze to remain on his face. "Why are you standing there?"

"Why are *you* in the hallway?"

This sounded like an impasse. She tried to break through it with as few words as possible. "I thought I heard something."

He sighed. A this-woman-is-killing-me sigh. "So, naturally, you rushed around the house without waking me."

"You might be overstating—"

"And that." He nodded in the direction of her entire body. She glanced down at her ribbed tee and silk pajama shorts.

Everything seemed to be in place, more or less covered. She wiped a hand through her hair because anything could be happening up there. "You don't like my outfit?"

"You're barely wearing anything."

She refused to look again. "I don't sleep in a parka."

"Maybe you should," he mumbled.

"What's wrong—"

"Come back inside." He stopped lounging and stood up straight after delivering his order.

"Stop interrupting me."

"I will if you come in here and put on a robe."

She wasn't sure why he thought those things were related. "The part where you bark orders is a problem."

He shrugged. "Complain to my boss, who is me. In case that wasn't clear."

She wasn't up for banter. She wasn't sure why she was up at all. "I'm coming back in my room because it's chilly, not because you ordered it."

"Whatever works." He gestured for her to move out of the way then walked behind her and shut the door to the hall. "Now. Tell me what happened."

She really wanted to return to her bacon dream. "I heard something."

"What?"

She knew he'd want details. She didn't really have any. "A thud."

"A thud or a thump?"

She spent exactly one second trying to figure out the difference then gave up. "Or a whistle."

More male sighing. "That's a totally different sound."

This time she sighed back at him because it was two in the morning and because standing there, barefoot and yawning, was starting to make her feel weird. "The point is something woke me up. A noise in the hall, though it kind of sounded like someone was in the room, which you had locked, so who knows."

"And after hearing someone break into the room—"

"I didn't say that."

"—you ran into the hall. The same hall that leads to the people who tried to get you to fall off the balcony." His eyebrow lifted, as if taunting her.

"Okay, you've made your point." He was right and she mostly hated that. "I was only out there for a second before you appeared."

"Because I heard you get up."

She wasn't sure how she felt about that. "Is that cute or creepy?"

"Maybe both." He pulled a baggie out of the elastic waistband of his pants, as if that were a totally normal thing to do. "I found this earlier."

"You're just randomly shoving things down your pants now?"

"I had it under my pillow. I didn't want it out of my sight, so I tucked it." He handed the bag to her. "A bracelet."

"You tucked . . ." She saw the sapphires. *Oh, shit*. "It's Izzy's bracelet."

"I found it in your drawer. It's in the baggie in case there are fingerprints on it that belong to someone other than Izzy."

It was as if he was throwing words at her. She hadn't understood a thing since he dug around in his pants for the baggie. Mind went blank after that. "Explain the drawer part."

"I check your room every night."

Uh-huh . . . "When?"

"While you're in the shower."

Maybe she was dreaming this. "I have so many questions."

"Then you come out . . . you know. Smelling like . . ." He made a humming sound. "Fruit."

"Fruit?"

"It's nice." He smiled. "Smells pretty. Your face is all shiny."

He stared.

She stared back.

The room spun a bit.

She finally blinked a few times to keep from jumping on him, because that had gone *so* well last time. "The bracelet?"

"Right." He cleared his throat. "I found it in your drawer. With your underwear."

She tried not to think about him touching her underwear. Tried and failed. She ignored the way her face grew warm. "This all happened tonight? Why didn't you say anything?"

"You seemed cranky. I figured it could wait until morning."

Her brain couldn't take much more. She focused on the thin bracelet. So dainty. Not very expensive but pretty. Distinctive and definitely the one Izzy wore at their impromptu tea. "Someone put it there."

He snorted. "I didn't think you stole it."

"No, I mean . . . who? Jay? He's the most logical suspect since he was with Izzy all day."

Beck shook his head. "Izzy came back here and was with Astrid and Anika out on the deck for a while."

"So, any of them could have picked it off her."

"Then planted it in your room to frame you."

Jillian thought about her probation and the possibility of going back to prison. "Whatever you're doing, this investigation of them that's supposed to protect me? Hurry up. My cousins are not going to wait for you to do your thing."

He glanced at the bed. "Maybe we should—"

Oh, no. They were not going there or anywhere near there. "Good night, Beck."

CHAPTER TWENTY-THREE

MOOREWOOD FAMILY RULE #32: *You can't change who people are at their foundation.*

THE NEXT MORNING, JILLIAN FOUND A PEACH PIE IN THE HUGE kitchen downstairs.

Day. Made.

She walked in there to hide for a few minutes. Then she saw the note attached to the chef-grade French oven. The thing was light blue and cost as much as a fancy new sports car. She recognized Fran's writing but didn't see her anywhere. If Fran and Stan were smart they went into hiding to avoid the Moorewood destruction splatter on the horizon.

Welcome home.

Yeah, she loved Fran and her cooking. The scent, sweet and buttery and delicious, brought back so many memories of running into this room and sneaking snacks. Jillian calculated the chance of grabbing anything else and having it taste even half as good as warm, freshly made pie. None. No chance.

"I missed this." Jillian pulled one of the barstools into the corner, away from anyone who might be spying or hanging around to poison her, and savored her first bite. The crust might have been the most mouth-watering and perfect thing she'd ever tasted. She let out a groan right as Beck stepped into the room.

He looked around until his gaze landed on her. Next came an eye roll as he walked over to her. More like stalked, looking all in control and exasperated. Big and confident . . . hot.

"There you are." He stopped in front of her. "If you were a different person I'd think you were trying to ignore me."

"I'm perfectly capable of being this person and ignoring you."

He eyed her pie.

Not in the mood to share, she pulled it closer to her stomach.

"After last night . . ."

"You mean, the bracelet?" She whispered the question.

"The tiny pajamas."

"Oh . . ." Her mind went right back to his lounge pants and how easily he hid stuff in them. "No. Nighttime clothing, or the lack thereof, is an off-limits topic."

"Our talk about us and our misfire needs to happen if I have any chance of sleeping again. Dealing with this, coming to an understanding, doesn't need to be so difficult. We're healthy adults."

Easy for him to say.

"We can pretend the awkward pass never took place." On a list of imaginary options, that's the one she'd pick.

His gaze traveled over her hands and up her body, ending in an intense stare-off. "Maybe I don't want to."

The eye contact and the closeness combined to choke off her breath. It came out in tiny pants. This was more *teenager* than she'd acted when she was an actual teenager.

She went with a hard swallow and then tried to blurt out something half rational. "I was on edge when I . . ." He knew. No need describing it.

"Uh-huh."

Maybe not so rational. "I should never have pushed. I'm your—"

"If you use the word *boss*, get ready for me to yell the house down."

"I am and you weren't interested in crossing that line between professional and personal. I get it and I respect your position. Consent matters. Everything stops there." The words sat between them. He'd forced her to say the demoralizing sentences. Out loud.

"Good Lord, woman." He followed that up with a guttural sound, kind of raspy and low. "Come on."

"I'm a big girl."

He grabbed her plate and held it away from her. "A big girl who needs glasses."

Her fork bobbed in the air. "What?"

"Are you serious right now? Do you really think I wasn't interested?"

"I can't do this with you." She stole the plate back. "Not this week."

"Right. The big revenge plan. I'd point out you've had opportunities to expose Jay and Anika, and you haven't."

"I'm playing the long game." And the pie was right there, so she scarfed down another bite.

"You told them you intended to change things around here in the next few days."

"Okay, the short long game," she said while chewing.

"Wow."

"Don't *wow* me. It's your fault. You told me to wait before upsetting them again. I'm on hold for the green light from you."

He balanced a hand against the cabinet on the wall behind her head. His mouth hovered over hers. "I'm trying to protect you."

"I'm pretty tough. I survived prison, mostly thanks to my revenge fantasies. You're here to make sure they don't kill me. And thanks for that. That leaves family drama, and I've been handling that nonsense since birth."

"For the record, you survived prison because you're a survivor."

Well, that was kind of sweet . . . in a weird way. "That's a great example of circular reasoning."

"Over the last few days I've seen you angry, hurt, excited."

"Let's leave that last one off." Her mind zipped back to her bedroom and that bumbling pass. The one she wanted to take back. More than that, she wanted to go back upstairs and this time have him say yes. She worried that made her pathetic but pretending he didn't give off a zing that had her body thrumming was a big ol' lie.

"We're going to circle back to us and the excitement part soon and discuss your terrible seduction timing. Not this minute because for some reason you're not ready, but later." He hesitated, as if daring her to say something. "Right now, I'm trying to make a different point."

"Fine. Get there." He seemed determined to talk her to death. So much for thinking he'd be quiet, easy to order around, and lethal. As far as she could tell the last one fit. Not that she'd seen him go off, but her family's annoying habits would likely push him there.

"You spent your whole life protecting them. I'm not a hundred percent sure I know how or why, but I have theories," he said. "Who you are is who you are. It's not something you can just break out of."

But she wanted to. She ached with the need to. "Get to your non-excitement, not-about-us point."

"I kind of did."

Well, that was anticlimactic. "I missed it."

He put his hands on her knees. "You know what they've done, and you've never turned them in. You could have when you were being questioned by the FBI years ago."

"I'd done too good of a job burying the evidence."

"Will it matter if I find something on them? If you had the firepower, would you use it, or is this really about controlling them with money?"

"I don't want to control the money." Okay, she did but not in the way he was suggesting. "I want to be free of them."

He didn't look like he believed her. His skepticism had her spinning and rethinking. What did she want? The real answer was what she could never have: a big, healthy, *normal* family. Cutting ties was the safest thing to do, but it would alienate them all. Was having no family better than having a grifting one?

Of course . . . but was it?

Beck nodded. "If you're sure, I'll set them up. No more delays. We'll catch them in the act."

"Of what?" Her thoughts scattered. Every plan she'd made in prison suddenly didn't sound right in her head. She felt shaky.

"Planting evidence. Coming for you. Whatever they plan to do next."

That all sounded logical. "Okay."

"And then we'll see what you really want."

CHAPTER TWENTY-FOUR

MOOREWOOD FAMILY RULE #23: *There's not a big difference between an ally and an enemy.*

OPERATION GREGORY. ANIKA WANTED TO TAKE THIS MEETING off the estate, away from prying eyes, but she couldn't really afford to start rumors or give the Tolson family another reason not to trust her. Being seen with Gregory would do just that.

She hustled him into the dining room during a quiet, non-meal moment of the day. No one was in there and no one needed to be, which made it the perfect clandestine meeting place. She gestured for Gregory to take the seat at the head of the table. Let him think he was in charge and all that. Men liked that shit.

She sat to his right. It put them close together, but not too close. "Thank you for coming."

"I was intrigued by the invite."

Anika had to admit the guy had charm. A chiseled face and disarming smile. Loads of confidence and an ability to handle bad news without flinching. The way he met Jillian verbal volley for verbal volley the other night, with humor and a mix of what looked like reluctant admiration and stellar self-control, impressed Anika.

His father had stolen, cheated, and lied his way into the pockets of almost every wealthy person in New England. By the time the FBI caught up with him, the list of charges against him and his fake brokerage firm made him look like a crime boss. The fact that he led law enforcement on a car chase worthy of the best action movie made him infamous. And very dead.

The entire scene was awful and newsworthy. It also saved Gregory and his family from years of public humiliation and protracted litigation. Talk about how the whole thing unfolded remained very hush-hush, but local gossip said the family handed over the bulk of its fortune, properties, and accounts in fines to stave off further legal action.

All of it led back to Jillian . . . somehow. Anika wasn't sure how, and she'd been through every article and video she could find, but the tension between Gregory and Jillian couldn't just be about sex. That would have to have been some *really* bad sex.

"Actually, I agreed because I was supposed to pick up Emma for—"

"Good." Whatever. Not the point. Anika didn't care about any of this. She cared about Jillian. And him. Mostly Jillian with him.

"I know this is awkward." She reached her hand across the table but didn't touch him. "Because of Jillian."

"Ah, yes." He leaned back in his chair and folded his arms across his chest. "What about her?"

Anika tried to let Gregory know he could confide in her. "It can't be easy."

"What?"

She shrugged. "You know. Sisters . . ."

His pretty blue eyes narrowed for a second before his expression relaxed back into his usual carefree stance. "Anika, may I be honest with you?"

She hated any conversation that started with those words. People requesting reciprocal truth usually pretended to do so before landing a conversation wallop of some sort. She smiled and agreed anyway. "Always."

"My guess is that I'm here for a specific reason. That you have something to say." He glanced at his watch.

So did she. She immediately evaluated its value, just as she'd been trained to do since she could walk. A Breitling Chronomat. The perfect watch for anyone who wanted to drop ten grand on a casual watch. Apparently the family hadn't spent all of its fortune paying those FBI fines.

But back to business. "Now that you're dating Emma, I thought we should—"

"Anika. The real reason."

Sweet talk failed. Tact failed. That left cold hard truth. "Fine. You and Jillian. Spill the details."

He laughed. "I guess I asked for that delivery."

Anika moved her chair closer to the end of the table and to him. This topic demanded some level of confidence. She wanted to show him that he could trust her. She'd listen and be objective. "You have a history. It's all secretive and difficult, but it doesn't have to be."

"It's also none of your business."

She was starting to wonder what either sister saw in this guy. He wasn't a sharer. If the rumors were true, most, if not all, of his potential inheritable family fortune was gone. That left few positives other than the pretty face, whatever income he made now, and the fancy BMW sedan he drove around town.

Anika inhaled and tried again. "It might be easier if you talked to me. Getting stuck between Emma and Jillian would be uncomfortable for you. I could help to ease that . . ."

"Discomfort?"

Now she suspected he was messing with her for fun. The jackass. "Sure."

"One question." He sat up, letting the front legs of his chair land on the hardwood floor. "What makes you think there was anything between me and Jillian?"

The dining room door swung open. Anika was about to yell about privacy when Jillian stepped into the room. She glanced at Anika then focused on her companion.

"Greg," Jillian said in a flat tone.

He nodded in greeting as he stood up. "Can you just not pronounce my full name?"

"Did you come to steal the silverware?" Jillian asked.

He didn't even sweat as she grilled him with sarcastic one-liners. "I have plenty of forks, but thanks."

Anika wanted to step in. She also didn't want to.

His smile widened as he gestured toward Anika. "She invited me."

Great. Now he'd dragged her into the conversation after ignoring her questions. He grew less attractive the more he talked. Anika liked attention, but not this kind. Being the target of Jillian's fury made Anika's whole body jerk and twitch.

"On that note"—Gregory clapped his hands together—"I should go because I don't want to interfere with your family time."

Anika wanted to reach out and grab him. They hadn't finished. Jillian looked pissed. Anika didn't like her odds alone with her cousin.

He stepped into the doorway and stopped, turning to look into the room again. "Jillian, we need to have a talk soon. We're long overdue."

Jillian snorted. "No thanks."

"Excellent." Gregory's smile only grew wider. "I'll be in touch."

When Anika stood up, Jillian shifted to block the now-closed door to the hall. "You're playing a dangerous game, Anika."

"I don't know what you mean." Anika did, but she clearly

never expected to get caught. Who used the formal dining room in the middle of the afternoon? With all the rooms in this place a clandestine meeting shouldn't be so difficult.

Jillian took a step forward. "If you have a problem with me, go through me. Don't hide shit in my room."

The stupid listening device. Anika knew that was a bad move.

"And don't try to use Emma or Gregory against me," Jillian added.

"How would contacting Gregory impact you?" This shouldn't get her any closer to her goal of getting answers, but Anika tried anyway. "Is there something between you?"

"Hatred."

Anika could hear emotion vibrating in Jillian's voice and see it in the stressed lines of her body. If she pushed any harder against the table her bones might crack. Anika decided to shove her a bit anyway. "Why?"

"It's history and not relevant to your life at all."

Anika doubted that. Every kernel held the possibility of leading somewhere. "If it's old news, then why are you afraid to discuss it?"

"I think you'll find that a lot of what happened in the past is better left in the past." Jillian shrugged. "Except for the identity of the person who turned me in. I need to know that."

Cryptic. Curious. In other words, a typical Jillian response. Anika didn't have the time or patience to deal with her today. But there was one question she wanted to know the answer to. "So you've said. Repeatedly."

"Then let's get to it, shall we?" Jillian crossed her arms in front of her. "Was it you?"

"Of course not." Anika appreciated the straightforward approach and had no trouble selling the answer.

"Why should I believe you?"

"Whether you do or not is your problem." And that was enough of that topic. Anika moved on to a more interesting one. "Now it's your turn. Did you have something to do with Gregory's father's death?"

A frown came and went on Jillian's otherwise unexpressive face. "It was a car accident, and if you remember, I was already in a cell when that happened."

All true but not really relevant to the question.

"Why are you spending time with Gregory instead of visiting with Harry?" Jillian looked around, acting as if Harry were hiding under a chair or behind a curtain. "Where is he?"

"At home." Anika had tried to call him three times and he never got back to her, so this was a touchy subject . . . and Jillian's frown wasn't helping. "Did you think he was here?"

"He was." Jillian's voice didn't suggest an attempt to lie. An interesting choice since lying was Anika's go-to strategy. "We talked. Yesterday."

Dread poured through Anika. It ran so fierce that she was stunned she stayed on her feet. "About what?"

Jillian dropped her hands to her sides and stood up straight. "Your relationship. His mother. You're going to make that woman's day when you break it off with Harry."

In no scenario was that going to happen. In a weird way,

it was also the least terrifying possibility confronting Anika at the moment. Jillian with Harry's mother. That was the nightmare scenario.

A recurring vision flashed through Anika's head. Harry walking away, getting into his car, and never looking back. Immediately finding someone else, someone more appropriate. Anika blinked hard to erase the images.

"Look, I get that you hate me, but Harry deserves better. He's had . . ." How did she even explain this without sounding pathetic? "I know you look at him and see a spoiled rich kid, but he's a good guy. He really doesn't care about your prison sentence."

Jillian shrugged. "Does he care about you being a con artist?"

Desperation welled up inside Anika as she searched for the right words to make Jillian understand. "Harry is willing to take on his mother and his aunt for the two of us . . . as a couple. Don't do this."

"Are you . . ." Jillian's mouth dropped open. And stayed there.

"What's wrong with you?" Anika had no idea what a stroke looked like but the mix of shock and confusion on her cousin's face, along with the sudden rush of blood to her cheeks, couldn't be good. "Do you need to—"

"Do you actually care about him?" Jillian sounded stunned at her own question.

Now Anika's brain sputtered a bit. "Well, I plan on marrying him."

"I don't mean marriage like the men in our family do it. I mean, really care. Do you feel something genuine for him?"

"I want the security." He wouldn't hurt her or . . . no, that wasn't quite right. He would be sweet to her. He always was, but the reason for marriage was far more practical . . . or it had been.

Like, love, ambivalence. Anika needed another category. Harry couldn't destroy her if his feelings for her were bigger than her feelings for him.

Jillian's shoulders slumped and her facial features seemed to soften. "Does he know the real you?"

Anika repeated the question in her head, looking for judgment but not hearing any. "If he did he'd run, right?"

"Right." Jillian blew out a long breath. "Look, I talked with Harry and he seems to care about you."

Hope shot through Anika, but she tried to beat it back. She couldn't need him this much, or at all. She had to be ready in case the opportunity fell apart. "You don't know his mother."

"Harry wants me to talk with her."

A wave of dizziness had Anika grabbing on to the back of the chair in front of her. "You?"

"Patricia agreed for me. For the two of us, actually. I don't get it either."

"Don't do it, Jillian." Anika tried to pull back from begging, but she could hear the hint of it in her voice. "I get that you think we need to stop . . . our work. But Harry is off-limits."

Jillian looked confused. "That's not—"

Beck walked into the room. His gaze traveled all over Jillian before he spoke. "Everything okay in here?"

"Yeah, we're good," Jillian said.

They were not good. Jillian stopped in the middle of the most important sentence of Anika's life.

Beck nodded. "Then I'll show this Greg guy out."

Jillian's eyes widened. "He's still here?"

"He wanted to stick around and talk with you." Beck smiled. "I'd rather throw him out."

"Wait . . ." He was gone by the time Jillian looked at Anika again. "Okay, then."

Gregory. Beck. Ugly. Cute. Anika needed a promise, some sort of assurance. "Whatever you have planned, aim it at Jay. Not me."

Silence fell between them. The grandfather clock on the wall ticked but no other sound passed between them for a few minutes.

Jillian finally sighed. "You have to tell Harry the truth. You can't lie to him your whole life. If you care about him, and strangely, I think you might, you need to come clean and start over. Give him a fighting chance to walk away. That's how you'll know it's real."

A thundering whoosh filled Anika's head. "He'll leave and find someone else."

"You have a choice, Anika. A real relationship or a lifetime of being like Jay."

In Jillian's place, Anika would have come back home with a flamethrower and driven them all out. So, a part of her did understand the anger roiling inside Jillian, but that didn't make her heavy-handedness any more tolerable. "I don't know why you think you get to decide for me."

Jillian blinked a few times, as if bringing her body out of a trance. "As much fun as this is, I have to go make sure Beck doesn't throw Greg into traffic."

No agreement. No understanding of her tenuous position with Harry. More uncertainty. Anika hated the feeling of being off-balance and ready for a blow.

"Always the rescuer." Anika would hate that role. "Doesn't that get old for you?"

"Honestly? I'm trying to break the habit."

CHAPTER TWENTY-FIVE

MOOREWOOD FAMILY RULE #5: *You can fake your way through most difficult situations.*

JILLIAN'S BRAIN TURNED ALL SQUISHY AFTER AN AFTERNOON of unexpected conversations. Harry loved Anika . . . or a version of her. Anika might actually like him back . . . a little, which was more than she'd ever liked any person. Ever.

Jillian hadn't seen that coming. But right now she had another mess to clean up, or at least tidy up some, before it bit her in the butt.

"Wait," she called out as Beck and Greg walked toward a gray sedan parked in the circular driveway.

She'd half expected to see a shiny McLaren like the one Gregory's dad had gifted to him for college graduation. It had been superfast, ludicrously expensive, and very hard to find. So exclusive, there were only about a hundred in the US. Clearly an appropriate car for a twentysomething with more hormones than brains. Jay immediately had tried to figure out how to steal it. Jillian remembered more than one dinner conversation about it.

Beck glanced at her over his shoulder. "It's okay. He's leaving."

"I need to talk with him."

"That sounds like a bad idea," Beck said, then kept walking even though Gregory had stopped.

Leave it to Beck to think he got to decide.

Gregory turned around to face her with a big smile on his face. "This just got interesting. If you're giving your bodyguard a performance review, I'd have to say his manhandling needs some work."

As if she'd side with Greg over Beck on anything ever. "Don't make me change my mind and let him kick your ass."

"What's the plan here, Jillian?" Beck asked.

"Greg and I are going to have a long-overdue conversation in the library." She walked back inside, hoping at least one of them would follow her. When she didn't hear footsteps, she took a quick peek over her shoulder.

"You heard her. Go." Beck gestured for Gregory to follow her.

Gregory walked past her and toward the right room. He'd been here before. He knew where to go. She stepped in front of Beck before he could follow.

"Alone," she said in a whisper.

Beck made a low rumbling sound that bounced all over the marble entry and came out as a near shout. "Not okay."

Gregory being Gregory turned around and came back to them. Stepped up beside Beck and acted as if he were part of the conversation. "What do you think I'm going to do to her?"

"What did you do to her before?" Beck asked, his voice low and menacing.

Gregory whistled. "You tell your bodyguard a lot of private information."

She'd had enough. She walked to the door leading to the library and stared at Gregory. "Inside."

Beck leaned against the doorframe. "Are you sure?"

She tried to soften her voice because the tension rolling off him was not good. She needed his gun in his holster. "He's not going to hurt me."

Beck glanced over her shoulder, into the belly of the room. "I'm a little more afraid for what you might do to him if he says something asinine, and he likely will. You're mighty fierce when you're angry."

Some people might be offended by the comment. Sounded like foreplay to her. "You're the one who thinks I'm nice."

He snorted and sat down in one of those pretty-to-look-at-but-don't-use fancy chairs in the hall outside the library. It groaned in protest. "I never used the word *nice*."

Jillian counted to ten before going into the library and shutting the door behind her. She hadn't been alone with Gregory in years, and she preferred it that way. Distance let her forget him and what he did.

Gregory leaned against a wall of bookshelves on the far

side of the room and watched her walk toward him. "He seems very protective."

"He's a bodyguard. The career basically has the definition right there in the name."

Gregory shrugged. "If you say so."

"I do." Because she didn't want Gregory judging Beck or talking about him, or even thinking about him. She was determined to keep Beck out of the mire and muck that sucked down this family and everyone they knew.

She debated where to sit and if to sit. All that confidence she carried back with her from prison ran out of her. Any feelings for Gregory had died long ago. Well, the good ones did. He'd seen to that, but his presence was a reminder of a time when she'd been outsmarted. Vulnerable. Really pissed off.

She pulled out the desk chair and dropped into it. She swiveled until she faced the man she thought of as an enemy. "What are you doing here today? No bullshit. The truth."

"Anika invited me. She acted like she wanted to be my friend." Gregory made a face at that. "It's clear she wants to dig up dirt on us. Use me to put a wedge between you and Emma."

Huh. That all sounded genuine and believable. No made-up garbage meant to throw her off. No obvious scheming. "Okay, I give up. What game are you playing, Greg?"

"Gregory, and I'm not."

That's what had her mentally scrambling. "You answering any question with even a twinge of honesty sets off an alarm in my head. You don't do honest."

He pushed away from the bookshelves and walked over to the desk. After a few seconds, he sat down in the chair across from her. "Maybe I'm trying to show you that I've changed."

Not possible. No one could change that much. "Sure. You're a choirboy now."

He watched her for a few seconds before talking again. "For what it's worth, I'm sorry."

"Did you steal something when you were with Anika?" Jillian waved her hand. "If it's one of those fancy pens, keep it. They're fake."

He didn't break eye contact. "I'm sorry about what I did to you."

Nope. She'd been there. He'd relished hurting her. Didn't show one once of remorse. "What are you doing right now?"

"Taking responsibility for what happened between us years ago."

"I don't buy it. You have an angle. You always have an angle."

He shifted in his seat. "Can I be totally honest?"

This was new, which made her even more skeptical. "Do you need me to explain what the word means before you make the pledge?"

"You're right. My father wanted to go after your mother's money. He befriended your dad, and they did some deals together—"

"They stole from people. No one from the yacht club is lurking around. I'm not wearing a wire. There's no need to clean up the language." Her dad had been tame compared to Gregory's, but they played together, caused chaos together . . . and died only a few weeks apart.

"They were very like-minded, your dad and mine. Open to taking things that belonged to other people. In my father's case, stocks and money." Gregory glanced at the bookshelves then looked at her again. This time his eye contact didn't waver. "Dad clearly thought he had an easy way into your mom's millions. She turned him down, but he was looking to go around her. He tried to convince your dad to transfer money."

"Con the con man." Something about that part appealed to Jillian.

"My dad thought he'd take control, show some fake monthly statements. Convince your mom that he knew how to handle her finances then take over all of it, all the while using her money to cover his short-term losses and hoping for a turnaround so he wouldn't get caught."

Jillian actually knew all of this. The FBI had filled her in, told her what they knew about how Gregory's dad operated. That's when she knew what he'd tried on her mom all those years ago was what he'd been doing to clients forever—earning their trust then siphoning off their money. Gregory's betrayal was different. So personal and deep. It happened years after the attempted con of her mom and fourteen months before the FBI showed up.

"After your mom died, my dad watched. He realized you controlled the money and told me to come on to you, date you. He thought he could get to you through me, which would lead to your mom's accounts," he said.

They'd finally gotten to the part she dreaded. "And you obeyed Daddy."

She wanted to forget what happened next but couldn't. They dated for a short time, but long enough for her to believe him. Long enough for the joy he took in telling her how little she meant to him to make a lasting impression. One that she couldn't erase.

The only good news was that the memories of sleeping together, the sex, no longer played in her mind. That ultimate humiliation—her wanting him and him wanting her family's money—finally faded. One of the few benefits of prison.

Lesson learned. "Jackass."

He nodded. "I'm not denying it."

No, that was too easy. After years of belittling her, explaining his behavior away by saying she got hysterical about casual sex, now he coughed up the truth and an explanation?

She wasn't buying any of it.

Before she could call the meeting to a halt and let Beck toss him out, Gregory spoke up again. "I didn't want to scam you, and I never intended to hurt you."

That was not her memory at all. "That's interesting because you were really good at it."

"After years of doing anything to get Dad's attention, good or bad, I'd had it. I needed to make a good impression and show him I was worthy." He sighed as he shifted again. "But the rules for gaining his affection were pretty high."

He sounded like one of her cousins. "So, you're the victim here?"

"Of course not." He rubbed his hands together and his foot tapped against the floor. He was in full fidget now. "Everything that happened . . . I did it. I want to blame him, but I was a willing and, yes, eager accomplice against you."

She started to stand up. "Are we done?"

"Jillian, please."

She sat back down but didn't say anything. This was on him. She was fine to fester in private, hating him from a distance. She excelled at that.

"What I did to you was really shitty." He opened his mouth as if he intended to say something else but closed it again. "Looking at you back then messed me up. The night you figured it out . . . the crying." He wiped his face before looking at her again. "It's why I got defensive and lashed out."

She'd been too busy reeling to notice anything about him back then except for that laugh. He told her the truth and laughed at her.

"I see you and I'm reminded how easy it was for me to act like my dad," he whispered.

Her mind screamed to end this. Wall off all the hurt, bury the memories for good, and never examine them again. But she couldn't. He was back to his old games and hadn't even ventured very far to find a new victim. "And now you plan to try your sweet-talking scam a second time, on Emma."

"No." The color drained from his face. "God, no."

Such a firm answer. From the pained expression, someone else might believe him. Someone who hadn't listened to him gloat about getting the upper hand. "Save the acting job."

"Your sister reached out to me. Ask her. She contacted me after my father died." He shook his head with a small smile on his lips. It was as if he mentally stepped through the memories as he spoke. "She didn't have you. Your dad was dead. She was conflicted—hated him and loved him—and guessed I would understand that grief."

More guilt. This time hers. Leaving Emma vulnerable was the greatest regret, one of many, but the big one. It left her blindsided when Dad went in for questioning and died. Jillian had been so busy protecting and saving her sister that she'd failed to prepare Emma.

Gregory's drawn face looked like he'd been battered. "I know you don't believe me, but I really care about your sister."

Jillian had heard all of these words before. Yeah, they sounded more sure now, but he was older. Maybe his grifting talents had become more refined.

"And her bank accounts." That's what it all came down to. Money. How to get it, where to steal it, and how much to stockpile. "Dating her, scamming her, would be a good way of rebuilding the family accounts, right? Your dad got in trouble, but the rest of your family forfeited almost forty million dollars to avoid a similar fate. That didn't come close to compensating the victims of the scams for all they'd lost, but it was huge money."

"True."

"You gave up most of the fortune because you *had* to. The FBI made that a condition of not going after the entire family, dragging the litigation out for years." She knew every detail. Down to the penny.

"My dad was a bad person. So was yours." The chair creaked under him as he shifted. "I don't want to be like either of them."

The words slapped her. They stung because she'd thought the same thing so many times. Her whole life, actually. But she refused to buy this act. She'd been pushed down and taken advantage of. Too much to just roll over when he came along looking and sounding all apologetic.

"I have a new career. A legitimate one that I love." He smiled as he talked. "My firm refurbishes yachts and resells them."

"Lucrative but not forty-million-dollars lucrative."

"I don't need that much money," he said.

Need had never stopped his father, or hers, or most of the people they were related to. "Because you intend to use Emma's money."

He let out a dramatic exhale. "She knows about my family. She knows about my finances."

Jillian leaned in closer. "Does she know what you did to me?"

"I've admitted to being shitty in past relationships."

"How chivalrous of you." She really wanted to punch him.

"I was doing you a favor, actually."

That was the Greg she remembered.

His gaze grew more intense. "After all, naming you might lead her to figure out what *you* did. You eventually got your revenge. Didn't you?"

Jillian's breath left her body in a gigantic *swoosh*. She didn't know he knew. She hadn't told anyone outside of those who had to know—except Kelby, and that conversation had not gone well. He'd been disappointed in her. Exasperated at her choices and horrified she'd dragged another family into the mess.

"Am I the only one in the room who's going to be honest?" Gregory sounded more resigned than angry.

That made no sense to her. If he really knew what she'd done he should be furious. On a rampage. She immediately pivoted because trying to hold it together and maintain eye contact, all while keeping her lunch in, was sucking all her energy. "Leave my sister alone."

"She's a grown woman."

Jillian hated that. She wanted Emma to find someone else. Literally anyone else. "I'll tell her what you did."

He didn't blink. If the idea of showing who he was panicked him, he hid it well. "Are you ready to tell her all of it, Jillian? What I did and what you did in response?"

Hell, no. Not at all.

The hard knock on the door told her Beck wanted in. She didn't hate the idea. As far as interruptions went, this one was well timed.

He opened the door without waiting for permission and nodded his head in Gregory's direction. "Emma's looking for him."

"I can announce myself." Emma walked around Beck and came into the room. She wore a smile that didn't quite reach her eyes when she looked at Gregory. "I hear you've been busy visiting with the female members of the family."

"Not all, but most." Gregory stood up and went over to Emma. Kissed her on the cheek. "I was going to tell you when we met up for dinner."

"Everything okay in here?" Beck asked.

They were all looking at Jillian. She nodded. "We're done."

At least they were until she could figure out Greg's game and match it.

"Good." Emma wrapped an arm around Gregory's. The two of them left the room without saying another word. But he'd said enough. Implied a lot. Apologized, which Jillian thought was garbage. Sounded like he knew about things he shouldn't know, which could be a huge problem.

The pent-up energy ran out of her, and she sprawled in the chair. She told Beck what Gregory did back then. She left out the part about what she did in response. Her secret.

"I didn't tell you earlier because if you kill him I'd have to break in a new bodyguard, and I don't have time." She managed to keep her voice light, play along, even though part of her brain was off and racing through a massive list of potential problems and issues.

"As if I'd get caught." He nodded toward the door. "Want me to go run him over with my car?"

"Yes, but less so than before." She liked how protective Beck was. That, for once, someone sided with her. Unconditionally. But right now, she wasn't the one in potential trouble. "I need to make sure he's not scamming Emma."

"I'll run a check on him. Financials, known associates, the works."

She'd done her version, but his sounded much more intensive. "Oh, right. You have a big security company at your disposal."

"I'm very impressive." He cleared his throat. "And while you're dealing with things from the past you want to ignore, I haven't forgotten about our bedroom mix-up."

Mix-up? Is that what they were calling it? "We'll talk about that if we all survive the lunch with Harry's mother tomorrow."

"Fine, but after that, no more running."

She stood up. "I never run."

He snorted. "Right."

"But I can walk very fast."

CHAPTER TWENTY-SIX

MOOREWOOD FAMILY RULE #29: *Never let anyone outtalk or outcon you.*

BEVERLY LANIER TOLSON ARRIVED EXACTLY TEN MINUTES LATE for their prelunch meeting. No apologies or excuses offered, just a curt hello and nod of her head when Beck escorted her inside the library.

Jillian now knew the definition of *fashionably late*. She also knew how underdressed a purple T-shirt dress and white sneakers could feel in comparison to a spiffy blue Chanel suit and hair styled in a perfect chignon that didn't move even when Beverly sneezed.

No, Bev didn't come to play. She could only be described as a woman on a mission. Pursed lips. Leather purse dangling from her arm. Pumps that looked low enough and comfortable enough to wear all day and kick some ass while doing it.

She wore a thin diamond tennis bracelet and a sapphire

necklace that looked like it should be kept in a vault. At least one of those was likely to disappear during the family lunch.

Anika sure knew how to pick a target.

Without another word Beverly sat down on the small settee across from Jillian. "Thank you for seeing me separate from the luncheon."

Jillian crossed and uncrossed her legs, feeling like she should go find an evening gown and slip it on for this conversation. "My aunt is running a little late, but we both know you have things you'd like to talk about."

Running late meant purposely waiting so she could make an entrance. Aunt Patricia was not the type to let Bev dictate the conversation or take charge.

"Very much so, yes." Beverly looked around. Her gaze fell on the paintings and the desk before skimming to the water view. "I've always loved this house."

That seemed like a safe topic, especially since Jillian didn't remember meeting Bev before now. "You've been in it before?"

"I still mainly prefer our house in New York and try to spend most of the year there, but I have a nostalgic fondness that pulls me back to Rhode Island. We summered here for decades and several years ago finally bought a little place to stay for long vacations."

The *little place* in question sat twenty-five miles away in Barrington. A four-story waterfront mansion she bought for the bargain price of fourteen million dollars and immediately renovated for millions more.

Yeah, Jillian had done her homework before this uncomfortable meeting.

"Your mother hosted a ladies' brunch a few times." Beverly made a very proper *tsk-tsk*ing sound. "Honestly, I don't think it was her sort of thing at all. You know how it is."

Jillian actually had no idea and sensed getting filled in would tick her off, but why not try. "Explain it to me."

Beverly fluffed up the embroidered pillow next to her. "There are people who are from here and can trace their family back for centuries. People who live here. Those who summer here. The ones who work here. The . . . what do they call them? The townies."

She managed to be condescending without really saying much of anything. A skill but not one Jillian planned to emulate. "My grandparents owned the house. It's been in the family for a very long time."

"And they were wildly accepted by society. Everyone at the club adored them. Lovely people, your grandparents." Beverly's voice rose in a flurry of excitement over the memory. "They used to host charity events in the ballroom upstairs. They once held this outdoor soiree. We were on the lawn and a parade of yachts went by." Beverly let out a happy sigh. "Just extraordinary."

Jillian suddenly felt really sorry for her mom and for Harry. "My mom was probably here for the yacht *thing*."

"Indeed." Beverly smiled, clearly warming to the rich-people talk. "She went away for boarding school. A deeply religious one, if I remember correctly. All about punishment and marrying well, but she returned home."

"Excuse my late arrival," Aunt Patricia said as she glided into the room in a fancy blue dress with ruffles down the front.

"Patricia." Beverly shifted in her seat but didn't stand up. "It's been a long time."

"It certainly has."

The short, not really friendly but not unfriendly pseudo-greetings were followed by a flurry of air kisses and gentle shoulder-patting non-hugs.

Patricia kissed Jillian on the cheek before sitting next to her. "Where were we?"

"Right." They needed to find a new topic before Jillian gave herself a migraine from rolling her eyes. She looked at Bev. "So, Harry and Anika."

Beverly frowned. Not just any frown. This type usually came with eating rotten food or seeing something violent. "Oh, dear."

This woman could give drama lessons.

Patricia reached a hand across the small table toward Bev. "Are you okay?"

Beverly shook her head. "You know we can't allow this relationship to continue."

The royal *we*. Jillian thought that might make an appearance. "We?"

"Do *we* get to decide that?" Patricia asked.

"The relationship is doomed." Beverly's gaze traveled back and forth between Patricia and Jillian. "Surely you see that."

Patricia made a little *hmpf* sound. "That seems unduly negative."

Beverly matched Patricia's *hmpf* with one of her own. "There are issues that cannot be overcome."

Jillian wasn't convinced she was needed for this conversation, but she played along. "Like?"

"You can rub and rub but sometimes stains won't wash out." Beverly acted out the words with her hands, as if the demonstration were somehow needed.

Jillian had been called many things in her life, and some of the most negative came from people who lived in the house with her, but never a *stain*. That was new. "So, my criminal background is the problem."

"Well, prison is hard to ignore. It . . ." Bev had the good sense to wince. "It says something about a family."

Yeah, that she needed a new one, though Jillian doubted that's what Bev meant. "Do tell."

"Look, I'm not judging." Beverly refluffed the pillow. "And the reality is, you were in prison for financial crimes, not real ones."

Uh . . . "The prison felt real."

Jillian felt a smack from the tip of a leather pump against her bare shin. She glanced at Patricia, who hadn't moved. Apparently, somewhere during the past three years, Patricia had perfected the art of kicking without shifting.

"I understand what we're dealing with." Beverly moved the pillow to her other side. "I've done my homework."

"What does that mean, exactly?" Patricia asked before Jillian could.

"The way the tax laws are written makes it very difficult for people with money." Beverly appeared to be off and running on some sort of white-collar-crimes-aren't-crimes tangent. "You get pertinent information and use it, because of course you do, who wouldn't? Then everyone starts squealing about insider trading."

Jillian prayed for a migraine to hit so she could leave. "That's not really what—"

Another kick. This one not as gentle.

"You didn't take anyone else's money," Beverly continued. "You didn't actually steal anything."

That sounded wrong. Technically and actually.

In less than three minutes, Beverly had managed to write off and excuse a list of felonies as no big deal. Jillian was willing to bet Beverly would be fine sending a townie to jail forever for smoking a joint.

"You tried to trim your tax obligation, as you should—that was your financial responsibility as the person in charge of the family and business finances—and people got fussy." Bev let out a dramatic sigh that carried with it a note of *how dare they.* "It's a game and your only fault is that you didn't play it as well as you should have. I'm sure you know better now."

Jillian wasn't sure if she should be impressed with Bev's

novel criminal defense arguments or appalled by her, in general. She went with the latter. "So, I'm not the issue?"

"This is about family."

Jillian couldn't imagine the Moorewoods scoring well on that topic.

"Could you be more specific?" Patricia asked.

Bev in full Beverly mode glanced around. "Do you have someone who brings you tea?"

Jillian was tired of this, of getting kicked, of her entire family. She had no idea how Beck just stood there without making a sound. "Could we circle back to your point about family?"

"Anika didn't divulge the information about your past. She tried to hide it. I fear that doesn't bode well for her honesty." Beverly arched one of her perfectly sculpted eyebrows in Patricia's direction. "Don't you agree?"

Patricia didn't physically react to the verbal slap. "Maybe she was afraid of being judged for her cousin's actions. I mean, who could do such a thing?"

Jillian was pretty sure the older women saw her sitting *right there.*

"We can't be too careful." Beverly did a second look around the room. "So, no tea?"

Jillian could not imagine being a kid and having this woman for a mother. She half hoped some nice nanny had raised Harry. "I'm confused about your position on Anika."

"The Barnabys had a painting by Salvator Mundi go missing after a house party. Lauren Loman's diamond-and-emerald Harry Winston necklace disappeared. The Pearmans'

Qianlong vase was substituted with a copy. The Hoffermans' matching Rolex watches. Gone."

Patricia froze. "That's a lot of misplaced items and, as far as I can tell, unrelated to our discussion."

"We're talking about the people who come in contact with family, who add to the family's lineage. We made our choices but the next generation . . ." Beverly looked at Jillian. "Yours, specifically. Young people are dating and engaging in friendships without any regard to the future. They do not make careful choices about who they bring into the house and, by extension, who they expose the family resources to."

Jillian still wasn't clear if Bev knew the Moorewoods had made all those items disappear, which is what Jillian was sure happened, or if this was some meandering tale about Anika not being who Bev would have picked for Harry. Because that sort of stern position about her offsprings' dating habits had gone over so well when she threw it down with her older son.

"Are you saying you think Anika was responsible for the loss of those items?" Jillian asked.

This kick rammed into Jillian's calf. She flinched but refused to even look at Patricia. The woman weighed about a hundred pounds but had the foot of a professional soccer player. When had that happened?

"Of course not." Beverly snorted. "I'm saying she might not be careful about who she's exposed to . . . she might allow negative forces to drive her judgments. Honestly, she's not right for Harry."

So, this was a meandering tale. At least Jillian felt as if she'd caught up on that part, but there was something Bev wasn't saying. "Forces?"

"Let's just say I don't think this is a love match on Anika's part. Not that I can blame her for seeking security. That's wise, but Harry is not her answer."

The comment suggested Bev was a bit more street smart than she looked. Jillian reluctantly admired that. Women needed that kind of advantage when it came to relationships. She'd learned that the hard way.

"Anika is a wonderful catch. Beautiful and charming. Smart and efficient," Patricia said.

Jillian was pretty sure Patricia ran out of words at the end because *efficient* didn't make a lot of sense. And the rest was just nonsense.

Beverly gasped. "Yes. I'm not saying otherwise. That's not really my point."

Jillian hoped they were getting to one. "What is your point?"

"Well . . ." Beverly leaned in a bit closer. "I'm not sure how to say this."

"Out loud would be good." Jillian lifted her legs as she spoke to keep Patricia from firing off another warning kick.

"Anika's father." Beverly sat back in her chair, as if settling in for a long story. "He's been married several times. There have been many girlfriends in between. An engagement or two."

Beck coughed, which clearly was meant to cover up a laugh.

Beverly's chin rose higher. "Frankly, Jayson's bouncing around in relationships shows a misunderstanding of the importance of family. I fear he passed that on to his children, and his lifestyle will influence Anika's. At the least, they would have learned the lack of commitment by watching him."

The comment ticked Jillian off. Sure, she could piss all over her family and Anika, especially, but Bev could not. "Anika isn't responsible for her father's love life."

"This is about priorities. Harry needs a certain type of woman. Focused, not frivolous. Someone supportive, who can be a true partner." She sighed. "Men make mistakes. He can't afford to have a wife who doesn't understand that. One who runs off at the first sign of trouble. He needs a woman bred for forgiveness and understanding of men in business."

Bred?

"He's lost in his feelings for Anika." Beverly shook her head. "He can't think this through logically." She turned her focus to Patricia. "We both know love of that nature can be fleeting. Sometimes it can be purchased."

"Please tell me you're not thinking of trying to buy Anika off." Mostly because Jillian feared it would work.

"Harry is quite determined to defy me about this relationship. He's made that clear. I'm sorry to say he's as stubborn as all the other men in our family." She picked up the pillow again. Turned it around. "Saying *I told you so* after the fact is not going to be sufficient in this case, I'm afraid. We must think of the assets."

"Again, Anika is not her father." It hurt Jillian a little bit to say that. Good thing she never took a vow to remain completely truthful when talking about her family.

Beverly smiled for the first time since entering the room. "She seems lovely."

Congratulations to Anika for pulling off *lovely*. "Then I don't understand your objection."

"I'll be frank." Bev touched her fingers to Jillian's wrist. The move should have come off as grandmotherly but carried an air of control. "Money."

She whispered *money* like some people said *cancer*.

"I can't have him being so loyal to Anika that he turns his back on his family and his responsibilities to us."

Patricia let out a snort. "We could say the same thing about Anika. Why is Harry good enough for her?"

Beverly's eyebrow did that arching thing again, making her look like a comic-strip villain. "Excuse me?"

Jillian had a sudden vision of Patricia and Bev rolling around on the floor, wrestling in their expensive outfits. If Patricia landed one good kick, Bev was done. "May I suggest we let Anika and Harry figure this out? We may find that with a little more time together they'll decide they aren't right for each other."

"No." Bev didn't appear to like that suggestion at all. "I simply can't take that risk."

Bev had something to lose here—another son. So, Jillian

loaded her biggest weapon and fired. "As someone with a younger sibling, I've often found that telling her not to do something is the exact way to get her to do it. After all, we don't want to push Harry and Anika into making a drastic decision they aren't ready for and don't intend to make."

Beverly's eyes narrowed. "Like what?"

"Eloping in Las Vegas."

"They wouldn't dare," Bev said in a low whisper.

Bev looked so horrified by the idea that Jillian almost laughed. She somehow pulled herself together to carry on with this annoying conversation. "They would if Harry thought he needed to protect Anika or prove something to other people. But without that motivation this thing between them could wither."

All of the color drained from Beverly's face. "I need to use the powder room."

"Certainly." Patricia helped Beverly up and pointed her down the hall.

Jillian waited until Patricia came back in and shut the door to unload. "What was that about?"

"Bah, who knows." Patricia slipped a cheese stick out of the edge of her bra and ripped off the plastic cover. "Beverly has her own opinions on things. Outdated and ridiculous, but they're hers."

"I meant you showing up late to the meeting you agreed to."

Patricia stopped munching. "You didn't need my help. Right, Beck?"

"She does like to be in control," he said.

Jillian sent him a quick glare before turning back to her aunt. "Don't drag him into this."

"But he's right. You could have told Bev that Anika was only after her son's money." Patricia held the half-eaten stick. "It's what she wanted to hear."

Okay, but . . . maybe. "I talked with Anika earlier and told her to come clean with Harry. She knows she has to do it."

Patricia looked at Beck and nodded. "*Told*, as in demanded."

Beck nodded back. "Uh-huh."

What was this? "The two of you working together is a force for evil. Stop it right now."

Patricia sighed. "Now she's deflecting."

Beck hummed before responding. "Seems so."

"Did everyone take psychology classes while I was in prison?"

"You don't see it, dear." Patricia grabbed Jillian's hand and held it. "You say you don't want to be responsible for this family yet you keep putting yourself right in the middle of everything."

"Interesting," Beck mumbled.

Jillian didn't like anyone in the room right now. "Shut up."

"You'll figure it out." Patricia gave Jillian's hand a squeeze then let go. "The hard way, I fear."

CHAPTER TWENTY-SEVEN

MOOREWOOD FAMILY RULE #33: *Food eases the tension for difficult discussions.*

THEY NEEDED TO STOP HAVING FAMILY MEALS.

Jillian made that decision ten minutes into the group lunch with Beverly. It amounted to a nightmare with a side of soup. Not pleasant at all.

The participants today were a select group. Everyone on Jay's side of the family except Tenn, who, as usual, was left out. Harry showed up in a linen suit that miraculously didn't wrinkle. He really had a gift for not wrinkling.

Beck joked about skipping the affair to do his laundry, but Jillian was not about to go to any family event without him. No, he was stuck with her . . . and she'd figure out why she felt that way later. He refused a seat at the table and chose to stand guard at the door instead. Kelby took the chair to her right and grumbled under his breath for the first five minutes about not being hungry.

All in all, a meal with the usual amount of Moorewood entertainment and grief.

As soon as the food hit the table and the water and wineglasses were filled, and for Beverly the wineglass refilled, the lunch lurched to an uneven start. Beverly jumped right in, possibly not knowing that she'd start them off with a bang . . . or possibly knowing. Who could tell? "Jillian and I were having a nice chat before lunch."

Jay nearly dropped a platter of burrata and tomato salad.

His gaze flicked to Jillian before he plastered on a smile and glanced at Beverly. "You should have told us you had arrived early. We all could have joined in."

"That would have ruined the purpose for the meeting." Beverly took a sip of wine before plowing ahead. "It was a private discussion."

"Beverly." Jay stopped long enough to clear his throat. "I hope you understand the pressure Jillian is under."

"She's still a bit out of sorts." Astrid dropped her voice to a whisper as she leaned in toward Beverly, as if the rest of them weren't right there, in listening range. "It's not something we like to talk about."

That was news to Jillian. "Really? It feels like you bring up my supposed mental state pretty often."

"I can explain," Anika blurted out.

Astrid froze in the middle of eyeing up Bev's diamond

bracelet. Harry held a bowl of couscous in front of him like a shield.

Beverly didn't seem to notice any of it. "What is it, dear?"

"The reason I didn't mention the prison sentence earlier. Why I tried to soften the impact for Harry." The words rushed out of Anika. "I'm sorry for both of those things."

"Oh, pish." Beverly dismissed the comments with a flick of her hand. "I was angry at first, but on second thought your reluctance to vomit up family details is quite refreshing, actually."

Jillian got stuck on *pish*.

"Of course it is." Jay gestured for everyone to start passing the food and drink and act like other humans might act at a meal.

Grilled shrimp and lobster salad made the rounds. Jillian saw the dish pass by but wasn't fast enough to grab any food. She was too busy watching Astrid make a move.

"Your bracelet is beautiful," Astrid said to Beverly while brushing a finger over the linked diamonds, likely undoing the clasp.

"Astrid." The warning in Anika's voice was pretty clear.

"It was a gift from Harry's father," Beverly said as she broke contact by ladling the salad dressing from a silver gravy bowl. "But I'm afraid the small talk is about to end."

Harry looked a little green instead of his usual pale shade of beige. "What are we talking about?"

"I knew about Jillian." Beverly reached for a homemade

biscuit, clearly enjoying herself as she filled her plate and headed for the bottom of her second glass of wine. "For heaven's sake, I read the newspapers. A Moorewood being hauled off by the FBI was news. The gossip carried on for several months, though you all did an admirable job of killing it."

"It was a dark day in the household," Jay said with a heavy sigh.

Astrid nodded. "A complete embarrassment."

"You all know I'm sitting right here, right?" They either weren't listening or just didn't have a stop button. Jillian didn't see how she'd force down lunch. Looked like another trip with Beck to hunt down french fries waited in her future.

"The disappointment must have been unbearable." Bev made taking a pat of butter, then a second one, look dramatic. "I remember being relieved poor Sonya wasn't here to see this ending."

Jillian was ready for a new topic. "I thought you didn't care about my criminal past, Beverly."

"That phrasing is a bit too blasé, dear." Beverly stopped buttering and grabbing food long enough to send Jillian a scolding look that all mothers seemed to have in their arsenals. "But your financial issues aren't the type that would raise concerns about a relationship between Harry and Anika."

"Are we talking about that?" Anika asked.

Some beige-like color came back into Harry's face. "That's good to hear, but even without your permission we would continue seeing each other, Mother."

Jillian could hear civility come to a screeching stop. No one else seemed to notice.

Beverly made a face. "Jillian asked me not to discuss this issue now, so I won't."

The entire family looked at Jillian. *Gee, thanks, Bev.* "I tried to suggest it wasn't our business. That Harry and Anika should talk and work out their issues without us."

Beverly slowly set her wineglass down. "I'm afraid I can't do that."

Oh, Bev.

"Patricia, could you . . ." Jillian looked around and realized Patricia wasn't actually in the room.

Coward.

Beverly pointed to the water pitcher and Harry dutifully filled her empty glass without saying a word. "You are all perfectly lovely, but I'm afraid I can't support this relationship."

"What?" Anika sounded breathy and far more frazzled than usual.

"Jillian, what did you do?" Astrid asked.

Beverly drank a sip of water before talking again. "This is about family and loyalty. About following through with promises and marrying for life, regardless of the consequences."

Jillian bounced back and forth between not liking Bev, tolerating her, and being terrified by the control she wielded over people she wasn't related to. "This is probably a private conversation. Not best suited for a luncheon like this."

Harry sat up straighter in his chair. "That's okay, Jillian. I'm fine having it now. Better now than later."

The poor guy looked like he wanted to stand up, but Anika pinned his hand down. Her grip was tight enough to turn Harry's fingers white.

"Of course we should continue to socialize, but more than that isn't possible." Beverly took a bit of salad and made all of them wait until she chewed and swallowed before finishing whatever thought was in her head. "Jillian and I agreed on that."

Wait. Bev did not just . . . but she did. "When did I agree?"

Jay slowly lowered his knife and fork to his plate. "I would love to know the details of that agreement."

"Me too," Kelby muttered under his breath.

Anika blinked about three hundred times before forcing some words out. "I don't see why this is a family discussion."

"That's exactly the problem, dear." At least three people started to talk but Beverly being Beverly cut them off by glaring. "Beyond money, there are questions about similar values and upbringings."

"What money?" Astrid asked.

Beverly patted the table near Kelby's plate. "It's good to see you again, by the way."

Jillian made a mental note to ask about that. Beverly and Kelby didn't move in the same circles mostly because Kelby found people like Beverly exhausting and obnoxious.

Beverly continued because, really, she had the most captive audience ever. "There are ways for me to enforce restrictions. Harry is a vital part of my family, and I don't wish to take those steps, but I will if that's what is needed to convince him."

Harry stood up. "You can't be serious."

"I think we have some confusion here." Jay shoved his plate away from him and stared down the long table at Jillian. "What did you say during your meeting?"

"Almost nothing." Not an exaggeration, actually. Jillian had sat there, mostly confused and trying to figure out why Beverly viewed not paying taxes as an inconsequential crime.

"Every family has that one relative." Beverly chuckled after she dropped that gem. "In our family it's Great-Uncle Bernard."

Harry looked more confused than usual. "He drove over his wife and claimed he thought he hit a deer."

Jillian had no idea how that fit in, but the horrifying snippet did make Harry's family way more interesting.

"You can't believe whatever Jillian told you." Jay sighed. "I love my niece and am so grateful to have her home, but this is a hard time for her. She says things that . . . frankly, aren't correct."

Beverly's head shot up and the amusement left her face. "Why are you blaming Jillian? You don't even know what we talked about."

Jillian silently scored a point for Bev. Also vowed never to get on Bev's bad side.

Beverly tut-tutted. "I've made my own observations over the years. This is not about your family. Not really. I've had specific goals in mind for Harry since he was very young. A path that would be best for him to follow."

"Do I get a say?" Harry asked.

Beverly glanced in Jillian's direction and gestured toward the seafood salad. "This is delicious. I must have my cook get the recipe from yours."

Jillian felt a bit rattled by Beverly's delivery. She said things, munched on her food, and acted surprised when everyone else at the table started mumbling and shifting in their chairs. It wasn't that she was clueless. No, she knew exactly what she was doing. She drew a line and dared anyone to cross it.

"Mother."

"This is settled, Harry." Beverly's tone suggested she meant it. "We've talked about this privately and now with the Moorewoods."

Jillian missed the *talking* part. "Maybe we should—"

"What's settled?" Anika asked.

Beverly smiled. "Your relationship with Harry. This is as far as it will go."

CHAPTER TWENTY-EIGHT

MOOREWOOD FAMILY RULE #24: *Sometimes you need to drop the hammer.*

THE LUNCH BUMBLED ALONG FOR ANOTHER SEVEN MINUTES until Harry insisted they talk about his relationship with Anika and Beverly demanded he take her home.

Jillian stopped Beverly on her way out. "Beverly, wait a second. Astrid?"

Astrid wore a *who, me?* expression. "Hmm?"

Jillian admired the innocent act. It was tough to look that clueless. "I believe you have something that belongs to Beverly?"

Astrid pretended not to understand. "I don't know what . . ."

"Her bracelet." Astrid had pulled off an impressive lift when Beverly put her fork down. One minute, a shiny bracelet rested on her wrist, the next minute bare skin. Astrid had really improved because Jillian almost missed it, and she'd been watching all during lunch, waiting for the inevitable. "Didn't you find it?"

Anika paled. "Astrid?"

"Yes, of course." Astrid smiled at Beverly. "It fell off while you were talking. I was about to give it to you." Her smile flattened a bit as she handed the bracelet over. "Here it is."

Beverly refastened it on her wrist and off she flounced. The five-foot-three equivalent of a wrecking ball.

Jay escorted them to Harry's car. So, at least for a few minutes, they had a yelling reprieve. Jillian made the most of it by stealing a shrimp off the seafood salad platter.

Beck sat down next to Jillian at the table, which was in disarray and had its chairs pulled out. He didn't touch the food, but who could eat after that display.

"That might have been the most stressful lunch of my life," Kelby said as he reached for the water pitcher.

Beck shook his head. "I missed the bracelet grab. The two times I thought Astrid would take it, she didn't."

"Amateurs." Jillian knew the lunch fallout would get much, much worse. "You think that was bad? Wait until the next half hour."

Beck looked lost in the meal wreckage. "Rich people are weird."

"Amen to that," Kelby said.

"Jillian!" Anika screamed as she ran back into the dining room with Astrid nipping at her heels.

Jay stopped in the doorway, all red faced, the muscles around his mouth straining. "Explain yourself, young lady."

Astrid nodded. "Yes. Right now."

"And you." Anika turned on her sister. "You stole her bracelet? She's my future mother-in-law, or that was the plan. You must learn to control yourself."

"Don't talk to me that way."

Anika let out a sound somewhere between a yell and a groan then faced Jillian. "What did you say to her to ruin everything?"

"I can only imagine the lies," Astrid said, clearly still stinging from losing out on the bracelet.

"No lies, actually." For most of her life Jillian had viewed Anika as the potential problem on that side of the family. She was street smart, devious, committed, and very charming. She knew how and when to use her looks to get her way, and when to tone them down to blend in. But as she grew up, she figured Jay out. She dealt with him in careful pieces, fighting back when necessary.

Astrid was a different story. She'd hooked her future to Jay's, and Jillian couldn't think of anything more depressing.

"Jillian, you're playing games." Anika retook her seat from lunch. "This is a disaster. She's threatening to make him end it."

It was more than a threat, but Jillian didn't point that out. "I admit, Bev was a revelation to me as well."

"Stop with the sarcasm and the bullshit," Jay said, all charm gone.

Astrid joined in. "Yes, explain how the money fits in."

"Maybe you could stop thinking about yourselves for one second." Anika set down her wineglass with a thump and stared at her father and sister. "You're more concerned about how this impacts you than the destruction of my relationship with Harry."

"It's not as if you care about him. You can find another target," Astrid shot back. "I mean, his money is impressive, but the rest . . . no."

"Enough bickering. I want to know what she said." Jay switched his attention from Anika to Jillian. "Well?"

"Bev did most of the talking."

Anika groaned. "Don't call her that because then I might accidentally call her that, and then I'll never be able to fix this mess."

Kelby cleared his throat. "It's time, Jillian."

That stumped her. "For what?"

"Just tell them your plans." Kelby shook his head. "No more deadlines. Give them the bottom line and get it out in the open."

Patricia picked that moment to enter the room. "I agree. Enough dangling, dear. They deserve to know your requirements."

"I was waiting for the person who turned me in to step up and admit it." At first, anyway, but now Jillian waited for the official okay from Beck before she dismantled their lives. She looked at him now, hoping for a sign.

He nodded. "Do it. Honestly, the situation can't get worse."

"I already denied turning you in to the FBI." Anika slumped in her chair as she spoke. "I'd gladly name the person if I knew, just so we could move past this and get back to running the business."

"Scamming." Jillian tried to imagine the money they'd all make if the family put this much energy into running a legitimate business.

Jay winced. "Stop using that word. It's unseemly even in private."

That was too ludicrous to respond to, so Jillian turned back to Anika. "I know you didn't like listening to Bev at lunch, but she might have made things easier on you. I told you that you had to tell Harry the truth."

"Because you decide. You're the boss now," Astrid said in her most sarcastic voice.

"Yes, I am." A memory of Patricia and Beck and their comments on her being controlling floated back to Jillian. She pushed that aside, took a deep breath, and plunged in. "I control everything."

"You've said something like that before and, while you might find it delightful, it's an overstatement." Jay had a smug look on his face, as if he'd figured out a work-around. "You are not the only one with power and money here. You've admitted to using family funds to pay off the FBI, which is an outrage, but there's still the money we've earned on jobs before, during, and after your time in prison. You weren't the only one planning ahead. So were we. There is a tidy nest egg, and that keeps you from being the only one with leverage here."

Yeah, about that . . . "No."

Jay frowned. "Excuse me?"

"If you had agreed to our original deal, I would have divided the pot of grifter money between everyone on your side, Jay, and disseminated it." Jillian had their attention, but she wasn't convinced they understood her use of the past tense. "I also would have set up quarterly payments from the inherited funds and legitimate business interests. The combination of your equal portions of the grifter fund and the quarterly payments would have guaranteed you each a very comfortable lifestyle. Lavish with no need to con."

"Why didn't that happen?" Astrid asked.

"Because one of you turned me in." When they started bickering and denying, Jillian talked over them. "And you never stopped grifting, which was a prerequisite to all of this. Since you didn't abide by any of the terms I imposed, you didn't get the big pot of money or the quarterly income."

"Okay, fine." Exasperation echoed in Anika's voice. "Let's say we agree to your terms now. One of us will cough up an apology and we'll . . . minimize our activities. What happens then? What is the monetary deal you want us to consider?"

And now for the bombshell. "Nothing. The grifter money is gone."

Astrid's eyes widened. "Wait . . ."

"You mean all of it? That can't be. We're talking about years of work," Anika said.

Jay shook his head. "Exactly. It's not possible."

They were going to hate this part. Jillian tried to walk them through it so there would be no confusion. "When I said I paid the fees and taxes from the grifter pot, I meant that I *emptied* the grifter pot and closed the account. It was part of the deal with the prosecutor. I handed over *all* of that money."

"We're talking a significant amount of money, and it couldn't just disappear," Jay insisted.

Jillian winced for him. "Well, actually . . ."

Jay talked over her. "And we earned money while you were gone. We've also sold paintings and other lucrative items that we'd held on to for years, all to ensure our ongoing liquidity as well as our deniability to the FBI. We didn't keep anything with questionable lineage that could have led to trouble. A few things maybe but not much. It's mostly all liquid now. In cash."

He meant anything they'd stolen, but Jillian was impressed he made the black-market sales sound so fancy.

Astrid sighed in what looked like relief. "Jay is exactly right. We didn't tell you, but we dumped assets just in case the FBI came back to dig around in those faked sales documents you drafted."

They were so close to being right . . . and yet so far. Jillian tried to close the gap. "You did sell assets and get money. I actually did know, allowed the sales to happen, and then took all of the proceeds without you knowing."

"Oh, shit." Beck didn't even try to whisper.

"The money you earned while I was gone, all those assets you turned into cash, all the grifts over the last few years, it's all mine." No one said a word, so Jillian kept going. "I had separated the accounts. The FBI took one, which left only the trust, which is mine."

Anika's mouth dropped open. "You mean . . ."

"You did all that hard work intending to screw me, but it benefited me."

Anika's mouth stayed open. "You stole our money?"

"Yes, I did. All of it." Jillian intended to make reparations for the stolen items in the form of donations to worthy causes and return anything left to return, if she could figure out how, but that didn't change the facts. She took every single dime they created.

Jay stammered a bit but finally choked some words out. "I deposited . . . but how did . . ."

"The only way for the money to look legitimate and not attract the FBI's attention again was to wash it through the trust. Make it appear to be income from the sale of legitimate trust assets or from the sale of inherited items." She smiled. "So, you put the money in, and then it went to the trust. I kept it."

"Give it back!" Astrid yelled.

"No." That was never going to happen. They reneged on the deal, and this was the price they'd pay. "This is why I fought so hard to keep control over the trust even while in prison. I allowed minimal access in order to get all of the money. You were conned. By me."

"You can't do this." Astrid was almost breathless as she talked.

"I can and did." Jillian decided to unload every painful fact. "In fact, since Kelby paid for all of your food and other items during the last thirty-nine months through the trust, and you didn't repay any of those living expenses, you actually owe me money."

"Doug somehow convinced Jay to give him almost four hundred thousand dollars, which is also due to be repaid to Jillian and the trust," Kelby added. "There are official documents evidencing all of the debt."

The relative calm that came with confusion and shock exploded when Astrid shoved her chair back and stood up, facing Jillian across the table. "You bitch. You stockpiled all the assets and money for you and Emma and fucked us."

Jillian realized the repetition helped. They seemed to be understanding the breadth of their loss now. Finally. "Yes, that's exactly what I did. As I told you before, you all could complain to the police or the FBI but then you would have to explain where all the money you *earned* came from, and where you got all those stolen goods, and in doing so would reopen all the old claims, and this time the spotlight wouldn't be on me. The documents I created show I'm the innocent party here. I had no idea what you all were up to."

The room broke out in a new round of yelling and cursing.

The louder it got, the more animated Jay became and the quicker Beck moved to Jillian's side.

"You sure know how to put on a show," he whispered.

"Thank you." Jillian held up both hands to get everyone's attention. "I'm still talking."

"What can you possibly have left to say?" Anika asked.

Jillian planned to give them one more chance. "While I'm not obligated to forgive your debts or give you anything, I will. I might also set up the quarterly payments for you all, but you must uphold your side of the bargain."

"How big will the payments be?"

"Oh, Astrid, never change." Jillian didn't mean that at all. Astrid absolutely needed to change. Her emphasis on money at all times was exhausting. "The answer really isn't relevant until my other condition is met."

"Jillian, be reasonable," Jay said in his best *I'm trying to con you* voice. "Anika can't just tell Harry she targeted him. Especially not now, after what you did. We need to be able to make money."

"There are other ways to make money." Jillian shrugged. "You could try earning it legally."

Astrid snorted. "Oh, please."

Jillian felt like she'd said this a hundred times, but she tried it again in a slightly different way. "It's time everyone moves out and moves on. If you don't want to stop grifting, fine. If you don't want to fess up to turning me in, also fine. But I won't bail you out, none of you get the allowance, and no matter what, you can't live here. You'll be cut off."

"How long until this nightmare happens?" Jay asked.

They'd already had more than three years, but Jillian wasn't that petty. "The moving vans will be here in two days, ready to escort you all out, except Aunt Patricia."

Astrid cut through the mumbling and name-calling. "If someone admits to turning you in, are you going to make them penniless?"

Very tempting. "I just want to know why they did it."

"And we're all supposed to just sit around and wait for someone to confess?" Jay asked.

Jillian shrugged. "I sat and waited for more than three years. Now it's your turn."

A HALF HOUR later Jay, Astrid, and Anika crowded into the den they used for private conversations.

Anika couldn't believe they'd ended up here. Jillian came home and everything exploded. Everything. "I didn't think she was serious about taking us all down."

"We're talking about dismantling generations of hard work." Jay shook his head. "How could she do this?"

Anika looked for any positive angle . . . and kept looking. "Jillian and Kelby took Sonya's inherited fortune and tripled it. Diversified assets. All of that artwork . . . the jewelry. So much money and we don't get any of it."

"But we should. We could if we changed our strategy." Astrid sighed. "I do have a plan."

Jay waved her off as he always did. "Not now, Astrid."

"This is her way of flushing out the person who turned

her in." Anika couldn't blame Jillian for being pissed about that but stealing all the money went too far. "Was it you, Jay?"

"Stop." Astrid moved between Anika and her father. "We are losing sight of the issue. Jillian thinks she won."

"She did." Anika didn't know how her side of the family still didn't get that.

Astrid smiled. "Not if she's back in prison."

CHAPTER TWENTY-NINE

MOOREWOOD FAMILY RULE #41: *Handling fallout is delicate work for which not everyone is suited.*

AFTER UNLEASHING A FAMILY HOLY WAR IN RECORD TIME, Jillian did what any half-intelligent person would do. She hid. She didn't really have a choice. Beck wanted her out of any room containing knives, glass, and Moorewoods. No amount of bacon was worth listening to all that familial bickering, so she agreed.

She sat on the edge of her bed and finished typing out the texts to Emma and Tenn that delivered a highly edited version of the clashes with Beverly and the bloodbath of an aftermath. Both of them responded, expressing concern. She promised not to leave Beck's side for even a second.

She watched him move around the bedroom, back into his area, and then return to her. He looked at his phone and checked something on his computer. He didn't act even a little retired now.

"You can sit for a second."

At the sound of her voice, he stopped pacing about and looked up at her. "If I say DEFCON, do you know what I mean?"

Oh, good. A quiz. "Only because I saw it in a movie. It's that chart that tells us how worried we should be about an attack against the US."

"Close enough." He glanced at his phone again. "We're at DEFCON 2 and might be heading toward DEFCON 1."

She shifted on the bed, drawing her legs up in front of her. "DEFCON 1 is the good end, right?"

"It is not."

He hadn't blinked in a really long time. She started counting the seconds and gave up. "How worried are you?"

"I'm calling in reinforcements. A few members of my team will patrol the grounds. We'll have a night crew. It shouldn't be too intrusive because they're good at what they do."

It sounded like an armed camp to her. "I'm trying to get people out of the house, not invite more in."

He didn't respond for a few minutes. Something on his phone snagged his attention. He made a strange grunting sound while he read. It was the most bodyguard she'd ever seen him.

"Do you have somewhere you need to be?" she finally asked.

"You mean this?" He held up his cell. "I run constant checks for listening devices and—"

"Really?" They'd hit on a topic more interesting than her family. She crossed her legs and balanced her elbows on her thighs. "That's kind of cool."

"You should assume I'm constantly running surveillance. I also set up a keystroke program on my computer." He finally put the phone away. "I was checking on that."

He packed a lot of words into his sentences. She tried to unpack the scariest one. "Does surveillance mean cameras?"

"I put them in these rooms and a few other places in the house after someone tried to use my computer. My keylogging program let me see what they did, which mostly amounted to trying to figure out my password."

She'd stepped into a spy novel. "They're coming after you now."

"Let them." He shrugged. "My laptop camera came on, but the person was smart enough to put something over the lens to block my view. But I admit the whole mess ticked me off and upped the stakes. Now we have cameras."

That was quite a game, and no one bothered to clue her in. "Where was I? Where are the cameras? I have so many questions."

"Me too." He stood in front of her with his hands on his hips.

Uh-oh.

"I'm wondering why you didn't tell me you planned to

use a blowtorch to burn down your family." He whistled. "That was quite a spectacle."

She had to lean back a little to see his expression. "Too much?"

"I think I mentioned previously that it's easier to protect you if you warn me when you're going to paint a target on your back."

Only Kelby had known exactly what was coming for the Moorewood clan and how harsh it would be. He'd warned her to tread carefully. She clomped her way over that advice and landed them here, hiding in her room while the smoke cleared. "I'm not great with sharing."

"That's not a shocking statement."

Her defenses kicked in. "Neither are you."

"No one is contemplating killing me."

"I find that hard to believe," she mumbled.

He sighed at her. Not a subtle one either. "At least now I get why I'm really here. You never intended to give them options. You wanted to see them sweat then pummel them."

"A dramatic way of putting it, but correct."

"You poked a lot of misfit dangerous bears today. I can't believe you once thought you could do that without safety reinforcements."

For most of her life, she'd thought of Jay and her cousins as savvy and uncontrollable, not dangerous. The brakes, the railing . . . those should have been wake-up calls, but part of her wanted to believe they would never physically hurt her, which sounded ridiculous now that she thought it through. "I really was going to wait, as you asked. My thought was to fill you in on all the naughty details so you could make a contingency plan for our safety before I unloaded on them."

He nodded. "See, that sounds logical. What happened to that?"

"Beverly got them all riled up."

"Uh-huh."

"Fine. I was ready to spill it. Kelby gave me the opening, and not to cast blame or wiggle out of the spotlight, but you gave me the go-ahead." Jillian was pretty sure she'd slipped into rambling. If he'd yelled or said something she would have stopped, but he stood there, staring. His expression unreadable, which was really annoying. "Have I finally disgusted you?"

"Never."

A quick response. No waffling.

She couldn't believe he was that forgiving, that understanding, of all she'd been through. "Come on. I'm not exactly an innocent bystander in all of this."

He reached down and pulled her to her feet with his hands lightly framing her waist. "I'm impressed with your shell game. They deserved to lose everything. I would just like you to get your revenge without them killing you."

Killing . . . right. She tried to concentrate on what he was saying, but the bed was right there, and he was all big and grumbly hot in front of her.

"What I said in there, my final ultimatum, wasn't about

revenge." She pretended the breathiness meant she needed to exercise more.

"Jillian."

The sexy scrape of his voice had her grabbing on to his forearms. "Okay, a little. But it was more about teaching them a lesson. They create human roadkill without even stumbling. This time, they're the roadkill. Mine."

"That all makes sense to me. I'm surprised you waited this long to level the final blow. But taking their money and boxing them in, forcing them to burn assets just so you could turn around and take the sales money, too? Absolutely brilliant and pulled off with military precision."

"Why, thank you. It's nice to have one's skills appreciated."

"But I'm really not buying the lack of vengeance part." His mouth hovered close now. His breath blew across her cheek. "You could give them a bit of money, kick them out forever, and tell them you're done with them. That would end things quickly and cleanly. They'd balk, but I'm here to fight them off, so uncomfortable and tense but doable."

She was done talking about them. She wanted to focus on him. "How long are you going to be here?"

"We'll see." His fingers clenched on her waist. "Instead, you financially ruined them and made them all sit there and listen to how you screwed them."

"So, I do or do not suck now?" He was almost whispering, so she whispered back, not wanting to break the moment. "I think I hear a tiny echo of judgment."

"Listen closer because you don't." He pulled her in, until his mouth grazed her ear. "I'm suggesting that you talk a tough game, acting like you don't care about them. But that scene downstairs happened because they hurt you. They don't realize, of course, because they're failed humans and have no genuine people skills, but I see the harm they inflicted on you. The harm you pretend isn't there."

Her brain scrambled. "I, uh . . ."

"I'm saying you're more complex than you want to admit." He pressed a small kiss to that sensitive spot right at her hairline. "And I like it."

Bodyguard, bad choices . . . who cared? "Maybe we can hide up here forever."

"We do have a bed."

She could hear the amusement in his voice. It touched off her own. "That doesn't sound like bodyguard talk."

He looked at her. "My role has morphed. I view myself as a sort of hybrid bodyguard."

She kept losing the thread of the conversation. "Hybrid with what?"

"I'm not sure yet. I'll let you know when I figure out how to deal with it."

That sounded good to her. "You know, despite everything, I seriously debated redistributing the money. I thought if they behaved—"

"Not possible with this crowd."

"Yeah, I see that now. I'm not sure they even know how to act." She gave in and leaned her head against his shoulder, liking the feel of him cuddled around her. "That conversation had to happen, but I am sorry I made your job harder."

"I like this job."

She smiled into his shirt. "Even though I made a mess?"

"For the first time in my life I'm liking things a little messy."

CHAPTER THIRTY

MOOREWOOD FAMILY RULE #19: *Assess new information with an open mind.*

"HEY."

"Hi." Jillian sat on the deck by the pool, overlooking the backyard. She wanted to lounge in silence, but at the sound of Tenn's voice she gave up on finding peace until everyone moved out, which better be soon. "You missed lunch, you lucky bastard."

"I've learned a few things over the years. Like when not to be here."

"My guess is your side of the family is in panic mode."

"Let's say they aren't at their best." He sat down and looked out over the pool's still water. A second later a smile spread across his face.

"Sorry about all the yelling and meeting in secrecy behind closed doors." She'd set that off. Didn't regret it but felt bad Tenn came back from signing the papers for his new place and walked face-first into the wall of tension.

"Not your fault."

"It kind of is." Like, totally was.

Beck walked out to them. His gaze fell on Tenn, and he grunted a hello before walking around the area, giving them some room. Jillian assumed that meant he thought she was safe with Tenn.

Tenn balanced his elbows on his knees. "I'm sorry you're stuck fixing everything again."

Yeah, that was the thing . . . "I'm not sure I'm going to."

Tenn's smile grew even wider. "You taking all the money and assets was genius. Like showing them how they don't get to benefit from lying and scamming anymore."

"You continue to be the smartest Moorewood."

"Honestly, I think it was past time you acted and unleashed on them. You were clear on the rules years ago and they ignored you."

He sounded resigned, so she wanted to be clear. "This mandate won't impact you. You've never been a party to the scams. I fully intend to provide you with an allowance from the family funds, and you are welcome on the estate anytime, for as long as you want."

He shook his head. "Thanks, but I have a job and an income. I'm good."

"I know, but—"

"You don't owe me anything, Jillian."

She thought back over the years and all she'd seen and

heard. The times she didn't speak up. She had an excuse while she was younger, but not after college. "I don't know about that. Seems to me the whole family could have treated you better."

"Nah." He shrugged. "Your side was fine to me."

"I fear your expectations were set pretty low." All of the Moorewood kids suffered from that. They should have demanded more in terms of acceptance and affection. The Moorewood men didn't understand the concept of unconditional love at all.

"My mom gave me a way out of here and away from Jay. I didn't take it." He rubbed his hands together. Stared at them while he did it.

Jillian figured no part of this conversation came easily for him. For her either. The two of them rarely sat down and discussed family failings on a deep level. Now that she had the chance, she asked the question that had tormented her for years. "Why didn't you go with her? Your mom. Leave Jay and all the yelling behind years ago."

He kept flipping his hands around. Studying his nails and knuckles. "It's pathetic, really."

"Try me."

"I thought if I hung around, tried to be the son Jay wanted, he'd . . ."

"That he would accept you." That's about what she thought. An understandable but terrible answer because Jay would never change.

"That he would grow to *like* me." He dropped his hands,

letting them hang between his legs before looking up at her again. "But he's made it clear I'm a disappointment. He told me again this morning how Mom trapped him into marriage."

"That's not true. Jay targeted women, not vice versa." Jillian wondered if he'd ever stop.

"I know." He nodded. "Well, I do now. Mom told me she had to get out, escape, before she lost herself."

"Sounds familiar." Jillian wished her mother had possessed that gene.

"She wanted to take me, but Dad threatened her." He blew out a long breath. "I guess it was one of those *I don't want him, but you can't have him* things. A power move. So, she let me make the choice, thinking she'd go to court and risk everything if I wanted out."

"Your poor mom."

"She thought she was making things easier on me by having me stay here without a fight." A tiny smile came and went. "But it wasn't all bad. I know your dad was rough on you, and you had to clean up a lot of his mess, but he was nice to me." The smile came back bigger and brighter. "I loved your mom."

Being back, Jillian had realized how much she missed her mom. How often she thought about her. Jillian didn't understand her mom's choices, and she would never fully accept her mom taking the way out that she did even if she thought it was for the good of the family.

The life of martyrdom didn't make much sense to Jillian,

but she was starting to think that was okay. She and her mom were different people with different dreams. Jillian just wished her mom's road had been emotionally easier.

"Family . . . blah, blah, blah." That's what it sounded like in her head, so she said it.

He laughed. "What?"

"Beck could tell you what it all means." The guy who lost his parents young and never got over it but could talk honestly about their failings without any of the corresponding anger. He could teach them all a lot. "Just don't tell your sisters that you're getting money no matter what. They'll be all over you."

"I really don't want any more family secrets. The last one was too much." Tenn's eyes narrowed. "I didn't know Izzy was here."

"Did you say . . . what? She is?" Jillian's attention ping-ponged from Tenn to the back upstairs patio. Izzy came outside, looked around the table, and went back in. No talking. No stopping. No Jay. "Beck?"

"Yeah, I see her." He took out his phone, probably engaging in some of that fancy surveillance.

Jillian didn't understand why Jay thought it was a good idea to let his mark wander around the house without him. She could go into the wrong room. *That* room.

Jillian's attention moved back to the conversation Tenn had dropped. "What secret were you talking about?"

"I should have done something to stop it, but I'm not sure what."

His tone tugged at her. Anxiety swelled out of nowhere, rose up and threatened to swamp her. "Tenn, I have no idea what you're talking about."

"The FBI and the phone call implicating you." He said the words nice and slow. Separated each with a heavy breath.

The anxiety crashed in waves now. One shot after another. She leaned forward, trying to keep her focus as dizziness spun through her. "You know who made that call?"

"I thought . . ." He was stammering and shifting now. "I thought you were messing with the family, that you really knew. I was told you knew."

"How would I?" She could feel the pain creeping up on her, but right now he was her concern. He was a ball of move-ment. Whatever secret he had buried was trying to claw its way out.

"God, Jillian. I'm so sorry. I thought you'd forgiven me for not telling you right from the beginning." He shook his head. "I never meant to hide it. I mean, I did back then. I promised."

He stood and slammed right into Beck, who had moved to the door. Beck stayed cool and unruffled as he blocked one-hundred-eighty pounds of messed-up male.

"I'll take it from here, Tenn." Patricia patted Beck's arm as she squeezed by him into the middle of the battle.

Jillian's stomach dropped. Fell right onto the ground. "Aunt Patricia?"

Tenn looked green. "I don't—"

"I'm sorry, dear." Patricia put her palm on Tenn's cheek in

a sweet, totally out of character, loving way. "I lied to you, and I was wrong. About all of it—putting you in that position in the first place, trying to undo the damage. Requiring you to lie for me and keep my secrets."

"What are you two talking about?" But Jillian knew. Part of her sensed what was coming.

"Let me talk with Jillian." Patricia dropped her hand as she shot Tenn a crooked smile. "You go."

Tenn hesitated a few seconds before stepping around Beck and into the house.

A soft wind blew across the deck, but no one said anything as Patricia walked over and sat down in the chair farthest from the door. She patted the empty seat next to her while she looked at Jillian. "It's time I cleared up a few things."

CHAPTER THIRTY-ONE

MOOREWOOD FAMILY RULE #2: *Never take sides against family. Never snitch.*

JILLIAN SAT DOWN NEXT TO AUNT PATRICIA. SHE DIDN'T RE- member doing it or her knees buckling, but she landed on her ass and stared at the one older family member she trusted. She'd always been wary of the woman's power, but also half in love with the idea of a strong female leading this band of renegade scammers. "What's going on?"

Patricia touched a hand to her perfectly styled white hair. "I think you know."

A thousand thoughts screamed through Jillian's brain, but she ignored them all. "Tell me."

"I'm the one who turned you in."

Just like that. With an economy of words, her aunt flipped her world upside down. Jillian always assumed the answer was Jay, but she'd been wrong.

Beck whistled. "Shit."

"Beck, maybe—"

"No, you can stay." Patricia motioned for Beck to come closer before looking at Jillian again. "I'm actually surprised you didn't guess."

"That my own aunt would put me in prison? No. Didn't see that coming."

"It's not that simple, dear."

Jillian tried to hold it together, but her control, her body, ripped apart at the seams. "Explain it to me. Explain why Tenn is a mess right now. But first, tell me why you broke every rule you ever taught me. Was it about punishing me?"

"Not at all." Patricia took out a new pack of cigarettes and spun it in her hand.

The movement caught Jillian's attention. Her gaze shifted to those hands that had survived a lifetime, and the way some fingers bent and stiffened. Patricia complained that a woman's age showed in her hands. She could put on makeup and wear the right clothes, but her hands hinted at the passing of every year.

"Family members talk about you being ruthless but—"

"Jillian." Patricia let out one of those long, lingering sighs. "For once in your life, stop trying to control the narrative and listen."

Jillian flipped from frustrated, confused, and a little hurt to furious in the beat of a second. Probably had something to do with how much the comment stung.

"I've never claimed to be nice. The sweet old grandmother

bit is just that. A facade. I hate being a grandmother. What a waste of time. Honestly, my grandson is the reason I still smoke. He's so much like the other useless men in the family. Finland then Belgium? Why would . . ." She continued to turn the pack over in her hand, end over end. "Well, that's another story."

Jillian had only so much patience and Patricia was using up every ounce of it. "Prison, Patricia."

"You tried to lay down the law about going legitimate before the family was ready."

No. Jillian refused to take that guilt on. "They were never going to be ready."

"I meant me." Patricia's response came out more like a roar than real words. Her hand clenched around the pack, making the wrapper crackle. "You didn't consult with me."

The anger, the shock . . . the *how dare you.* Jillian heard it, turned it over, and sent it flaming right back at her aunt. "You condemned me to prison because you were pissed off that I didn't have your permission? I was doing what my dead mom asked me to do."

"I contacted the FBI to save you."

Jillian shoved her chair back. In that moment she needed some space from the woman whose complex range spanned from that of string cheese connoisseur to art expert, and who had ultimately betrayed her.

Jillian wanted to stand up but feared her legs wouldn't hold her. Every muscle, every cell, shook inside her. "It's taking all I have not to kick you off this estate."

"We both know you're not going to do that." Patricia sounded so sure, so absolutely convinced she could muddle through this and end up fine . . . like always.

"Maybe that was my former position, but not now." Jillian pushed up, amazed her body could move when her mind had shut down. She walked around the chair, faced the ocean— tried everything to burn off some of the energy whizzing through her.

"If you had consulted me I would have told you to wait. Because you were putting yourself in physical danger," Patricia explained.

Jillian inhaled, silently lecturing herself that she couldn't drop-kick an old lady into the ocean no matter how much she wanted to in that moment. "From you?"

"No, dear." Patricia looked almost disappointed that Jillian wasn't immediately understanding the story she shared now out of necessity and even then only in fits and starts. "The way to survive in a male-dominated family of grifters is to be better, smarter, and more ruthless. I've always done what I needed to do, without emotion and without a second thought."

Deflection? Defensiveness? Jillian couldn't tell. "I'm not sure what you're trying to say to me."

"I'm not the only family member who would, for instance, smother a disloyal jackass of a husband with a pillow or throw someone off a yacht."

"Damn," Beck whispered under his breath.

Patricia's determined expression and firm voice demanded

attention. "When you prematurely made your demands, you unleashed a new generation of ruthless Moorewood women who would do anything to protect what was theirs. They started with your brakes. That's not where it would have ended."

The words finally got through. Danger . . . not from Patricia.

"Anika?" Beck asked, showing the same distrust he'd had from the beginning.

But Jillian knew the answer and felt the steady thrum of hate aimed in her direction. "No, Astrid."

"Exactly. She convinced that boy at the garage who had a thing for her to help. He's lucky I didn't make him disappear." Patricia waved her hand in the air. "Astrid told me she'd done it, but you were already out driving. I couldn't stop the accident. After that, I knew her behavior would escalate."

"She threatened to do something else to me." Some of the fight drained out of Jillian, and she sat down again. "That's what you mean, right?"

"One of the benefits of getting older, and on the days where my knees ache I think it's the only benefit, is that people tend to forget you're in the room. They think you're napping or can't hear or whatever, and they say things." Patricia leaned in a little closer. "Sometimes the threats come out in the middle of a vicious diatribe with a half brother."

The pieces clicked together in Jillian's head. Still fuzzy but coming into focus. "Astrid told Tenn that she was going to do something to me. Hurt me in some way."

"When the brake tampering didn't solve the problem, she said she'd move on to something else. She warned Tenn not to depend on you or think you'd rush in and save him because you weren't going to be around much longer."

"That bitch." A lot of other descriptive words flew through Jillian's mind, but she landed on that one. The nicest one.

"Did Astrid say how?" Beck asked. "It would be nice to know in case she falls back on the same idea now."

"My sense was drugs." Patricia looked at Jillian. "An overdose . . . to mimic your mother's death. Astrid planted the seeds by saying how depressed you'd been since losing Sonya. But since Astrid's not particularly good at anything dealing with human emotions, her motivations came off as transparent."

"Making it look like Jillian killed herself?" Beck made a rough sound. "Anyone who knows Jillian knows that would be ridiculous."

"That's very sweet, dear," Patricia said.

"Sweet?" Beck sounded appalled by the word.

"You see Jillian the same way I do. Her cousins have always underestimated her." Patricia sank down into her chair. "Circling back to Tenn, he supported your request for the family to change back then and said it out loud, which Astrid did not appreciate. That's why she issued the threat and accidentally showed her hand."

Jillian could almost hear Astrid drop from that charming voice she used to woo others to the harsh staccato ranting. She would have turned on Tenn. He was an adult but vulnerable back then because of Jay's poor treatment.

"Tenn panicked, but I was there. I heard what Astrid said." Patricia finally set the cigarette pack down without opening it. "I told him I would warn you and handle everything. Before you got out of prison, he confronted me, and I told him I'd tell you on that first night, but I didn't. Then the balcony incident happened, and I knew we were entering round two of getting rid of you. I've been quiet, listening and skulking about, trying to figure out Astrid's plans so I could tell Beck."

Jillian thought about the warning to get a bodyguard and how Patricia had pressed Kelby on that topic. It all made sense now. Patricia possessed information the rest of them didn't. But there was a bigger point, one Jillian couldn't forget. "You should have warned me back then, before the call to the FBI, and given me a fighting chance."

"My solution was to take you out of the firing line completely." When Jillian started to object, Patricia talked louder. "I admit I messed up the timing. I assumed you'd finished hiding assets, so that the FBI would come, make your life miserable, and, incidentally, block Astrid from going forward with her plans. Even she wouldn't do something as stupid as hurting you with law enforcement crawling all over the estate."

"You used me, and you used Tenn."

"It's probably fair to say there was a part of me that was upset with you. After all, I've been in this game a long time. I'm very good at it and had not yet reconciled myself to being done when you made your demand."

In other words, she pricked the bull. Aunt Patricia was in charge and Jillian had the nerve to contest that. Forget the issue of the cost. "I went to prison."

"You did exactly what I knew you would do. Survive."

"There were days . . ." Memories of those first few nights rushed through her. The terror. The catcalling. The threats, both subtle and not. The absolute belief she would die in there. She thought that every day inside and even now woke up panting and sweating after dreaming about being dragged back there. "I can't . . ."

Patricia shook her head. "I don't have many regrets but what happened to you is one."

Jillian could only stare at her aunt. "I guess that makes everything okay, then. Thanks?"

"I was hoping you'd come out of prison having learned a lesson." Patricia's voice hardened. "You can't control everything and everyone around you."

So, her fault. No matter what the other side of the family did, they always justified their actions by backing a truck over her. "What choice did I have? My parents put me in that role."

"And you loved it. It made you feel wanted."

Jillian had shuffled through so many emotions in the past five minutes. She finally landed on pissed off. "You're wrong."

"Honestly, you've been maneuvering the family and getting into everyone's business for a very long time." Patricia opened the pack of cigarettes and pulled one out. "All that energy prevented you from having a life of your own."

"I didn't ask for the job." Jillian leaned over and snagged the cigarette. "The Moorewoods are a mess."

"And they're not your responsibility anymore. Your mom is dead, Jillian. Let the pressures she put on you die as well. Figure out what you want to do, what interests you." Patricia held out her hand and wiggled her fingers. When Jillian didn't immediately hand over the cigarette, Patricia grabbed another one from the pack. "You talked big back then about being done with the family and moving on, but you weren't ready. You *needed* them to need you."

"Not true." *Damn, was that true?*

"This time I will support your plan and you. I'll watch out for Astrid."

Jillian could almost smell a second prison term on the horizon. "Because that worked out so well for me last time."

"I'll handle Astrid," Beck said. "I look forward to it."

"I'm counting on that." Patricia smiled at Beck but it faded when she looked at Jillian. "And you? Break the cycle."

"Meaning?"

"Stop managing and fixing. They're grown-ups. It's time you figure out what you want outside of the family and go for it. Let them go."

CHAPTER THIRTY-TWO

MOOREWOOD FAMILY RULE . . . *There's no rule for this. Self-reflection isn't a Moorewood trait.*

BREAK THE CYCLE.

That one ticked Jillian off for hours. She stomped around her bedroom, muttering and coming up with new profane names to call her relatives, especially Aunt Patricia, before finally slumping onto the mattress.

Jillian had spent so much of her upbringing longing for a different life. She wanted her dad to be different. For Jay's side of the family to be different. She even wanted her mom to be different . . . stronger, more self-protective.

She remembered her mom once talking about donating most of the estate to take away any temptation by the older generation of Moorewood men to do more harm to their children. She was a woman locked in a self-imposed sentence at the estate, rarely venturing out. Refusing all invitations as the years passed by. Her disappointment with her husband growing every day.

The family operated on the thin edge between rigid self-control and hysteria. They reveled in chaos. Plunged headfirst into it. Jillian had put her body between them and the FBI, law enforcement, anyone who would destroy their perfectly crafted fake image. She blamed them, but now she wondered if her sentence was self-imposed, just like her mom's. A horrible decision she made for herself because she didn't know who else to be.

She liked to say she gave up everything for family, but now, looking back, she wasn't sure what she'd sacrificed. Time and years of her freedom, but the idea of doing what she wanted to do, being what she wanted to be . . . she had no clue what that meant. She'd stopped dreaming so long ago, satisfied to play family enforcer. She took on the role, complained about it. Wore the damn thing like a blanket.

Maybe Patricia was right. Maybe a part of her—small, but still there—needed to be needed. Maybe somewhere along the line she'd twisted love and affection into a drive for more self-sacrifice.

The whole idea made her queasy.

"You okay over there?"

At the sound of Beck's voice, Jillian looked up from her position sitting on the bed. He stood in the doorway between their rooms. Arms folded. Legs crossed. Looking formidable in a my-boyfriend-can-beat-up-your-boyfriend kind of way.

He wasn't that, of course, but the idea made her feel the first lightness of the day.

She patted the mattress next to her. "You want to take a load off?"

"With you? Any day."

The bed dipped when he sat down. The move had her thigh balancing against his. "You're a sweet-talking type."

He looked around, acting like she was sharing a big secret. "Don't tell anyone. I have a reputation, you know."

"No worries. You still look highly capable of firing a weapon."

He wiggled his eyebrows. "What makes you think I carry one?"

She'd seen the gun, but that wasn't the point. The mild back-and-forth banter amused her, and that's what he'd meant to do. Lighten her load. She was onto him now. Mr. Tough Guy was actually a good guy. He claimed he mostly hung out behind a desk these days, though nothing about his body would suggest he remained idle.

"It's been a rough day," he said.

"Apparently I have some character flaws I need to work on."

He made that familiar humming sound. "Who doesn't?"

"You."

"Some people think I'm bossy."

She laughed. "No, really?"

"I can be strident and difficult. I'm grumpy when people don't listen to my great ideas."

"I've noticed that."

He didn't move but somehow inched closer. "Patricia flimflammed her way through her points earlier, but I think she meant well. Hard to tell."

She leaned into him and rested her head on his impressive shoulder. "Probably because in all that talking she admitted to being a husband killer who sent one niece to prison in order to keep another niece from committing homicide."

"Yeah, that's what I got out of her explanation, too." He sighed. "Your family is never dull."

"Then there's the part where she blamed me for her decision to turn me in to the FBI. That line of thinking was harder to follow."

"That's not—" He stopped when she lifted her head and glared at him. "Okay, yeah. She did suggest that. It would be fair to say she thinks you talk a good game but also love being the one everyone runs to for help."

That rolled off his tongue a bit too easily.

"We all have our assigned and learned roles in our families, but that doesn't mean the roles can't change, Jillian. You have the power to switch the roles if you want to. You decide."

Thoughts and newfound realities rattled around in her brain. She needed a moment to *not* think, to just be. "I want to focus on something other than family and people trying to kill me for a while."

"On that note, are you ready to talk about our near miss yet? You know, since we're sitting on the same bed where it happened." His gaze bounced from the mattress to her.

She groaned and flopped back onto the bed, burying her head deep into the pillows. Crossed her arms over her face. She'd avoided this conversation for as long as possible. Reliving her horny teen moment didn't sound fun at all. "I thought we agreed not to talk about that."

"You know we didn't."

Why did she invite him to sit next to her? It was like a part of her wanted to revisit the humiliation. "It's embarrassing."

"I hope not, since I want it to happen again."

She dropped her arms and forced herself to look up at him. "Another near miss?"

"Oh, no. You're going to hit your target this time."

Uh . . . "Are we talking about the same thing?"

He leaned over until his hands were on the bed on either side of her hips. "You flamed out because—"

"There has to be another way to say that." But she did like him this close.

"I prefer the phrase I used."

"It makes me sound pathetic."

"You are anything but." His elbows bent and his body dipped a bit closer to hers. "The last time didn't work out . . ." His eyebrow lifted. "Is that language better?"

"So far but you sometimes take a wrong turn, so I'll give you a conditional maybe." She slipped her hands up and down his arms, over the sharp contours of his muscles. The friction of shirt against skin intrigued her.

"Your last attempt didn't work out for a few reasons," he continued.

"Oh, good. A list." And he sounded so serious about it that she snuggled down, cocooned in a pile of pillows and him, and let him verbally meander.

He tried to swallow his smile but failed miserably. "First, you were really upset that night, on fire and mumbling—"

"That's an exaggeration."

"So, the timing was all wrong. If I had caught that pass, you might have been regretful and all quiet and freaky weird the next morning."

"Freaky weird?"

His fingers danced over her chest, right along her collarbone. "Second—"

"Wow, you really do have a list." He needed to get moving through these numbers because it had been a day. The combination of touching and having his body press against hers shot right through her control and what was left of her good sense.

"We'd just met."

She snorted because that reason deserved a snort. "You know it still was only a few days ago, right?"

"I don't need a calendar." He dipped his head and pressed his lips to the line his finger drew up her neck.

"Right." Her breath hitched. Got lost somewhere between her chest and mouth, leaving her panting, squirming, and ready for more. "Forge ahead."

He kissed her under the chin then lifted his head to stare down at her. "The point is we both felt something, but there was so much going on around this house. We needed to get our bearings first. Figure out if this was a zing that would fizzle out or something bigger."

He traced the neckline of her dress, letting his fingers dip as they lingered over the tops of her breasts. He caressed like he protected—all in and hot.

She swallowed six or seven thousand times before she found her voice. "How big is the zing?"

"Big enough to knock me on my ass." His lips brushed over hers, light and fleeting. "You?"

"Same." She tried to catch his mouth for a real, blow-your-panties-off kiss but he'd moved to her ear, and whatever he was doing there sent a shiver racing through her. "Are you done with the list yet?"

"There's a third point, and it's the biggest reason nothing happened."

Her mind went blank as her legs tangled with his. "What?"

"I didn't have a condom." He raised his head and winked at her. "Big problem."

She could barely concentrate. Energy pinged around the room and her body heated to the point where she wanted to strip off whatever both of them were wearing. "That's not very prepared of you."

"Don't knock my Boy Scout skills." His hands skimmed down to her legs and up, just under the edge of her dress. "I don't go on assignments these days. Even if I did, body-guards shouldn't have sex on the job. It's a bad idea."

His hands circled to the backs of her knees as he pulled her legs up higher on his thighs.

She responded by wrapping them around his hips. "I'm hoping there's a *however* coming next."

"However, I'm not really a bodyguard. I'm a businessman now." He reached around to his back pocket and pulled out a condom. "A businessman gets the job done."

Forget the dating drought and prison beds. Forget the frenzied chaos raging through the household and the horror show Astrid might now be planning. Jillian was exactly where she needed to be . . . all over Beck.

She found him charming and delightful and sexier by the minute. "Look at you carving out an exception."

"I make the rules."

"Even better." She slipped her arms around his neck and tugged him in closer. "So . . ."

"The timing still might be wrong, but I wanted to be clear about what really happened before."

She could not possibly make the invitation clearer. Her body was one big flashing *go* sign. "Are you kidding?"

"You acted like I turned you down last time and started spouting off about me being your employee."

She put a finger over that hot, and what she was betting to be expert, mouth. "Can you stop talking for a second?"

"Yeah." He kissed her finger. Even sucked on it a little.

This could kill the moment, but she had a pretty basic question she needed to ask. Knowing now could prevent screaming later. "Are you married, dating anyone . . . anything like that?"

He made a face. "Good Lord, woman. I wouldn't be on top of you if I were."

A rush of relief made her dizzy. "We hadn't talked about it."

"Not in a relationship. Haven't been for a few years, and that one wasn't serious because neither of us was at a point in our lives to have time for serious, so it ended amicably."

"That certainly sounds healthier than my relationship with Greg."

"That wasn't a relationship. He used you."

She was ready to kiss now. "True."

He pulled back before she could land that kiss. "I've been working to build the business and ignoring almost everything else. Now we're stable and I have people I trust to handle tough jobs. But, and hear me when I say this, even if I still needed to work all the time, I would make an exception to date you."

Her heart nearly rocketed out of her chest. "Then the timing is good."

"Huh?"

"Right now." She leaned up and kissed him. Not slow. Not meek. More like wrapped her body around his and laid one on him.

He didn't hesitate. Those arms scooped her up. His mouth traveled over hers, conquering every cell it touched. The kiss overwhelmed and excited, and when he lifted his head his lips were wet and his hands were all over her.

He had ten seconds to strip her.

"You're sure?"

She loved his need for consent, but he had it. "Yes!"

His body touched hers . . . everywhere. Heat rolled off him and his hands framed her face. She could see him and nothing else.

"Then let's get you naked."

CHAPTER THIRTY-THREE

MOOREWOOD FAMILY RULE #38: *Always be gathering new intel.*

MORE THAN TWO HOURS LATER, JILLIAN LAY OVER HIS CHEST in an exhausted sprawl. With her head tucked under Beck's chin and his fingers tracing lazy patterns on her back, she fought the urge to drift off. She wanted to savor this. It had been a long time and she really hoped this was only the first of many nights together.

"How do you know Kelby?" She squeezed his biceps. The sleekness of them had her wanting to explore.

He was a big guy, muscular and tall, but if there was an ounce of fat on him she couldn't find it. And she tried. Managed to touch every part of him.

He let out a loud sigh. "That's the first question that pops into your head post-sex?"

"I've been holding it in." Kelby's vouching for him made

her open to trusting him. He earned that trust in the first hour after they'd met, which said a lot about him and how he acted since she'd been raised not to trust many people.

He hesitated for a few minutes, caressing her lower back rather than talking. She was about to say forget it even though she didn't mean it when he started talking.

"My life went sideways when my parents died."

She knew exactly how that felt. "Not a surprise."

"I wasn't in the car, but I put the pieces together from the newspaper articles, things the police said, and what their friends would tell me. Later, when I started handling security for a living and my research skills improved, I found insurance records and reviewed the police file."

She stayed quiet, not sure what to say. Just offered comfort and support by touching him and listening.

"They attended a dinner party. Sometimes Dad's jokes were more hurtful than funny. That night he embarrassed my mom. Joked with some of his friends about how the alcohol made her more attractive."

"Whoa."

"Yeah, he wasn't a great guy. He took her for granted. Not overtly affectionate. Not the kind of dad who plays catch in the yard." Beck drew in a deep breath. "At this party, Mom got angry and walked out. Dad followed, apologizing and insisting he was joking."

She felt Beck go still underneath her and held on even tighter. She hoped the gentle touch of body to body soothed him.

"The police think they started fighting again in the car.

Bottom line, Dad lost control of the vehicle and they crashed. She died instantly. He lingered but never woke up." Beck's lips brushed over her hair.

"I was furious with him for so long. He'd been on the road on sales calls, staying in hotels for a month, though now I think it might have been a trial separation. Then he came home and instead of being grateful he took a verbal shot at Mom at a party." With each word, his voice tightened and his muscles stiffened.

"Are you still furious?" She didn't know how he couldn't be.

"Sometimes. It still flares up, but most of the edge is gone." His built-up tension eased. "Thanks to a lot of therapy and support from Kelby and a few others, I realized my dad was a limited guy. Never really matured past the fraternity boy stage." Beck made his usual humming noise. "Hating him took too much of my energy and was an insult to my mom's memory. I had to let it go, though it took years to get there."

She ached to be that healthy. To see her father as flawed but not let those flaws take up so much of her headspace. "No wonder you immediately liked Tenn."

"I *was* Tenn. In a way."

And Beck changed. He grew up, made a career and a life for himself. Given the chance and enough support, he moved on.

The light that had been flickering in her head turned on full blast. Maybe that's what her mom really meant when she asked her to save the family. Give them the space and the assist they needed to move on . . . then let them go.

It seemed so simple. "That puts things in perspective."

"Like what?"

This moment wasn't about her. It was about him, so she kept the spotlight on him. She lifted up high enough to place a quick kiss on his chin. "Nothing. Go ahead."

"Kelby was a big-time college basketball player. Pretty well known and left the game only when an injury messed up his pro chances." Beck smiled as if watching a memory play in his mind. "He volunteered at a YMCA where I hung out."

The last puzzle piece. "He mentored you."

"First, he threatened to drop-kick me." He looked at her. "Those were his actual words. He believed I stole money from a club fundraiser. I didn't, but I was thinking about it." He brushed the hair away from her eyes as they stared at each other. "Then he gave me rules, structure, and attention. He cared when I messed up and when I didn't."

"Sounds like him." They had both needed Kelby over the years, and he had been there. Without question.

"I lived with him for a while. Trained, finished college, volunteered, because he insisted." The love, the admiration, was right there in Beck's voice. "When I was ready to go out on my own, he invested in my company. He's a silent partner."

The news hit Jillian with a smack. "So, he convinced me to hire his own company for protection?"

Not that she was angry. The whole thing made her laugh. Years ago, Kelby told her that he was investing some of his money in side businesses. Carving out something for himself, away from the family, and she encouraged it. Now she knew he'd invested in Beck.

"He's sneaky like that. But really, I doubt he even thought about the potential for conflict. When he called, his only concern was keeping you safe." Beck pulled her in tighter against his side.

"Are the two of you still close? I'm asking because he hasn't had you around here before."

He shot her an I'm-onto-you look. "The question you're not asking . . . yes, I knew about your family before he asked for my bodyguard help."

She shoved against his side. "And you accepted the job anyway? What's wrong with you?"

Though she couldn't imagine how any words Kelby used could adequately sum up the messy, yelling, scheming crew on this estate. They defied description.

"I'm a professional." He put his hand against his bare chest. The use of drama suggested he'd fit in fine with the Moorewoods. "I also knew he was in love with your mom. He never specifically said it, and I didn't put it together until I was here for a few days. I've been living in a different state for years, but I remember when she died. It wrecked him."

Someone else had mourned her with the same fierce love and grief as her children. That mattered to Jillian. "I guess we've been on the fringes of each other's lives for a few years."

"Sounds like it." This time he kissed her forehead. "I still can't believe he lives next door to you."

He may as well have said *Has Kelby lost his common sense?*, which was fair.

"Kelby had been stunned by that part of Mom's wishes and offered to refuse the bequest, but I insisted. So did Emma." But that was old news. Jillian's point had to do with the future. "After your role here ends, if it ever does, you should visit Kelby more. At his house. Next door. To me."

Yeah, that babbling wasn't awkward or anything.

Beck tightened his arms around her. "I'm hoping for a reason to be around here a lot. Maybe by invitation. But you have other things to worry about before we get there, and I need to make sure you don't get killed doing them."

"I know and I'm ready."

CHAPTER THIRTY-FOUR

MOOREWOOD FAMILY RULE #34: *Avoid pillow talk.*
It will screw you in the end.

THE NEXT MORNING ASTRID DIDN'T WAIT FOR ANIKA TO GET some food at the buffet and sit at the dining room table before launching into whatever new plan she'd hatched during the night. "We have a new problem."

"I'm not sure we can handle another." Anika had never meant a sentence more.

Every meal, every meeting, started this way lately. Jay and Astrid might blame Jillian's unexpected return, but Anika blamed them. The constant plotting and bickering. All the unnecessary covert discussions. Anika grew weary of being anywhere near her side of the family.

She'd spent the night with Harry, with him insisting he'd go against his mother's wishes, and her begging him to try one more time to win the older woman over. Anika had no interest in doing things the hard way—i.e., without the Tolson money. That meant they needed Beverly to come around, and that meant doing this dance the right way.

She'd almost convinced Harry to calm down when Jillian texted. That was enough to make Anika regret ever climbing out of that comfy bed. She came back only because Jillian called a family meeting, and after the revelations during the last family discussion, Anika feared not being present.

Unruffled and clearly only half listening, Emma didn't look up from her tea to respond to Astrid. "What's going on?"

Jay put down his knife and fork to jump into the newest round of anti-Jillian talk. "Your sister and her outrageous behavior. Stealing from us? It's ridiculous."

"She'd been pretty clear." Emma stared at Jay as she took a sip from the mug. "What did you think would happen when she came back?"

"There was some hope she wouldn't." If Astrid was trying to whisper or mumble, she failed at both.

Anika picked up on an interesting fact that her scheming sister and out-of-control father had missed—Emma knew what was happening at the house despite rarely being there. That could only mean that Jillian had sent out a text to warn her side of the family. Probably the kind of thing caring siblings would do for each other . . . not that Anika had personal experience in that area.

"Does everyone think this lifestyle is cheap?" Jay asked as he looked from Anika to Astrid and back again. "That jewelry? The clothes you wear? They don't just appear. You've all benefited from my choices."

Typical Jay. Spread the guilt around to make sure little, or none, stuck to him. Anika could almost guess his responses before he said them.

"You need to look a certain way to fit in around town. The club and all those events with Harry require a back-drop of wealth, which means spending money." Jay shook his head in his dramatic *why do I have to explain this simple thing* way. "Even Jillian knows that."

"Are you looking for sympathy?" Anika asked, knowing he was.

"Everyone is so busy pointing to me as the bad guy that you all forget your parts in this. You, my dear daughters, took that money and never asked one question about where it came from." Jay finished pointing at Astrid and Anika and leaned back in his chair. "Besides, Sonya would want all of us to share the windfall from her estate."

"Uh, no." Emma slowly and oh-so-carefully put down her mug. "That's a stretch by any review of the facts."

"Your mother cared about my girls."

Emma nodded. "I agree, but she could have divided up the money and shared it. She didn't."

"Which brings me back to my point." Astrid clanged a teaspoon against the side of her plate. "The new problem. Jillian and that bodyguard."

Not what Anika expected. "How is that relevant to anything?"

"What about them?" Emma asked.

"They're sleeping together."

Her family was so trifling. Anika couldn't figure out how Astrid and Jay thought this would save them now that Jillian had taken everything. "Don't assume that just because they're always together."

"I'm not." Astrid rolled her eyes. "I peeked in his door earlier and he wasn't in bed. Some bodyguard he is."

Emma looked appalled. "Why would you do that?"

Astrid kept right on babbling. "Then I looked in her room, as I've done every night since she's been home, and there he was. I guess no one warned her those old locks are useless."

Everyone greeted the news with silence. Emma still hadn't stopped frowning. And the way Astrid dropped the revelation, as if breezing in and out of people's private rooms was a perfectly reasonable thing to do. It was breathtaking in a totally disturbing kind of way.

Anika didn't know how, but she, or someone—anyone else, actually—needed to have a word with Astrid about boundaries before she became even more of a mini Jay. "You went too far. You invaded Jillian's privacy."

"I'm doing this for all of us." Astrid thumped her finger against the table. "She's going to have us begging for lunch money if we don't control her."

"We are not living like that," Jay said. "I've worked too hard for too long to accept Jillian's scraps."

They were off and running now.

Everything about this breakfast setup annoyed Anika. Emma was making it pretty clear which side she was on, and it wasn't theirs. Astrid was . . . good grief, Anika didn't know what to do with her sister except try to make her see how absurd this all was. "What does Jillian's sex life have to do with any of this?"

"She's begging to go back to prison." Astrid said it out loud. Just put it out there.

Emma's eyes bulged. "*What?*"

"She's playing dangerous games. Not being careful. That's what got her in trouble last time." Astrid fiddled with her spoon. "She's meeting with Harry in secret. She had a heated talk with your new boyfriend the other day, Emma. Did you know that?"

Emma rolled her eyes. "I was there."

"Were you in there for the whole talk?" Astrid sat up straighter, clearly itching for a fight. "Even her poor body-guard was locked out of that one. I saw him stomping around outside the door. She's making threats. Moving money. Opening old wounds." Astrid listed off Jillian's supposed sins. "This can only lead to a bad place."

Emma stood up, leaving the tea and a plate of uneaten food behind. "I'm going to find her."

Astrid smiled. "Knock first."

ANIKA WAITED UNTIL the dining room door slipped shut to unleash. "What the hell was that?"

"Planting the seed. Showing Jillian is careening toward trouble." Astrid sounded satisfied with her performance.

"You did very well." Jay reached over, not quite touching Astrid's arm, and rested his hand on the table. "Got Emma all riled up and concerned."

Anika saw the half-feral look in Astrid's eyes. "This is not the way."

Astrid stuck a hand in Anika's face. "You need to listen to me. Jillian thinks she ruined us, and we can't let that happen. Not that you care. You'll have Harry and Harry's money."

Jealousy? Was that the note Anika heard in Astrid's voice? "Didn't you hear his mother?"

"The rest of us have no choice but to fight back. We need to find a new way to handle Jillian. Your lame listening devices aren't enough." Astrid looked at Jay then preened under his nodding attention. "We need to be ready to come at her with an equal threat."

Anika choked back a groan. She was going to be so pissed if they put her in the position of having to save Jillian.

"I'm open to a better idea, if there is one," Jay said.

Anika had never been fond of Jillian. That wasn't a secret. But taking another run at her, doing something that might result in a long prison sentence? Anika couldn't work up any excitement for that plan. She was tired of all of it. The constant complaining, the never-ending scheming.

"I will not beg her. I will not abide by her rules. She needs to be caged. You of all people need her contained." Astrid smiled. "We need Aunt Patricia."

"For what?" Anika asked.

Astrid and Jay answered at the same time. "Leverage."

ANIKA HAD HAD enough family and talk of revenge for one day. Her future teetered on the edge, but Jay and Astrid cared only about how much they could hurt Jillian.

Typical.

Anika had finally found a way out, and a good one, and no one wanted to help her. Harry was rock solid. With that mother, he should have been twisted and mean, untrustworthy and a money hoarder. Unless he was hiding the traits, and he'd have to have Jay-level grifter skills to trick her, he was a good guy.

When they first started dating she thought he was . . . well, a nerd. Not all that exciting but very interested and weirdly punctual. She'd convinced herself the money made him hotter. Over time, it kind of did. With a little sun and a lot of attention—and months of time away from his mother—he could be a catch. And she'd gotten to him first, before some other woman moved in, fixed him up, and got her name on the bank accounts.

Not that she loved him. Of course not. That was ridiculous. But she did like him, and that was new for her. She didn't want him hurt by her lousy family and their twisted ways. And she really didn't want him to leave her.

Anika was grumbling to herself, working her mind into a rage, as she walked up the staircase. She stepped carefully and quietly because she'd been taught to sneak . . . and she wasn't the only one lurking in the hallway.

"Izzy?"

The other woman jumped when Anika called out her name. Literally smashed into the wall right next to the one room she shouldn't go into—the command center. The one room that should have a lock by now and would if the house hadn't turned into a nonstop rush of people.

Izzy placed a hand on her chest as the color came back into her cheeks. "You scared me."

Anika didn't say she was sorry because she wasn't. "What are you doing up here?"

"Honestly?"

That word didn't mean much to Anika, but okay. "I guess."

"I was being nosy. I had to use a bathroom and thought I'd try one up here." She smiled. "This house is so stunning. I've been dying to explore."

Interesting . . . "I'm sure your home is equally lovely."

"Of course, but you know how it is. When you live in a place, you take it for granted." Izzy walked up to her. "We'll just keep this between us. I don't want Jay to think I was being rude."

Anika watched Izzy lift her skirt the slightest bit and walk down the stairs. Anika wasn't sure what that little scene was about, but she knew it wasn't good.

CHAPTER THIRTY-FIVE

MOOREWOOD FAMILY RULE #20: *Clear up confusion before it threatens the mission.*

JILLIAN WATCHED BECK SLIP ON A T-SHIRT AND SHORTS AND seriously considered asking him to undress again. Morning didn't mean they had to jump out of bed. Not when all manner of Moorewoods were milling about.

After a quick knock, the bedroom door opened. Emma stood there, her gaze scanning the room. Taking in Beck, who seemed to be frozen by the window seat, and Jillian, who hadn't figured out how to sit up yet.

Jillian blamed Beck for this. "Still didn't fix the locks?"

He looked at her like she'd lost it. "I can't exactly leave your side to go on a lock-buying excursion, but I'll rig something up before I leave this room."

"Won't matter," Emma whispered. "Lockpicking is a family skill. New or old, various members of this household see a lock as a challenge and pick it, which is why I was trying to shore up the security on the office."

Poor Beck. He might know bodyguarding but he didn't know about younger siblings. "Baby sisters are a nuisance."

Beck stepped in front of the bed, putting his body between the sisters. Jillian assumed it was a reflex since he knew Emma and Jillian were working together behind the scenes.

Emma peeked around his broad shoulders to wave at Jillian. "Good morning, sis."

"You're too happy to live in this house."

"I'd think you'd be feeling good this morning. If not . . ." Emma's gaze traveled all over Beck. "Well, that would be a disappointment."

Jillian sat up, relieved she'd thrown on that tank top when she went to the bathroom earlier. Muscles she hadn't used in years begged for her to snuggle back down and skip morning completely. "I'm ignoring the innuendo."

Emma's smile fell. "Bummer."

"What's going on?" Not that Jillian didn't welcome unwanted intrusions first thing in the morning.

The last of Emma's smile vanished. "The threats seem to be ratcheting up."

Jillian wanted to ignore that, too. She pretended not to be worried but on the inside her nerves scrambled. The Patricia news shook her. She still didn't know how to parse it out and understand it.

"What threats?" Beck grabbed for his pants and slid them

on over his running shorts. An odd choice. It was hard to look in charge in puffy pants, but he pulled it off.

"Well . . ." Emma winced. "Can they send Jillian back to prison somehow?"

The word sent a shot of terror racing through Jillian. "If I got caught with—"

"Are they making plans to do that?" Beck asked.

"It's hard to tell because Astrid talks big. She admitted to coming into your room, so I'd put a chair under the door-knob from now on. Something to slow her down."

Jillian looked at Beck. "I knew I heard something the other night."

Emma sat on the edge of the bed. "Honestly, it's one of a few problems today." She hesitated before delivering her news. "The alarms I set went off."

At least, Jillian assumed that was news. "I feel like you forgot some words in that explanation."

"Computer alarms," Emma explained to Jillian. She clearly thought Beck needed less hand-holding through this subject. "If someone starts looking into us, checking our names, try-ing to get into account information, all that, I get notified."

"Where did you learn how to do that?" Jillian hated to ask but really did want to know. "Is there some sort of grifter night course I don't know about?"

"There are scary parts of the internet where you can learn very scary things." For some reason Emma smiled when she said that.

For the hundredth time since getting out Jillian thought

about how she wasn't the only one who paid for her prison sentence. "Ever thought of taking up pie baking or something equally not dangerous?"

"Literally never."

Beck leaned against the dresser. "I have the same sort of alarms on my system."

"But I looked you up after we met," Jillian said.

"Yeah, I know. That's my point. You looked, instead of asking me, and I knew." Beck winked at her before turning to Emma. "Can you track the searches?"

"Not yet."

Beck swore under his breath. "Maybe you should take some time away, Jillian."

"I did. Thirty-nine months."

Emma laughed. "You walked right into that."

Jillian tried to think of a benign option. "Could the computer searches be Doug, trying to communicate?"

"He knows how to get in touch with me, and he isn't." Emma looked less amused now. "The good news is he seems to be sitting still, which is a miracle."

"The tracker is on his watch, right? Couldn't he just take it off?" Beck looked like he wanted to say duh but he wisely didn't.

"Why would he?" Emma asked.

Beck's smartass expression didn't change but the sarcasm in his voice kicked up. "Yeah, why would anyone run from your family?"

"More likely he's hiding from Patricia, but then that would

make him smarter than I thought he was." Jillian voted no on that.

She hadn't filled Emma in on the Patricia-as-the-narc discussion yet. She didn't know if she'd ever have the energy she needed to relay those details.

Emma stared at Beck. "What are you doing to protect my sister?"

"I'm looking into everyone," Beck said. "So, if you're only pretending to date that Greg guy let me know and I'll leave him out of this."

Gah! Jillian had meant to signal him—not really sure how—to avoid this subject. But here they were. Deep in it. "You really know how to suck the life out of the party."

"The relationship is real." Emma treated them to an eye roll. "Jillian and I haven't talked about it yet. Totally on purpose, by the way, so thanks for dragging that elephant into the middle of the room."

"Oh." But Beck didn't look one bit sorry.

Jillian assumed this was his not-so-subtle way of having the Greg issue handled. He wasn't wrong, but she wished she was wearing pants or at least underwear before having this sisterly showdown. She had no idea how Emma was going to react. "You're not going to like most of what I have to say about him."

Beck looked ready to bolt. "Should I leave? I'm thinking I should go."

He started this. He had to stay here, listen, and survive it, too. Jillian pointed at him to remain there. "Don't move."

"Shit."

The words scrambled in Jillian's head. She tried to swim through them but didn't get very far. "Gregory . . ."

"Let me help by saying the way you and Gregory act with each other is a problem. I worried you had unresolved feelings for him until I saw how you snuck peeks at a certain bodyguard." Emma made an explosion sound. "That is your *want to jump him* look. What you feel for Gregory is something else."

Beck nodded. "Nice."

He charmed everyone. Emma and Beck both did. They had this ease that Jillian envied. "Do you two need me for this conversation?"

"I started the relationship, not him. I reached out after Gregory's dad died because we lived through a similar thing." Emma shrugged. "He understood me. I understood him."

Jillian knew from experience how Gregory could make a person *think* that, but he really set up the entire meeting as part of a ploy. "Okay, but—"

"I expected it would be a one-time thing and we'd move on. I didn't trust him at all."

"Let's keep doing that." But Jillian could tell those days were gone. Gregory had won Emma over, convinced her that he was worthy.

"I realized he was as messed up as we were. Maybe even worse." Emma made a hissing sound. "I mean, wow. He misses his dad and hates him. Loves him and blames him and is confused by all of it. You know what that's like."

Beck glanced at Jillian. "Notice how I'm not saying anything," he said.

"But it's clear Gregory doesn't want to be his dad. Not anymore. He wants to do better." Emma took in a deep breath. "His mom is very invested in the idea of his dad being a victim and is furious that Gregory won't play along."

Jillian had to give Gregory credit. He had Emma cheerleading for him.

"About his dad . . ." Jillian struggled to finish the sentence.

Lucky for her, Emma wasn't done oversharing. "I've taken it really slow."

Beck raised his hand. "May I leave now?"

Emma finished before Jillian could answer. "We haven't had sex."

"Really?" Beck sounded stunned at the revelation.

Jillian thought people should go at whatever relationship speed made them comfortable and all that, but she remembered Gregory back then. How quickly they'd . . . yeah, she had so many regrets. She also couldn't imagine the Greg she knew waiting. "How long have you been together?"

"Months. He's giving me time to learn to trust him." Emma squeezed Jillian's hand. "I think he might be the one for me."

When Jillian groaned, Beck cut her off. "You're making a weird noise."

"I'm aware." Jillian tried reason since nothing else seemed to work. "Emma, there's so much about Gregory you don't know."

"Do you still have feelings for him?"

Jillian gasped at that horrifying thought. "Hell, no."

"Good answer," Beck mumbled.

"I really don't. But there's mistrust and ill will between us, and for good reason." There was so much more. Jillian didn't really want to talk about any of it. Not with specifics. She wasn't proud of many of her choices back then. She thought she was doing the right thing but the way it had all spun out made her doubt.

"I'd like for the three of us to sit down and talk things out." Emma had that pleading *I need you* look. "Your opinion matters to me."

Oh, Emma. "Don't give me that much power."

"You've never been anything but a great sister."

"How am I supposed to argue with that?"

"You're not." Emma stood up. "And I should go. I don't trust Astrid without a keeper."

Emma left with the same flourish as her arrival. Smiling, with a jump in her step. She'd always been a pretty happy kid but looking at her now Jillian saw something else. Despite the odds, Emma had grown into a secure, determined woman. And she wanted Greg. Jillian didn't know how to process that part.

Beck stood in the middle of the room with his hands on his hips. "When are you going to tell her the truth?"

"That Greg treated me like crap?" Jillian wasn't sure how to slip that into breakfast conversation, and she had no intention of sitting down with Greg and talking things out.

"The part where you turned Gregory's dad in to the FBI to save your family?"

Anxiety rushed through Jillian then right out again. Of course Beck knew the truth. He watched her. He listened. He *got* her. "You figured that out, did you?"

He smiled. "Your sentence was pretty light. I assumed you gave the FBI something they wanted more than your family."

She didn't know what documents he'd seen. Most were supposed to be confidential. She was an unnamed witness, the confidential informant, against Gregory's dad and his fake brokerage scam that bilked people out of millions.

"Emma is going to be furious when I tell her." Jillian believed they could survive that part. It was the other thing. "I don't want Gregory to take it out on her."

Beck sat down next to her on the bed. "He won't do anything that hurts Emma."

"Don't buy his *I've changed* act."

Beck held up a finger. "Normally, I wouldn't. But I happen to know how compelling the Moorewood women are and how much a man might be willing to sacrifice to have a relationship with one."

Now, this was a topic she'd like to spend some time on. "We're in a relationship?"

"We're talking about that Greg asshole."

The sheet bunched around her as she crawled over him. Straddled his hips with her thighs and faced him. Put her face just inches from his. "I'd rather talk about us."

His grin could light up a room. "Then, yes. We are in a relationship. Get used to it."

"You sound sure." The things he did to her. The way he made her feel. She tried to imagine what this week would have been like without him here.

"Oh, I am." He wrapped his arms around her and pulled her in close. "I'm more sure about you than anything else in my life."

"You should take those pants off and prove it."

CHAPTER THIRTY-SIX

MOOREWOOD FAMILY RULE #31: *It's okay to have limits but don't let them mess up the job.*

ANIKA COULDN'T IGNORE OR INHALE HER WAY OUT OF THE desperate clawing sensation inside her. It threw off her breathing and made her mind race. She needed someone to know. Disrespecting Jillian behind her back, making fun of her, listening in to her conversations, ignoring her—all fine. Getting her thrown back in prison for what could be years based on trumped-up charges . . . not so fine.

If this was what having a conscience felt like Anika preferred not to have one. Doing the right thing kind of sucked. Jay drummed into her the idea that emotions showed weakness. She'd been taught from a young age to beat back her instinctual need to bond with other people and concentrate on herself and the family's needs only.

Any other time, yes. But like it or not, Jillian was family. That was the only explanation for why Anika went hunting for Beck. She didn't have to solve this problem. She just had to pass it off to someone who would.

She found him on the back patio, talking to a man she'd never seen before. Did he call for extra bodyguards? Just what this house needed. More people . . .

She watched Beck give orders. Not that she could hear them. He spoke in a low voice, clearly trying not to be overheard. She stood by her initial assessment of him as Ugly Hot but had to admit the more she saw him with Jillian, in the quiet moments when they thought no one was watching, the balance tipped. He became less Ugly and more Hot.

Good job, Jillian.

Anika waited, all impatient, doubting this strategy. Her nerves kept firing and her brain shouted for her to walk away. This wasn't her problem. Jillian should have known she'd stir up danger.

Now or never.

She approached him and touched his arm to get his attention. "Do you have a second?"

She'd barely applied any pressure and his gaze shot to her. He seemed to be on high alert. He frowned but then his expression changed. Turned unreadable. "Sure."

"I'm meeting with Harry soon." A meeting she'd called for but dreaded. She toyed with the idea of waiting this out, seeing how far Jillian would actually go. But Astrid's behavior, all sneaky and devoid of any consideration for anyone other than herself, had Anika rethinking. The sooner she told Harry *her version* of how their courtship started, spinning it in the least offensive way, the sooner she could get out from under Jillian's looming threat.

"You seem anxious." His gaze searched her face, as if looking for signs of lying . . . and who could blame him. "Is that because of Harry or something else?"

"You've been paying attention. You know this household is headed for an explosion."

"That's why I called in reinforcements." He nodded in the direction of the man he was talking to earlier who had walked away.

Anika still couldn't see the other man's face and decided she didn't care enough to try. If he was with Beck, he likely couldn't be paid off, bribed, or scammed.

She hated that trait in decent people.

"Dealing with Beverly and Jay . . . and now I have to explain things to Harry . . ." As soon as the words spilled out Anika forced herself to stop talking. Beck wasn't her confidant, but the way he listened lured her in, making her want to share. She doubted he even liked her. Jillian could have told him anything about her, and a lot of the terrible things would be true. "Look, I know you're busy, but I wanted to talk about Jillian."

"What about her?" Every muscle in his body snapped to attention. He hadn't moved but now appeared taller, larger, and a bit more threatening.

"As you know, there are a lot of people coming in and out

of the house and on the estate. Things can get moved around and go missing." Good grief, she could not stop babbling. "She just got home from prison, which makes her the most likely suspect if anything goes wrong."

"Anika."

It wasn't a warning but his tone told her to make her point. She appreciated the nudge because she'd gotten lost in her words for a second. "Right. Get on with it."

"That would be helpful."

"I'm worried someone might do something to harm Jillian. Someone with a lot to lose because of Jillian's actions."

There. Easy. Done.

"Do you mean Jay?"

"I'm not specifically pointing at anyone." Yes, of course Jay, but Anika feared Astrid might be even more dangerous. Hard to tell right now.

Beck didn't seem to have a reaction. She'd expected an interrogation, or at least some questions. He just stood there, assessing and staring. The whole thing made her a little twitchy and not much else did.

She tried again. If she was going to be helpful, she might as well go one more step. Then she'd fix what she could fix and she'd be done. "Jillian might not see it, but she's vulnerable. She's on probation. She can't get in trouble. That was one of her release terms. She could go back to prison . . ."

If the words shocked or upset Beck, he didn't show it. "Won't happen. Not while I'm here, and I intend to be here."

Before she could respond he slid his phone out of his pocket and read something on the screen that made his eyebrows slam together. He made a noise that sounded like humming, which didn't make much sense to Anika.

"Walk with me. I have to check on a problem." He started moving, his long strides eating up the space between them and the house, and not waiting for her answer.

She scurried to keep up. "Do you need to take the call?"

"It was an alarm." He guided them through the house without hesitating.

"Is this about Izzy and the command center?"

That got him to stop. "What are you talking about?"

She didn't have any allegiance to Izzy and didn't particularly like the strange woman, so why not spill. "I saw her lingering upstairs, right by the door. I need to tell Jay so he stops leaving her alone in the house for even two seconds. She seems to pop up at inconvenient times."

Beck nodded and started walking again. "And disappear at others."

"I know it's your job to play security and all, but there's something about her." Anika tried to get the words out but his sprawling gait had her a little breathless as they jogged up the stairs and hit the first landing.

Beck nodded. "You're not the first one to notice."

Anika didn't know what that meant, but it sounded as if he had Izzy handled. Good. One less thing for her to get stuck doing.

"Jillian is prepared. I'm prepared." He looked at her like he expected an answer.

She fumbled. "Right. Sure."

"Good." He headed for Jillian's room. "And Jay won't touch her."

Anika wasn't sure he understood the lengths Jay would go to, the depravity he could justify as necessary to secure the family's needs . . . or the wild card that was Astrid. "Yeah, well, he won't hesitate to sell her out again."

"You don't need to worry about that." Beck stopped with his hand on the doorknob to Jillian's room. "He's not the one who turned her in the first time."

That was big news. It was also one of Jillian's ridiculous requirements for sharing some of the money, so Anika needed more information. "How do you know that?"

"I know."

Huh . . . Sounded like he was guessing. "If you say so."

Beck pushed Jillian's bedroom door open but didn't move further into the room. "Hello."

He was looking at something on the floor. Anika peeked around him and saw her sister. Astrid had shoved the big bed to the side and was crouching down, pushing and rolling the carpet underneath.

An alarm. Now Anika understood his comment about the phone. He must have had some sort of warning system for Jillian's new room and Astrid tripped it. She really did suck at this stuff. "Astrid?"

Astrid shot up at the sound of voices then lost her balance and fell on her butt. "I was looking for Jillian."

Beck actually smiled. "Under the bed?"

Astrid held the end of the carpet up almost as a shield. "No, I was waiting for her."

"On your knees?" Beck moved into the bedroom and stopped only when he loomed over Astrid.

Color flooded her cheeks. "This is none of your business."

Jillian stepped into the doorway behind them, still half hanging out in the hall. "What's going on . . . oh."

"Astrid." Anika thought her tone should be clear—get up, get out, and stop listening to Jay's ridiculous ideas.

Astrid ignored the warning. "I came in to find you and dropped—"

"Whatever you intended to frame me with?" Jillian shook her head. "It's not going to work. I'm not going back to prison."

All the blood that had rushed into Astrid's face at being caught leached out until her skin looked paper white. "What? I would never."

"The security box under the floorboards," Beck said.

Astrid used her *fake confused* expression, and it needed work. "Is there one?"

"I can almost imagine you calling the police and crying about how worried you are because you found . . . what? Drugs?" Jillian shook her head. "Did you really think this would work?"

"Clearly," Beck said.

Astrid balled her hand into a fist and put whatever she was holding behind her just as she'd done as a kid when she got caught taking Anika's toys. "It's nothing."

Planting evidence. She'd actually done it or tried to. No remorse. No little voice in her head telling her to stop. Just pure obedience to Jay. Anika didn't know why she was surprised. Astrid made it clear she intended to destroy Jillian, and Jay didn't say anything to stop her.

Anika wanted to shake her entire side of the family.

Astrid's pathetic *fake confused* look faded as she looked at Jillian. "This is your fault."

Jillian laughed. "I'm to blame for you breaking into my room?"

Did they always sound this pathetic and damaged when they lied? Anika had not noticed it before. Well, a little with Astrid because she wasn't half as convincing or smooth as she thought she was, but this was amateur stuff.

"Astrid, get up." Anika used her best angry mother *do it now* voice.

"You don't—"

"Enough." Because Anika was done. Her slapping tone quieted the whole room. "I'll handle this."

Jillian snorted. "You?"

Anika knew it had to be her. She had to try to stop this, or at least deflect it. Astrid could not live her life as Jay's sidekick. Anika got stuck in that role as a kid and begged God, the universe—anyone who would listen—to set her free because she knew if she got caught he'd sell her out to save himself.

That was bad enough as a kid when the criminal penalties were much lighter, usually a warning at first. Astrid wouldn't be able to hide behind her age if she kept doing this. She'd likely go to jail as a result of some disastrous Jay scheme to save his own ass.

"So, she's not going to come clean or apologize?" Beck asked.

Astrid sat there, looking up at all of them. "I didn't do anything."

"Siding with Jay means siding against me." Jillian shook her head. "Choose wisely, Astrid."

Anika helped Astrid to her feet. After some pulling and tugging, she got Astrid to release the bag. Jillian had been right. Drugs. Likely a one-way ticket to a long prison sentence for Jillian since she was on probation.

Anika dropped the evidence on Jillian's bed. Let Beck figure it out.

They didn't say anything as they walked down the hall. When Anika stopped at one of the extra bedrooms and slipped inside, she half expected Astrid to keep walking, but she followed.

Anika didn't wait to unload. "What were you thinking? That could have backfired in a hundred different ways. What if you'd gotten caught with the drugs by someone in law enforcement or if Beck had called the police?"

Astrid closed the door behind them and leaned against it. She had her arms folded in front of her and an I'm-not-sorry vibe thrummed off her. "You never listen. Those drugs, having her violate her probation, was the best way out of this without casting suspicion on us. We can't reason with Jillian. We need to remove her."

Anika held back a scream but just barely. "That was a ridiculous plan."

"Oh, and listening devices and begging her forgiveness worked better?" Astrid scoffed. "Your solution was too tame. Mine showed vision. It was about more than planting drugs. It was about Jillian using them."

"What?"

"We need the police here, and not for money crimes. It's called misdirection."

"Are you done?"

"Portraying Jillian as messed up after prison is not a reach. We could easily sell it. Upset, depressed . . . just like her mother."

Anika felt sick. "You are not good at this. You go too far. First, the balcony disaster, now this."

"At least I acted." Astrid's eyes gleamed as she grabbed on to Anika's arms. "Imagine Jillian overdosing and being rushed to the hospital. We could tell the police how concerned we are, authorize a search, for her benefit of course."

Astrid made it sound so logical, which was what scared Anika the most. "You have lost your mind."

"She tied up the money. We can't shout about her stealing,

but we need to match her killing move with one of our own. Get her out of here for as long as possible, have everyone question her stability."

"Do you hear yourself?"

"What do you care? You don't like it here and you're off with Harry now. You're going to be fine. Rich. But what about me? Where does all of this leave me?"

Anika took in Astrid's drawn features. She could act but this didn't feel like a role. This was just the two of them. Astrid airing her grievances, the kind of thing Anika usually treated with an eye roll or ignored. Wrote off as her sister's childish behavior.

The stark truth hit Anika—she'd helped to create this mess. She'd added to Astrid's insecurities. Treated her like a second choice. "Jay shouldn't—"

"Don't blame him. Unlike you, he trusts me. *He* listens to me. He knows I'm capable."

"He uses you." He drove a wedge between them long ago, pitting sibling against sibling. Tenn wisely dropped out. Anika had played the game until she grew too weary, but the game might be all that Astrid had left. "I know because he did it to me, too. Showered me with attention and compliments. Insisted I was his favorite."

Astrid didn't say a word.

"You want to please him. You want him to put you first. To care about you." Anika took a step toward Astrid in more ways than one. "He doesn't know how. What he gives is conditional and it hurts when he snatches it away. Realizing that and not playing into it is the only way to survive being related to him."

"Everything was fine before Jillian came home. Before you abandoned me for Harry." Astrid's expression went blank. "Good luck trying to win him back."

Back? "What did you do?"

Astrid finally smiled. "I've had a busy day."

CHAPTER THIRTY-SEVEN

MOOREWOOD FAMILY RULE #15: *Don't be afraid to make new rules.*

THE DEADLINE HAD ARRIVED.

There was no need to stretch this out any longer. The more time passed, the more volatile the situation became. Astrid had tried to send Jillian back to prison. Jay pretended everything was fine while he ignored requests to stop grifting. Patricia . . . who knew what she had planned?

Beck assigned two new men to work the estate with him. A few threats and attempts at familial criminal activities and right away the bodyguard got twitchy. He still didn't understand she'd lived her entire life under this sort of strain. Waiting for the next problem. Worrying a scam would blow up and they'd have to hide, lie, cheat, or run.

Watching her mother slowly die from cancer, spending

her last days plotting to block her husband and brother-in-law instead of enjoying the life she'd led.

Jillian stood on the patio outside the library. She'd grown accustomed to the close proximity to fresh air and the sound of the water. Tenn was out by the pool, locked in a conversation with someone she'd never seen before.

She stiffened, ready to scream.

"What has you all bunched up?"

Beck. He usually popped up with a flair for terrible timing and in time to steal her bacon. This was a nice change. "There's a man out there in a black suit. Very serious demeanor."

"He's with me."

She squinted, trying to get a better look. The guy gave off a Beck sort of confidence. Smiled in his cool sunglasses. "He's cute."

Beck slowly turned to face her. "Excuse me?"

Jillian almost laughed. "He's flirting with Tenn, who appears to be flirting right back. You know what happens when people are under stress."

Beck hummed. "They do stupid shit."

"Yes, that." She took another peek and was pretty sure Tenn was putting his number in the guy's phone. "Some also get a little giddy."

"Giddy?" Beck said the word as if he'd never heard it before.

He could not be this clueless. "The mix of adrenaline and danger can lead to fun things, or so I've read. Happens in all the action movies."

Beck smiled. "Oh, that kind of giddy."

"Tenn could use some giddiness."

"After. When my guy's off duty." Beck's scowl returned.

She grabbed his arm before he could take off and be all sexy boss man. "He's protecting Tenn."

"That's not his actual job right now."

She lifted up on her tiptoes, with her mouth right over his ear, just as he liked it. "Pretend it is."

"Jillian?"

Jillian turned to face her sister. And Greg.

She fought the urge to throw him off the property. Then she saw their faces. Emma looked pale. Greg looked like a smug asshole, so no difference there. If he'd said or done anything to upset Emma, he would drown in that big ocean out there. Jillian had no problem going back to prison for that crime.

"What's wrong?" she asked, knowing the answer was Greg. Had to be.

Strain showed around Emma's eyes. "We need to talk with you."

Jillian didn't like that tone, the expression. None of it. If they were . . . if she was . . .

"Why?" She realized she'd barked out the word when even Beck looked at her.

"Tone it down a bit," he mumbled, but his mumbling was loud, so they all heard the suggestion.

"Gregory told me what happened between the two of you." Emma inched away from Gregory. She still stood next to him but the space between them suddenly seemed very wide. "He told me he conned you. Pretended to be interested because his father wanted to get to Mom's money."

"Shit." Beck wasn't any quieter that time.

"Emma was furious and broke it off with me." Gregory looked pretty pissed off about that. Not his usual smarmy, flirty self at all. "She told me she hated me."

Jillian knew not to celebrate the demise of the relationship she despised. Emma and Greg were here for a reason. No way would Gregory accept this loss without a fight.

"I told her there was more to the story and begged her to come talk with you," he said. "I want her to know all of it. No more secrets."

"Because you're so honest." Jillian felt a twinge of guilt. It was mixed up with her anger and distaste for Greg, so it got a little lost, but it was there. Beating and growing, potentially forcing her to expose the secret she wanted to keep to herself. The one Beck had guessed.

Greg didn't back down. "Because what I feel for your sister is real."

"I'm not convinced you know what *real* means." He'd already apologized to her for back then. For the pain and embarrassment. Jillian wanted to be grown-up and not care and just accept it, but she couldn't kick the feeling that he was taking responsibility now so he could win Emma.

Emma snorted. "Now I know how my mom felt. Scammed by the man she was dating and . . ." She shook her head. "I really do hate you."

Okay, the words didn't make Jillian feel any better the

second time. That pissed her off more than anything. She'd wanted Emma to walk away from Greg, but this didn't sit right. Being the cause, and not in an honest way, felt more like something Jay would do.

The protective instinct to reach out and coddle Emma was hard to shake. Jillian had spent a lifetime watching out for her baby sister, clearing the way, trying to make her load lighter. But Emma wasn't a kid and all that protecting had left her exposed and looking for something else.

Patricia's words came flying back to Jillian. *Break the cycle. Stop managing and fixing. They're grown-ups.*

"Jillian, please." The pleading was right there in Greg's voice. "You know there's more to this. We both do."

Emma stood next to Jillian now, having subtly chosen sides. "What is he talking about?"

There were a lot of things wrong with this scenario. Jillian didn't like that Greg was trying to explain away his actions by highlighting hers. She also knew this had the potential to drive a wedge between her and Emma. Whether she told the next part or not didn't matter. Greg said there was more, and now Emma would always wonder.

"This is manipulative and you're a jackass." She had a lot of other words for him but stopped there mostly because she had to survive a family meeting after this.

Greg didn't deny it. "I'm desperate. I promise the information stays here. It never goes one inch further." His shoulders rose and fell on a sigh. "We call a truce and the anger we feel for each other stops before Emma gets hurt."

Emma grabbed Jillian's arm. "What is he talking about?"

She looked at Beck. He didn't say anything. Didn't have to. His *you know the right thing to do* expression dropped the last of her defenses.

Jillian sat on a chair and dragged Emma down to sit in the one beside her. "The reason the prosecutor agreed to pursue only the one charge against me and offer a short sentence was that I made a deal that pulled the spotlight away from us."

Emma's gaze traveled between Jillian and Gregory. "What does that mean?"

"She had to give them something bigger than your family's schemes and misdeeds to keep all of you from getting buried in lengthy prison sentences and fines," Gregory said in a tone that didn't give any indication about what was happening inside of him.

He wasn't wrong and that still confused Jillian. "How did you know?"

Gregory shrugged. "Hints the prosecutor dropped. How convinced he was in his case. The timing. It was the only thing that made sense."

Jillian hated every part of this. Telling it now and what she did back then. Mostly she hated Greg, but she knew that wasn't entirely fair. "I was skeptical of Gregory's dad and his brokerage business. The claims about wild returns on investments didn't make sense. I'd overheard him joking with Dad about how easy it was to make money if you bent the rules. A theory he likely assumed Dad would agree with, but Dad didn't control our money."

Most people got to hide the worst thing they'd ever done. Jillian didn't have that luxury.

Guilt rushed up on her. She felt the same choking sensation as when she'd found out her dad died. She'd never really gotten any satisfaction out of what she did. She'd searched for it, silently pleaded for it, but that bit of revenge against Gregory and his family didn't lessen her humiliation or fix her broken family. It just added one more burden to her already heavy pile.

She'd justified her actions with lofty explanations to her attorney and to Kelby back then. Neither of them fought her, except to say she shouldn't be in prison at all. A part of her knew that's exactly where she deserved to be. She paid a penance, just not for the crimes she actually committed.

She took a deep breath and walked through the rest of it. "There are a lot of details and legal negotiations, but I basically handed over information on Greg's dad. Pointed the spotlight at him. Provided evidence. Made it clear he was a much bigger fish than anyone named Moorewood."

Gregory's dad deserved to be found out and whatever money he'd stolen secured for his victims. But she didn't lie to herself and say that's why she'd made the choice. She'd wanted to hurt his family . . . and she did.

"How could you . . ." Emma's nails dug into the armrests of the chair.

"It made sense to me back then." Jillian did it for a host of reasons but none of them really mattered now.

"You made yourself into a martyr for us but then . . .

Jillian, the man died." Emma glanced at Gregory. "Their family lost everything."

Jillian felt sick. She'd spent a lifetime putting her body in front of Emma's. Now she had to admit that she enjoyed being on the receiving end of Emma's respect. Losing that hurt more than Jillian wanted to admit, mostly because the *martyr* tag stuck.

Emma reached a hand toward Greg. "I had no idea."

He slipped his fingers through hers and sat down at the table next to her. "I did, and it didn't matter when it came to how I felt about you."

Emma made a face. "What? After the car crash and everything that happened, do you forgive Jillian for pointing to your dad?"

"It's not that simple." Gregory's voice lightened but tension still pulled around his mouth. "It's more like I'm willing to start over. Understand what she did, if she'll understand why I put her in that position in the first place. Honestly, my family struck first."

A few days ago Jillian would have viewed the conversation and him not lashing out as a setup and waited for him to unleash his revenge. Watching him now, seeing how gentle he was with Emma even while she wavered in her defense of her family to support him, Jillian reluctantly believed him.

Maybe Beck had been right. People could change.

CHAPTER THIRTY-EIGHT

MOOREWOOD FAMILY RULE #35: *Sometimes a con fails. Move on.*

ANIKA FOUND HARRY OUT FRONT. HE STOOD IN THE ESTATE'S massive circular driveway, looking down as he moved the small stones around with the tip of his shoe.

Lost. That's the word she'd use to describe him.

"What are you doing out here?" She swallowed, trying to fix the wobble in her voice.

Harry slowly lifted his head. The look on his face said . . . nothing. She couldn't pick out anger or sadness. Part of her wanted to believe Astrid didn't sabotage the relationship, but she did. Anika could feel the walls closing in, preparing to slam into her.

"I talked with Astrid." His voice was flat. Lifeless.

"Okay." Anika tried to sound cheery. "Come inside and we'll—"

"No."

This was bad. Really bad. He never interrupted her, but now he cut her off as if he couldn't stand to hear her talk.

"I don't know what my sister said, but—"

"She told me the truth. That you were only going out with me for money."

So, she told *a* truth, not the big one. Not the worst one. That gave Anika some hope.

He shifted, scraping his shoe against the rocks again. "She tried to make it sound like she'd been trying to talk you out of playing this game, but I got the impression she was enjoying dropping the bomb."

"She's not . . . you can't listen to her."

He put his hands in the pockets of those slim pants she'd bought for him because the pleated ones didn't flatter him at all. "Was she lying?"

Say it. That voice in her head, the one honed by years of practice and all those lectures from Jay, called for her to turn on Astrid. To keep lying so that she wouldn't lose him. But his face. His expression had changed. Now he looked vulnerable and frustrated, a little sad and hovering on the edge of anger.

Anika balled her hands into fists and silently willed her brain to keep playing along. The game was simple and so were the rules. She needed Harry so she could escape, find a new life. The idea of starting over with another man, another target, made her physically ill.

"Anika?"

She could lie. Just lie. Say the words. "Harry, I . . ."

"So, the answer is no." He shook his head. "It makes sense. Look at you then look at me. Why else would you choose me?"

"Don't say that." At first, yeah. She saw him one way, but not now. He was decent and smart. Loyal and loving.

Oh, shit. She really did care about him. Not just about the money and what he could give her. Him. The realization nearly dropped her to her knees.

She blamed Jillian for putting the idea in her head.

"You wanted someone to rescue you." His voice sounded stronger now. More defiant.

She hated that word. *Rescue?* This was about a new partnership, which she now had to admit sounded like a *real* relationship. "No, not really."

His usual welcoming smile had disappeared. "You pursued me because of the money."

"You asked me out."

"Anika, come on."

"Okay, fine. Our relationship started out as one thing, but now . . . it's not that way. I care about you." She didn't even stumble over the word. It felt right, sounded fine in her head.

"Bullshit."

She'd never heard him swear before, and she didn't like it. It didn't fit him. "My feelings grew. I didn't expect that to happen, but it did."

He shook his head. "My mother was right about you."

Anika rushed toward him. "No. Please. We can make this work. I want to make this work."

He stepped back before she could touch him. "Goodbye, Anika."

CHAPTER THIRTY-NINE

MOOREWOOD FAMILY RULE #1: *Family comes first. Always.*

THEIR FAMILY STARTED WHEN A CON MAN SCAMMED AN HEIR-
ess into marriage. Years later, through kids and disease, grifting and aging, death and disappointment, they landed here.

Jillian swallowed a gulp of lukewarm tea as she looked
around the dining room at her family members. She'd
planned for their destruction and hoped for their despair.
Coming home and finding such a mess changed everything.
Her cousins had fumbled around, lost to varying degrees.
They'd turned from kids trying to please into adults with
limited honest-life skills. Still stuck in their old ways and
determined to get in trouble.

Then the issues piled on and her focus scattered. She'd
been forced to look at her life, her choices, and admit that

in addition to blaming everyone else for the things that happened to her, she needed to take responsibility for her part in the family disaster.

She always insisted she'd forfeited her life for them. The reality was harder to swallow. She could have walked away at any time, not been in control, said no to playing the role of martyr. She didn't.

Her mom filled her head with talk of family loyalty. She'd believed marriage lasted a lifetime and gave up everything, including personal happiness, to make that happen. Jillian had no interest in repeating those mistakes. She never saw the family business as anything but a burden, but she got to choose how she wielded her power . . . and that brought them to today.

Everyone crowded into the room and took a seat, including Kelby, Izzy, and Gregory. The former two needed to be there and the latter was like a bug that refused to be squashed. Jillian gave up trying.

"Jillian, it would be better if we limited this meeting to family only." Jay turned to Izzy and started to pull out her chair. "We can meet after—"

"She stays." Jillian looked at the folder Beck dropped in front of her. "Thanks."

"This is a mistake," Jay said. His not-so-gentle warning suggested he'd better not be ignored.

So, Jillian ignored him and continued. "Izzy, we're here to talk about some family issues, most of them relating to finances."

Astrid lowered her wineglass to the table with a smack. "What are you doing?"

Ignoring Astrid proved even easier now that Jillian knew how little her cousin cared about her safety and well-being. Jillian kept her attention on the woman who had been a question mark since they met. "Izzy, I couldn't figure out why you just walked into my bedroom that first morning home, or why a few of us have found you wandering the halls upstairs at random times."

Jay's arm froze in the middle of resting it on the back of Izzy's chair. "When?"

"I thought I explained." Izzy dropped her hands to her lap. "I was just—"

"Snooping." The contents of the folder proved it. Jillian knew because Beck didn't keep her in the dark. She knew exactly what he'd been investigating for the last two days.

Izzy frowned. "That's a crass way of putting it. I know you've been away, but I'm sure you've been taught the proper way to treat a guest."

"Bah." Patricia topped the comment off by slipping a cheese stick out of her bra and opening the plastic with a rip.

"Oh, forgive me. Can't you hear me?" Izzy started shouting at Patricia. "I can speak louder."

Patricia separated the cheese stick into two pieces. "If you don't stop yelling I'm going to—"

Jay's usual calm demeanor slipped. "Patricia!"

Fun as this was, and it kind of was, it was time to move this along. "At first I thought you were investigating Jay. You know, checking to see if he was who he said he was. That would be a smart choice for any woman with significant resources and assets."

Izzy let out a nervous laugh. "Women need to be careful."

"No doubt, but that's not what's happening here. I know that because I asked Beck to do what he does best." Jillian smiled at him to thank him.

"Stand around looking menacing?" Anika asked.

"No, his other skill." Jillian opened the folder and started reading. "Elizabeth Wayne. Unfortunately for Jay, not the Batman type of Wayne. The regular, doesn't-have-any-money type from New Jersey."

Some of the color left Izzy's face.

Jay was a bit slower to catch on. "What are you talking about?"

Beck walked around the table to stand behind Izzy. If she wanted to run she'd have to make a human-sized hole in Beck, and Jillian didn't see that happening.

"I thought maybe you had lied about the extent of your worth because you were looking for a husband, or whatever. Trying to secure a better future, which is not a terrible thing, so long as you're honest about it, but you weren't."

"None of that applies to me. I don't understand what you think is going on, but I assure you I've been honest in my dealings with Jay." Izzy's voice sounded so clear.

But she wasn't actually Izzy, so . . . "Incorrect. You're actually running a con on Jay, which is priceless. Like, you don't even know how priceless it is that you're trying to fool him and steal his money." Jillian laughed because ever since Beck had told her what he'd found she'd laughed about this. The con man getting conned.

Izzy gasped on cue. "That's not true."

"You've done it before, under different names. Admittedly, Jay was a big leap from the others in terms of what you perceived to be his net worth, but that was just one of your many mistakes. I blame that on the fact you're a novice." Jillian glanced at the file and thought about the information Beck and his team had found. Passports. Fake names. Divorced and widowed men who no longer had their bank and brokerage accounts. "Jay was only your third target."

Jay was smart enough to stay quiet. For once, Astrid did, too.

"See the big guy behind you?" Jillian pointed at Beck. "He has a buddy in the hall and, because I'm in a giving mood, they're going to usher you off the property instead of taking you directly to the police."

Astrid seemed to wake up a bit. "What is going on?"

"Izzy, real name Elizabeth, isn't an heiress. There is no big house in Boston. She's not visiting friends in Rhode Island. She's in a short-term rental and playing you, Jay."

Anika made a noise that sounded like *wow*. "This is too good."

"You're scamming *me*?" Jay sounded stunned. "How dare you?"

Jillian really wished she was recording this. The illustrious, well-informed, always-ready-with-a-lie Jay had been played.

"You don't understand." Izzy shifted in her seat to face

Jay. She grabbed on to his arm. "It started out as one thing, but once we spent time together and I started to feel—"

Jay pushed back in his chair, putting distance between them. "No."

"Damn." Tenn shook his head. "This is unbelievable."

"This is the wrong audience for that excuse," Jillian suggested. In her defense, the woman formerly known as Izzy couldn't know. The whole thing impressed Jillian with how good a job Emma had done planting stories and social media profiles to give the family credibility to anyone peeking in from the outside. "I suggest you learn a lesson and find a different career because if anyone ever does come asking, I will squeal."

"And I'll be tracking you to make sure you behave," Beck said as he touched Izzy's shoulder. "Time for you to leave."

"No." Izzy shrugged off the touch and moved closer to Jay. "You have this all wrong. What I feel for you is real."

"Here we go." Beck managed to lift Izzy out of her seat. She flailed and cried. Insisted she really cared about Jay and didn't mean to snoop. All in all, it was a loud three minutes until Beck had her up and out to his man on the other side of the door.

The sounds of her yelling grew fainter. In the silence, no one said anything. Jay sat there, slumped in his seat mumbling to himself.

"Well, I guess we should be happy she didn't steal anything." Astrid's gaze shot to Beck. "She didn't, did she?"

Jay snapped out of the stupor that threatened to suck him under. One second quiet. The next in full red-faced fury. He turned on Astrid. "You did the background check."

"I used . . . Emma is the one—"

"Nope." Emma lifted a hand in a way that said *don't even try.* "Do not blame me. You do security checks, and we all know it because you tell us how great you are at doing the work."

Now, this was interesting. Jillian hadn't thought about additional fallout, but she welcomed it. "Holy crap, you set Jay up."

"That's ridiculous." Astrid's voice came out high and pitchy. Totally fake.

Jay smacked his hand against the table with a whap. "Why would you take that risk? What were you thinking?"

"She's your right hand. The only one you can trust." Anika sounded like she was quoting Jay on something, but she didn't elaborate.

"That's right." Astrid went all in, ignoring the looks she was getting and Jay's escalating anger. "And I did it to prove how valuable I am. I would have stopped her before she caused any real damage, but that's not the point. I'm the one who can protect you . . . or not. My choice. I'm the one with the smart plans and new ideas. None of you respect that. None!"

Beck let out a long exhale. "This family is something else."

"No kidding," Kelby said.

They were all such a mess. Jillian had been gunning for

revenge for so long. She'd stoked her anger while slowly building a plan to suck them dry financially. But she saw now she didn't need to swoop in take her revenge. They'd chew up and destroy each other whether or not she yanked the money.

Old Jillian, like, the Jillian she was even two days ago when she told them all about the amazing grift she pulled off against them, would relish the opportunity to fix them. She'd issue orders, take over, try to make them conform to her rules. But Beck was right. Patricia was right. All Jillian's babysitting did was give the other side of the family a common enemy and keep them from getting one step healthier.

Worse, all that redeeming and shuffling had become her reason not to move forward. She'd been treading water and blaming everyone else. They all needed to move on.

She stood up because she did need them to listen. "Okay, it's time."

"For what?" Jay asked.

"Closure."

Astrid started shifting around in her seat. "I demand a family vote."

She was so damn exhausting. Jillian was about to point that out when Tenn jumped in. "That's not a real thing."

"Exactly," Emma said. "Jillian is in charge. A vote is useless."

Jillian hoped that was a good sign. Emma hadn't exactly been impressed with Jillian's big secret or the way she'd sacrificed Greg's family. Jillian understood. Emma felt something for the bozo. And, really, Jillian still beat back the guilt that came with remembering those days of negotiating with the prosecutor and admitting what she knew about Greg's family in an attempt to save her own.

"You won't win a vote," Kelby pointed out.

"Wrong." Astrid looked smugly satisfied. "Our family— Jay, Anika, Patricia, Tenn, and me. That's five votes." She held up five fingers as if the room needed an example. "You have three, and you might not have Emma."

"Jillian has my support on all Moorewood matters." Emma sounded grumpy and frustrated. Gregory must have heard the unspent energy in her voice, too, because he put his arm around her, as if to console her.

"I'd vote with Jillian," Anika said.

Okay, that was unexpected. Jillian stared at Anika, knowing something bad had happened. Something that made her switch loyalties . . . to the extent she had any.

Tenn nodded. "Me too."

In this imaginary vote that Jillian never intended to let anyone take, she just won. She wasn't sure how, but the room tipped in her favor. Probably had at least a little to do with her having check-writing authority.

Patricia ripped her cheese stick into smaller strips. "I voted against her once. Never again. I side with Jillian."

Anika's eyes narrowed. "When did you vote—"

"So . . ." Jillian rushed ahead. She didn't intend to out

Patricia. That would only further derail an already derailed conversation. "The rules have changed."

"What about you, Gregory? You and Jillian have a past and issues. Now you're with Emma." Astrid poured herself a second glass of wine. "It feels like we should talk about that."

Jillian hated Astrid for making her defend Greg. "We have an . . ."

Greg smiled. "Understanding."

"Sure." If that satisfied Emma, fine. Jillian would be happier if he disappeared, taking the memories and her guilt with him, but fine.

Jillian had thought about all the deals she'd offered her family. The one from years ago. The one she spelled out when she announced they were all leaving the house. Now she had a new plan, one that guaranteed any relationship they all forged from here, no matter how rocky and dysfunctional, wouldn't be dependent on her or on ongoing payments.

"I've had some time to think about what's important and how I want to live my life, and that is a good thing for most of you at this table."

"I doubt it," Astrid muttered.

"All of the Moorewoods present will receive a one-time, never-again payment." She'd already worked this possibility out with Kelby then abandoned it, but now she knew it was the right answer.

"How much?" Astrid asked.

Leave it to Astrid to jump right to the numbers. In a way,

Jillian admired that. "Everyone, excluding Doug because he's on his own, will get the same amount."

"That's not fair. Doug should get a slice," Patricia said.

"If he does, the rest of you will get less."

Patricia waved her hand in the air. "Actually, he made his choice when he took that car. Go ahead."

Jillian suspected that would be the consensus, so she pushed on. "Everyone will split the pot. The total in the pot will be equal to the amount Mom inherited from her mom decades ago. Keep in mind she inherited the bulk of the estate from her father, but her mother also had a nest egg. A much smaller one. That's the amount I mean."

"So that we're clear." Jay piped up for the first time since realizing Astrid had tried to sell him out, or test him, or get his attention . . . or whatever her failure with investigating Izzy was about. "Does that total include the house?"

Jillian made a mental grab for more patience. He was so trifling. "You never change, Jay. And no."

Astrid raised her hand as if this was a question-and-answer session. "Is the amount adjusted for inflation? I mean, as an example, ten million dollars would be a lot more today than back then, so the pot should be significantly bigger."

Beck swore under his breath. "Wow."

"No." In an effort to cut off more questions that annoyed her, Jillian skipped ahead to the punch line. "Eight million. Divided between Jay, Astrid, Anika, Patricia, and Tenn."

Jay just sat there. "One of the paintings we sold was worth that alone."

"Okay, but she means that amount plus the ongoing quarterly payments from the trust," Astrid said, proving she really was Jay's kid.

Jillian was ready for both of them to move out.

"No. Just the eight million, which is a lot of money even when divided by five since it's a gift and tax-free to each of you." Not enough for this crew, sure, but that was as far as Jillian was willing to go. The answer was this deal or nothing.

Astrid gasped in the way only Astrid could gasp. As if she were being hit with a stick. "That's not fair."

"Come on," Tenn said. "It's more than generous. We're not entitled to anything."

Astrid didn't appear one bit shamed. "Emma and Jillian have the separate trust with the house and investments and will keep getting family money. That's more like seventy million."

"Damn," Beck mumbled in typical, very loud, Beck fashion.

"All true. Congratulations on your solid math skills." Jillian was happy to make that clarification because it made the vein on Astrid's forehead pop.

"She could give you nothing," Kelby pointed out.

"One more thing." Jillian was pretty firm on this one. "Everyone moves out. Specifically, Astrid, Anika, and Jay. You have one week. You get the check as you exit the property for the last time."

Anika, who had been surprisingly nonconfrontational

and weirdly supportive during the entire chat, spoke up. "A week? That's tight."

"What do you care, you have Harry," Astrid said.

"Thanks to you, I don't."

Well, damn. Astrid had done something. Something bad. Jillian should have guessed. Anika's tone, all sullen, was off. She looked . . . sad.

"You little idiot!" Jay stood up, in full fury now. "Harry was our safety net."

Anika groaned. "Harry's money was never going to be yours."

"Anika, I'm sorry." Jillian meant that.

At first she felt sorry for Harry because the poor bastard loved Anika. But Jillian got the impression that at some point during months of scheming and planning, Anika started having feelings for Harry. She likely didn't understand them and fought them to near death when she had her first twinge, but they existed now, and Astrid had ruined any chance of Anika figuring it all out.

"Oh, please." Astrid waved off the concern. "She'll find someone new tomorrow to bone and steal from."

"You're vicious," Tenn said.

Patricia looked at her great-niece right before she could launch her response. "Stop talking, Astrid."

Astrid, her manipulation, that was for *that* side of the family to figure out. Jillian had done her part. "Now you know the deal. That's it and the terms will not change, except if anyone asks any questions or asks for more. In that case, the pot will decrease."

Jay shook his head. "While I appreciate you want this over, this solution is not going to work. It's not enough money, Jillian."

"Jay." Aunt Patricia waited until Jay looked at her. "Start packing."

CHAPTER FORTY

One Week Later

JILLIAN'S GENERAL RULE: *A family shouldn't need a bunch of stupid rules.*

THE CLOUDS CLEARED, GIVING WAY TO BRIGHT, WARMING sunshine. The noise in the house had grown to a thunderous crescendo during the week with furniture being moved around, cars pulling in and out. Today, for the first time, silence greeted Jillian.

She slipped outside, yoga pants in place and coffee in hand, and curled up on one of the patio loungers. She relaxed as the scene from the last few days played in her head. Her family really only ran at one speed, and this week it was fast and into a wall.

Ah, family.

The choices they made after being given this new and

absolutely final chance were their own. She really was done saving them . . . except the usual family saving that non-grifters engaged in, like rides to the airport and uncomfortable holiday dinners. She was ready for that level of family angst.

A shadow fell over her and Beck's voice rang out a second later. "You should wear that shirt every day."

She'd bought it at a truck stop gift shop right after getting out of prison. Her first purchase in years other than candy bars. "I think *In Dog Years I'm Dead* is the perfect reflection of the last few days."

"Could be." He sat down next to her. "Jay finally left the estate this morning. He packed his clothes and valuables while my people watched. Then he took the car and ran."

Not a surprise. Getting caught as the target of a con was the ultimate embarrassment for Jay. So was having to take a check from Jillian, which he hadn't done but she knew he planned on sneaking back to ask for it . . . along with china, silver, and various paintings she hadn't sold because they were *too hot*. The answer would still be no. He'd get one check only.

He'd need a nest egg to move on and carry out his schemes. He'd circle back and negotiate her to death. That's who he was and the man wasn't going to change now.

"Good thing I switched all the account passwords, moved accounts, changed banks to ones not run by his friends, and installed locks on everything I couldn't nail down." She'd done that before the family meeting, just in case.

"But he has the car."

"He can keep it." She'd have to check and make sure he didn't somehow put the insurance in her name, but she didn't care about a vehicle. "It's a price I'm willing to pay."

Beck stretched out next to her. "Not to say I told you so, but Astrid is on a plane to Italy."

That was an odd bit of information. "Italy? Did she just pick a country at random?"

"I've poked around a bit."

"You're good at poking." The man could *poke* for hours without stop. It was an impressive trait. One of many.

He smiled but didn't further the innuendo. "Doug now is in Italy, not Finland or Belgium. He and the expensive car, which is in the garage of a fancy apartment that I'm assuming is being paid for with the last of the money Jay set aside for him. Doug's watch with the tracker, however, still appears to be in Finland."

She wondered how Beck knew all those details since Doug was supposed to be in hiding, but then Beck seemed to pick up tidbits and put puzzles together without much trouble. He understood people. She was thrilled he understood her and had no signs of letting it scare him off.

"He never sold that ridiculously expensive car and now he'll have the pile of cash Astrid brings with her." He sounded grumbly about the latter. "I still can't believe we let her leave. I don't trust her at all."

"Hurting me no longer benefits her." Jillian made sure everyone knew that if anything happened to her and Emma the entire estate went to charity. They got nothing more than the checks she'd already handed over. She'd also kept the records showing their cons and would pull them out and incriminate them if they tried to seek revenge or send her back to prison.

"You're an unstoppable force but you shouldn't underestimate her."

Jillian really liked that first part. "I don't. Hell, Doug and Astrid working together is a scary thing. Two novice grifters who think they're more experienced than they are. They'll be in jail in no time."

"What are you going to do when the call for bail comes in?"

"Not answer."

"This is a nice change. The new *they're grown-ups and not my problem* thing." He winked at her. "It's very sexy."

Her stomach tumbled when he said things like that. "Thank you for noticing."

"Oh, I notice everything about you."

She cradled her coffee. "I'm trying to be different, less controlling and not dependent on the family for my identity."

The change would take some time. She was moving by inches but determined to change her focus. She'd spent her entire life simultaneously trying to escape from the Moorewood name and using it as an excuse to not go after the things she wanted from life. It was time to retire the martyr part of her and the scared part.

"Any word from Anika?" Beck asked.

Jillian groaned as she tilted her head back and looked at the bright blue sky. "She's going to be the death of me."

"What did she do now?"

She could hear the amusement in his voice and chose to ignore it. "While I admire her spirit and continue to be stunned that she actually fell so hard for Harry, her drive to win the poor guy back will kill us all."

"She is tenacious."

"She wrote him a poem." Jillian winced when she thought about the awkward lines. "It read like a ransom note."

Beck laughed. "That bad?"

"Let's just say emotions are new to her, and it shows." Jillian shook her head. "I had to rewrite parts for her out of fear she'd scare the crap out of him and then I'd never get her out of this house."

"Since you agreed to let her stay on in the guesthouse, one could suggest you like her living here."

"One shouldn't try unless one wants to be punched." Jillian ignored the part about how Anika badgered her until she agreed to speak with Harry on her behalf. Harry now lived in an Anika-induced haze thanks to endless visits, gifts, and wooing. "I still don't know how she convinced Bev to go back to New York and leave Harry here."

"Actually." Beck lifted his hand. "I helped with that."

Of course he did. She'd wondered but now she knew . . . but she specifically didn't want to know details. Not now anyway. She'd weasel them out of him later. "You're such a softie."

"Says the woman who agreed to let Aunt Patricia and her cheese sticks stay at the estate."

"In the other guesthouse. The smaller one, which I know is petty." That was the requirement Jillian had imposed. Tenn could stay in the main house when he visited and had his own rooms there. Emma could have a whole floor of the main house. Patricia, well, Jillian still needed a little space from her great-aunt, but she wasn't about to throw her out. She couldn't imagine the scene Patricia would cause. "She can only put me in prison once, right?"

"I wouldn't underestimate her either. She's terrifying and clearly fine with killing." Beck sighed. "But she wasn't wrong about everything. You do need a life outside of this family."

Oh, Jillian was *really* into the nonfamily thing right now.

She hadn't seen it coming but she'd gone from the ultimate dating slump thanks to prison to hitting the dating jackpot. "Any chance you're talking about yourself?"

He winked at her. "That's up to you."

Beck had been right about a lot of things. Seeing everything unfold as an outside, objective observer gave him insight. Seeing through her. She didn't want to be like Anika and take it for granted and lose him.

She put down her coffee and dove into the one topic she'd been tiptoeing around for days. "Ever think about opening a Newport office?"

"I could be convinced." He reached over and took her hand in his.

"I think I'm going to keep the estate, at least for a while. I love the house, and my memories of my mom are here. I can always think about subdividing some of the acres later and selling off the rest."

"Sounds smart. There's no need to rush into a decision."

"I'm going to take some time and figure out what I want to do, what dreams I gave up, and then figure out how to make those happen." She brushed her thumb over the back of his hand. "Until then, I'll work with Kelby to tie up any loose ends regarding the assets and then I'll get back to co-running the now fully legitimate family businesses."

"Sounds like you've got it all worked out."

"Not all." This was the risk, the one step she vowed not to take again after Gregory. But Beck wasn't Gregory, and she refused to be her mom. "I mean, there's this command center set up in the house that I'm not going to be using any-more. Have any ideas what I could do with that?"

He sat up a little straighter. "It just so happens I've been looking for a Rhode Island command center."

She didn't try to hide her smile. "How convenient."

"You've been more unexpected than convenient."

That sounded kind of sweet. "I'm a woman of mystery. Just so you know and can't say I didn't warn you, the space comes with a big house, a great view, and a pain in the ass family that's almost under control."

He smiled back. "How could I say no to that sales pitch?"

No to being alone. Yes to breaking the cycle. She liked the sound of that. "Then we have a deal."

"Let's hope it goes smoother than your last deal."

She looked out over the grounds and the water. "I'll make sure it does."

ACKNOWLEDGMENTS

I STARTED THIS BOOK YEARS AGO. BACK THEN IT HAD A DIF-ferent spin, more heist and less family disaster. I like to pretend the market wasn't ready, but really, my idea wasn't fleshed out. I put the vagabond chapters aside, wrote a few thrillers under my pseudonym, Darby Kane, killed off lots of bad fictional people (they deserved it and I loved killing them . . . still do!), and pretended to move on from the Moorewoods. But they stuck with me. I wanted to tell their (completely) dysfunctional, (hopefully) funny, and (mostly) wacky story. I loved creating a group of related people with almost no life skills who live in a big house and are headed up by a woman who got stuck in a family role she didn't want but one that came to define her. You wouldn't want to be related to most of these people, but I hope you enjoyed reading about them.

A huge thank-you to my patient and talented editor, May Chen, for helping me take a mash-up of "this might be something" and turning it into a book. Every insight you provided made this better. We cleaned it up, revised, revised again . . . then one last time, and now I really love this train-wreck of a family.

Thank you to everyone at HarperCollins, from the production team to the art team to the sales and marketing teams. Really, to anyone who touched this book in any way. You all make magic. And a big thank-you to my agent, Laura Bradford, for seeing a tiny flicker of potential in this and helping to get it out there for the world to see.

As always, thank you to the readers, librarians, booksellers, bookstagrammers, and fellow authors out there who support my work. My mortgage company also thanks you, but I adore you. You have my humble and very real gratitude.

Thank you to James, my husband, for putting up with my chatter about this book for three years. You're a keeper.

ABOUT THE AUTHOR

HELENKAY DIMON is a former divorce lawyer with a dual writing personality. Her work has been optioned for television and featured in numerous venues, including the *New York Times*, the *New York Post*, *Cosmopolitan*, the *Washington Post*, the *Toronto Star*, PopSugar, Goodreads, The Skimm, and Huffington Post. In addition to writing thrillers as Darby Kane, she is now writing stories centered on family hijinks with a bit of suspense and humor, and she hopes you'll go on this new writing journey with her. For more information go to helenkaydimon.com.